A BURNED

"Peter McLean's debut novel is an absolute gem that hits the ground running, a gritty, grungy, funny, sweary noir thriller with added demons. Don Drake is a wonderful creation. You wouldn't trust him with your life – he can't even be trusted with his own life. It's a wonderful, headlong read and I enjoyed it immensely. Very near the top of the half dozen best books I've read this year."

   Dave Hutchinson, author of Europe in Autumn

"Snarky, pacy and hellishly fun. *Drake* is just the sort of hero, with just the sort of life, to make you feel good about yourself. Dark and delightful, like a naughty treat, this is a rollicking story."

   Francis Knight, author of the Rojan Dizon series

"McLean has crafted a refreshing urban fantasy, with a wonderfully flawed, foul-mouthed protagonist who, despite some dubious life choices, is not quite beyond redemption. Imagine Mal Reynolds had dabbled in the occult and this would have been the result. *Drake* features equally complex female characters, ensuring the Burned Man is one series I shall be certain to follow."

   Susan Murray, author of The Waterborne Blade

PETER MCLEAN

DRAKE

A Burned Man Novel

ANGRY
ROBOT

ANGRY ROBOT
An imprint of Watkins Media Ltd

Lace Market House,
54-56 High Pavement,
Nottingham,
NG1 1HW
UK

angryrobotbooks.com
twitter.com/angryrobotbooks
Just one last hit

An Angry Robot paperback original 2016
1

A catalogue record for this book is available from the British Library.

ISBN 978 0 85766 510 2
EBook ISBN 978 0 85766 512 6

Set in Meridien by Epub Services
Printed in the UK by Printondemand-worldwide.com

*For Diane
All the way around
and back again*

CHAPTER 1

He saw my warpstone and raised me an angel's skull, and there was no way I could cover that bet. I had a Knight-high flush and the Tower, which is a fair hand in Fates, but that warpstone was all I had left. My palms were itching like badgers in heat. I looked down at my cards and the face of the Knight of Cups looked back up at me. He looked drunk and happy in his painted tarot world, the lucky sod. I was just drunk, and in London.

Someone laughed, away on the other side of the smoky club. I heard glasses clinking together and the rattle of dice at another gaming table. Across the table from me Wormwood was starting to look impatient. He poked another cigarette between his thin, grey lips and lit it with the butt of the last one. He mashed the old one out in the overflowing ashtray beside him without looking and coughed a streamer of acrid smoke into the already thick air. A strand of his long hair was stuck greasily to the three-day growth of stubble on his cheek.

He rested his free hand on top of the skull and stroked

it with fingers that were nicotine-stained to the colour of dark mahogany.

"Well, Drake?" he said. "I ain't got all bleedin' night."

I cleared my throat, and the waitress wiggled up beside me with the bottle and poured another generous slosh of whisky into my glass. Very expensive, very old single malt whisky. I nodded a thanks at her. She was pretty, I thought. Nice tail. Another night I might have tried it on with her, but this was proper serious now and I needed to concentrate on the game. I knocked the whisky straight back and set my glass down on the table.

The Tower, again. This was the third hand tonight that I'd drawn it as my trump, and if that didn't suck for an omen I didn't know what did. I glanced at the two decks of cards on the table, the thick one for the suits and the slimmer deck of major arcana which were the trumps in the game. I half wondered if Wormwood was cheating somehow, but that was a dangerous kind of thought to be having here. I reached up to loosen my tie a little, and stretched out my aching neck until it cracked. Wormwood was drumming his fingers on the skull now, and his huge, horned minder was starting to give me that look that said I'd better not be taking the piss. I found myself wondering where exactly you bought a dinner jacket to fit a nine foot tall demon, and what sort of tailor wouldn't think that was a bit odd. I realized my attention was wandering again and forced my eyes back to my cards.

"Right, look," I said, trying to put the enormous minder out of my thoughts. "I'd be about ready to call you on that but, um..."

"But you're skint," Wormwood finished for me. "Aintcha?"

He grinned at me. Wormwood had one of the most repulsive grins I've ever seen, and he stank to high heaven. I could smell him from where I was sitting, with three feet of card table between us and enough cigarette smoke in the air to kill a beagle. It wasn't that unwashed body stink like homeless people get, it was much worse than that. Wormwood smelled of rot somehow, of disease and other people's misery. And cheap cigarettes, I thought. Mostly he smelled of lots and lots of cheap cigarettes.

"Yeah," I admitted. "I'm afraid you've cleaned me out."

"Tosser," he said, and his mean little eyes glittered as he looked at me. "Now I might," he went on, "be able to do something about that."

That made my gambling muscle twitch. I started to reach for my glass before I remembered it was empty. I glanced around the club instead, trying to play it cool. There were maybe twenty punters in tonight, a mixture of us and them. Mostly them. Wormwood's club was private, obviously, and certainly not open to the general public. Hell, it wasn't even *visible* to the general public. You'd walk straight past it if you didn't know exactly where to stop in the alleyway, and precisely which bit of damp, graffiti-covered brickwork was the glamour that covered the front door. Even if you did know, Wormwood's place was strictly invitation only.

"Oh?" I said. "How's that then?"

"I might sub you," he said. "Enough to finish this hand, anyway."

"Why would you do that?" I asked him.

He shrugged. "I know you're good for it," he said. "Anyway, I like you, Drake."

No you don't, I thought. *You don't like anyone.*

I had a Knight-high flush and the Tower, and I really, really wanted that skull. There were all sorts of things I could do with an angel's skull. I met his eyes, trying to feel him out. If I folded now I'd lose the warpstone anyway. If I went for it, if I won, I'd walk away with both and a good pile of cash besides.

What've you got, you little bastard?

The waitress was filling my glass again. She really did have a cute little tail, I thought as she wiggled away. Demons weren't really my thing as a rule, but in her case I'd be more than happy to make an exception. *Idiot. Like she'd have you.* I swallowed the drink and coughed, feeling the shot of ancient whisky burning its way down my throat to chase all its little friends deep into my guts. There were a fair few people watching us now, I noticed. Well I say that, but *people* might be stretching it a bit. This was Wormwood's club, after all.

I looked around again, taking my time. The crowd had shifted and the only ones of "us" I could actually see now were an elderly hoodoo man I recognized, his black face glistening with sweat under the brim of his silk top hat, and a woman in her fifties wafting a peacock feather fan slowly up and down in front of her face. I didn't really know the hoodoo man but I'd seen him around a lot and I had always liked the look of him. He was such a cool old guy, you know? I didn't know the woman at all. Other than that it was all "them", horned or scaled or feathered or spiny or some nasty combination of any of those. All of them were very well dressed and various degrees of drunk, but in that well-behaved sort of way that only posh people seem to be able to manage. The club was invitation-only to them as well, and Wormwood didn't let just any old demon in. There was a bar downstairs for the hoi polloi.

My gaze drifted back to the hoodoo man in his white tie and tails and his silk top hat. He had a glass of rum in one hand and now his other arm was around the waitress with the tail, I noticed. I wanted to be irritated by that but somehow I just couldn't quite bring myself. *Good luck to you mate*, I thought instead. He was stroking her hip with fingers that glittered bright with diamonds. He winked at me, and I found myself grinning back at him.

Ah, if my old man had just been a bit more like you, I thought. *Oh sod it, why not.*

"All right," I said at last. "Sub me then, and I'll call."

Wormwood nodded. "Deal," he said.

I laid my hand out on the table. Wormwood took a long, careful look at my cards, and slowly shook his head. He turned his own hand over to show a full house and Judgment. *Bastard.*

"It ain't your lucky night, Drake," he said.

I shoved my chair back from the table and lurched to my feet, feeling the hot rush of the whisky hit me all at once. I wobbled on my heels, holding on to the edge of the table to keep myself upright.

"Easy now," said Wormwood's minder.

I took a deep breath, my guts twisting into a sick knot as it sank in. I'd lost the hand, I'd lost my warpstone, and now

I owed Wormwood big time.

"I'm all right," I muttered. "I just need some air."

"Right you are then," said the minder, affably enough for a nine foot monster with horns.

"Go home Drake," Wormwood said as he lit yet another cigarette. "I'll be in touch. Like I said, I know you're good for it."

Of course I wasn't good for it. Not by a long way I wasn't. I was so not good for it, in fact, that I had to walk home from the club. It comes to something when you can't even afford a pissing taxi. I hate walking. I'm pushing forty after all, and that ought to be enough exercise for anyone in my book.

South London is bloody awful at three in the morning when it's cold and raining, but at least this part of town is sufficiently bad that even the muggers don't dare go out after midnight. The Veils are so thin here that all sorts of things can slip through from the other side, and frequently do. Wormwood's club wasn't situated where it was for no reason, after all. Damn but it was cold out there after the snug warmth of the club.

At least I had the pavement to myself. I weaved my way down it with my hands buried in my coat pockets, the collar turned up and my hair stuck wetly to my forehead. The cold rain was starting to sober me up, and that was the last thing I wanted just then.

"Bloody Fates," I muttered to myself. "Bloody Wormwood. Arsehole."

I stumbled into an alleyway to take a piss, huddling out of the rain behind some big industrial-sized dustbins. For some reason I can never go properly when I've been drinking whisky, and I must have stood there longer than was sensible. I realized it had got very, very dark. Something cleared its throat behind me.

"Go away," I said.

The darkness shifted around me, feeling as thick as treacle now as I zipped up and turned to face the throat-clearer. I couldn't see a thing anymore but I knew roughly where it must be, and I knew damn well it was looking at me.

"Are you going to keep to our deal, or are we going to fall out?" I asked it.

The darkness shifted once more, wavering, and then began to clear until I could see the opposite wall again. I watched the patch of gloom slouch off down the alley, if a patch of gloom can be said to slouch. It was just a cheap glamour of course, but it was preferable to having to look at the thing that was hiding inside it. I knew that from personal experience.

I'd made my deal with the night creatures of this part of South London when I first moved here, and the terms of that deal were very simple. So long as they didn't bother me, I wouldn't come and bother them. They knew they wouldn't like it at all if I did, and they had been more than happy to accept my deal. Sometimes I just had to remind one of them who was boss, that was all. That would be me, in case there's any shadow of a doubt. I shook my head and headed back into the street, bumping my shoulder on the wall as I went. Maybe I hadn't sobered up that much after all.

I made it home in the end. Home was my office, above the Bangladeshi grocers on the high street. Classy, I know. At least I had my own front door at street level, with my own sign on it and everything. The sign said "Don Drake, Hieromancer" in nice big gold letters. Well it had done anyway, until some wag had spraypainted out the word "Hieromancer" and written "wanker" underneath it instead. I kept meaning to do something about that, and I kept not getting around to it.

I leaned my forehead against the door as I fumbled through my coat pockets for the key. It went in the lock at the third attempt, and I stumbled though the doorway and half-crawled up the bare wooden stairs to my office, dripping water as I went. I had a couple of rooms out the back where I actually lived, and another where I worked, but I kept the booze in the office. I threw my sodden coat over the sofa, sank down into my scruffy leather swivel chair and opened the bottom drawer of my desk.

There was a half-empty bottle of whisky and a couple of relatively clean glasses in there. The whisky was much cheaper stuff than Wormwood served, but it was a hell of a lot better than nothing. I ignored the glasses and drank it straight out of the bottle, which, when you thought about it, was glass anyway so what fucking difference did it make? It's not like I had anyone to share it with.

I swallowed and let my eyes close. *Fuck it!*

The phone jarred me painfully awake. I was slumped forward over my desk, my fingers still curled around the empty bottle. I fumbled out with my right hand, realized that was the one holding the bottle, and winced as it rolled off the edge of the desk and shattered on the hard wooden floor. I groaned and let the machine pick up. There was a beep and a little click and rattle as the old-fashioned cassette tape mechanism came to life.

"Good morning, Mr Drake," said a woman's voice. She sounded very professional and a bit pissed off, as though phoning the likes of me was somehow beneath her dignity. It probably was, to be fair. "This is Selina from Mr Wormwood's office. Mr Wormwood would be pleased if you could telephone him this morning to discuss the repayment of your debt. Good day."

I frowned. Wormwood? What the hell did he want... *Oh no...* My sodden memory turned over in the throbbing mess of my head, and I felt like crying. *My warpstone.* I had gambled away my warpstone, I remembered now, and not only that, but I owed Wormwood the equivalent value of an angel's skull as well. I dreaded to think how much that might actually be, and if we'd agreed a price last night I'd been too drunk to remember it now. That warpstone had been the last artefact of power I had left. The rest... yeah. Let's just say I've always been better at drinking than I have at playing Fates.

I slowly hauled myself up into a sitting position, and had to clutch a hand to my stomach as an acid rush of half-digested whisky burned its way up my throat and into the back of my mouth. I gave serious consideration to throwing up before I winced and swallowed it back down again. Maybe I've never been that good at drinking either, come to think of it.

Of course the warpstone wasn't quite the *last* artefact I had left, but if I ever consider gambling away the other you have my permission to shoot me though the head on the spot. I dragged myself to my feet and shuffled through to the workroom to look at it.

My sign downstairs wasn't entirely truthful, of course. Well, the wanker part might be, I suppose, but not the hieromancer. Hieromancy is divination through reading the entrails of a sacrifice, in case you didn't know, and while I could do that, it wasn't exactly my main line of work. Even a man with my talent for bullshit would struggle to earn a living from interpreting the insides of a pigeon, after all. No, the real money is in sendings. Summoning and sending is one of the oldest disciplines of magic, and it's always been the most dangerous and the most taboo. It's also, it ought to go without saying, the most lucrative. That was what really paid the rent and bought the booze.

I pushed open the door to my workroom and looked at the Burned Man.

"Morning," I said.

"You look like a lukewarm turd," it said. "What's up?"

The Burned Man was a nine-inch tall fetish that stood on the altar at the far end of my workroom. Tiny iron manacles encircled its wrists and ankles, linked to chains that were bolted firmly into the solid oak top of the ancient altar. It was the most powerful thing I've ever owned, or ever even set eyes on for that matter. The floor of my workroom was carefully inscribed with a grand summoning circle from the great classical grimoire *Lemegeton Clavicula Salomonis*, the *Lesser Key of Solomon*, and through the Burned Man I could use that circle to summon demons and send them to do my bidding. Certain people, not the sort of people you'd have round for tea exactly, would pay a hell of a lot of money to get you to set a demon on someone.

"I'm in the shit," I admitted.

The Burned Man snorted with laughter. "No change there then."

I pushed my hands back through my hair and sighed. The only trouble with the whole set-up was that the Burned Man wasn't quite as bound as I might have wanted it to be. Oh sure, it did what I told it to, it had to, but it had a bitch of an attitude problem all the same. Not to mention a smart mouth.

I shrugged out of the crumpled suit jacket I had fallen asleep in last night and chucked it in a corner, well outside the circle. There were dried sweat stains on my white shirt, I noticed. Classy. I pulled my tie off too, wrinkled as an old typewriter ribbon after my night face-down on the desk, and dropped it on the floor. My hands fumbled with the buttons of my stained shirt.

"What's the matter this time?" the Burned Man asked me.

I looked at it again as I took my shirt off. It was only little, as I said, but it was horribly lifelike. Every millimetre of its tiny naked body was blackened and blistered, its skin cracked open in places to show the livid, weeping red burns beneath. It was thoroughly revolting, and the bloody thing was always hungry.

"Wormwood," I said. "I owe him, and I can't pay."

I approached the altar and crouched down, offering my scarred chest to the Burned Man.

"You've been playing Fates again, haven't you, you pillock," it said. "Were you drinking too, by any chance?"

I grunted as it lunged forward and sank its tiny, needle-like teeth into the flesh beneath my left nipple. It started to suckle, blood running down its chin from the fresh wound.

"Is a bear Catholic?" I muttered, wincing against the pain. "I need you to sort it for me."

The Burned Man let go of my chest and stared up at me.

"With Wormwood?" it said. "*The* Wormwood? Wormwood the archdemon? Are you mental?"

"How many Wormwoods do you know, exactly?" I snapped. "Yes, that one."

"Oh dear," it said. "Oh dear, oh dear, oh dear. You ought to pay better attention to who you're playing cards with in future. No."

It stretched forward and bit into my chest again, a little harder than it really needed to in my opinion. Horrible thing.

"You have to," I reminded it. "I own you, Burned Man. I command it."

It whipped its head back again without opening its mouth first, spitefully taking a tiny chunk of bloody meat out of my chest. I yelled in pain and half-raised my hand to swat it before I remembered that would have been ten kinds of a stupid thing to do. I had to remind myself that this was just the fetish of the demon it represented and not the real thing. The real thing didn't even bear thinking about. I let my hand fall and glared at it instead.

"Bugger off," it said, around a mouthful of meat.

"I command it," I said again. "I need an angel's skull. Sharpish."

The Burned Man sniggered. "If I could summon up *things* you wouldn't be broke, would you?" it sneered. "You don't get to command me to do things I can't actually do, it doesn't work like that."

I sighed. The hideous little thing was quite right of course; it didn't work like that at all. I stood up and pressed the heels of my hands into my eye sockets with a groan. I could feel warm blood trickling down my chest from where it had bitten a chunk out of me. My head was pounding, and I was seriously starting to reconsider the whole throwing-up thing.

"So what am I supposed to do?" I said.

It shrugged, rattling its slender iron chains.

"Nothing you can do," it said. "You can't pay him and that's that. You'll just have to 'fess up and see what he says."

"How much," I asked slowly, dreading the answer, "is an angel's skull worth, exactly?"

When it told me, I puked all over my shoes.

By the time I'd showered and tidied myself up a bit, put some fresh clothes on and swept up the broken whisky bottle it was almost noon. My head still felt like there was a marching band inside it but at least I seemed to have finally stopped being sick. I came out of the bathroom and glared at the closed door to my workroom. I'd had to shut the Burned Man in so I couldn't hear it sniggering any more. I picked up the phone and called Wormwood's office.

"Hi Selina," I said when she answered, trying for the charm offensive. "Don Drake here, how's it going?"

"Mr Drake," she said. "I trust you are recovered from last night."

"Ah you know, bit of a thick head but OK otherwise," I lied, and forced a laugh. "You know how it is."

"I'm afraid I really don't," she said, and I could almost hear the sour expression on her face. "Mr Wormwood is in a meeting at present. I'll inform him that you telephoned."

"Yeah, about that," I said. "I was thinking, well, it might be better if I stopped by his office and saw him in person. We've got a few things to discuss so, you know, maybe face to face might be better?"

Selina sniffed disapprovingly. I had a sinking feeling that she knew exactly what I had to say to Wormwood.

"He's a very busy man," she said, and I heard the sound of a keyboard clicking as she checked his diary. "I can squeeze you in for fifteen minutes this afternoon at four. At the club, not the City office."

"Four's good for me," I said.

"I very much doubt that," she said, and hung up.

I blinked stupidly at the phone for a moment, and put it down. So much for my charm.

I had the best part of three hours to kill before I had to start walking to the club. I couldn't face the thought of eating, and although I was tempted to have a quick drink to steady my nerves, I didn't think my stomach was up to it yet. I did fleetingly think of dropping in on Debbie, but as on-off relationships go ours had been pretty much at the "off" stage for a while now. Besides which, if she decided to surprise me and turn it back on again I didn't think I'd really be up to that either.

"Sod it," I muttered, and snagged my spare coat from the back of the bedroom door. "There's always Big Dave."

I headed out. There was a café down on the high street next to the Bangladeshi grocers. A proper café, not one of those American coffee chains that seem to think it's OK to charge you four bloody quid for a bucket of froth. I stopped to lock the door behind me, and noticed that some twat had scratched "drunken" in front of the "wanker" underneath my sign. Someone must have seen me come home last night then. *I really must do something about that sign*, I thought. *Yeah I must, but not now.*

I walked into the café to be greeted by the ever-present smell of bacon and burnt grease.

"All right, Rosie?" said Big Dave from his seat behind the counter.

"Just a coffee, Dave," I said. "Nice and strong, there's a good lad."

I sat down by the window and picked up the newspaper someone had left lying on the plastic tablecloth. "Rosie Lee" is cockney for "cup of tea", in case you didn't know, and I hate tea. I never touch the stuff. I'm strictly a coffee man, so Big Dave calls me Rosie. London humour, huh? You get used to it. In case you're wondering, Big Dave's real name is Dave, and he's a big lad. That's about the standard of the banter around here.

Big Dave brought me over a chipped but nearly clean mug of thick black coffee, and I gave him a quid. That's what a café should be like, none of this crapachino business, thank you very much. I sipped my coffee and flipped through the abandoned newspaper, killing time. I had the place to myself for the moment, but I knew it would be getting busy with the lunch crowd fairly soon. The lingering smell of bacon from the breakfast trade was bad enough, I didn't think my stomach would stand to watch people actually eat the stuff for lunch as well. I knew they would be, it was just about the only thing on the menu. I busied myself with the paper and tried not to think about it.

"'Ere Rosie," Big Dave said after twenty minutes or so. "Have a butchers at that!"

I looked where he was pointing, out of the window and across the road.

"Bloody hell," I said.

She was drop-dead gorgeous, there's just no other way I can describe her. I mean proper, full on, words-fail-me gorgeous. She was tall and blonde, wrapped in a tight black leather coat, and her gleaming hair was tied back in a long braid that fell forward over one shoulder to rest against a truly perfect curve. She was standing outside the newsagents opposite the café and staring intently across the road at the grocers.

"What I wouldn't give for a piece of that," Big Dave muttered to himself, but I wasn't really listening to him.

I was staring at *her*. Now then, it's confession time – for all my bullshit, I'm not actually that great at magic. I mean yeah, I can do some divination and banishings and a few other bits and pieces, but all the really big stuff I do comes from the Burned Man, not from me. Sorry, but that's just how it is. One thing I *can* do by myself though is see glamours and auras, and two things about that stunning blonde really hit me. The first was her aura. Now, auras are largely pointless things unless you're a magician and you know what to do with them – everyone's got one, but they're usually just a dull sort of blue fuzz around people. Most of the time I don't even bother looking for them. Hers on the other hand was a brilliant white, and so bright I could see it quite clearly from where I was sitting without even really trying. That, to put it mildly, was bloody odd. The other thing I noticed was that there was absolutely no glamour on her at all – she really was that lovely.

"Do you know her, Rosie?" Big Dave asked.

"What? Nah, never saw her in my life," I said. *More's the pity.* I have to admit I'm a sucker for blondes.

"Well she's looking at your gaff," he said.

He was right, I realized. It wasn't the grocers she was staring at, it was the window above it. That was my office window. I was just working out what to make of that when a doubledecker bus drove past outside, and when it was gone, so was she.

"You snooze you lose," Big Dave said, helpfully. "You should have got out there and given her the chat while you had the chance, shouldn't you?"

"Mmmmm," I said. I wasn't sure about that, to be honest. Lovely she might have been, but something about that white aura was bothering the hell out of me.

I realized my coffee was nearly cold, and anyway time was ticking now. On the plus side though, my hangover seemed to have cleared up while I had been sitting there.

"Do us a bacon roll to go, mate," I said.

Big Dave busied himself for a couple of minutes and I left munching out of a paper bag full of bread and hot grease, feeling better than I had in days. Proper coffee can work miracles sometimes.

It was ten to four when I turned into the alley that led to Wormwood's club. I had been there often enough that I knew the right place to stop without having to bother looking for the glamour. I moved my hand over the exact piece of graffiti-covered brickwork and muttered the words of entry under my breath before I walked into the wall. It felt cold and sticky like a huge spider's web as I walked through it, but that was all. There was a plush little bar on the other side where the hoi polloi not actually invited up to the club itself tended to hang out at night. Right now though the main lights were on, making it look grubby and squalid. Nightspots always look crap in the daytime for some reason. I don't know why, but they do. Someone should do a study on that, get themselves a nice fat research grant.

The bar was deserted except for Wormwood's minder. He'd swapped his dinner suit for a pair of faded jeans that strained over his enormous thighs, and the largest knitted black sweater that I'd ever seen. If anything, he looked even bigger than I remembered. He was bald as a coot, and his two huge horns bulged out of his forehead. The sleeves of his sweater were pushed up over forearms that looked as thick as my legs. I nodded at him.

"Afternoon," I said. "I've got an appointment with your boss."

"You're Drake," he said. "Yeah, I had a text off Selina to say you'd be coming by." He took his mobile phone out of the pocket of his jeans and held it up to show it to me, in case I wasn't sure what he meant. He looked proud of it. "Come on up."

He led me up the staircase with its thick red carpet, and into the upstairs club. The bright lights were on up here as well, completely ruining the usual atmosphere. I took a look around, wondering how on Earth this place managed to look so classy at night. I tell you, there's a social studies PhD thesis waiting to happen on the shitness of nightclubs in the daytime. I wish I'd thought of that while I was still a student.

Something too tall and far too thin was standing behind the bar polishing glasses. Wormwood himself was sitting in an armchair near the windows, smoking and reading the *Financial Times*. He had cigarette ash on the lapel of his expensive looking black suit, and he still hadn't shaved or washed his hair. Come to that I don't think he ever did. He looked up and saw me.

"Drake," Wormwood said with a nod. "Don't mean to be rude but I ain't got long. What have you brought me?"

I cleared my throat. I could feel Big Dave's bacon roll turning over in my stomach as though it was suddenly crawling with maggots. I knew this wasn't going to go well. I'd been trying to work out what I was going to say all the way over here, but my thoughts had kept wandering back to the blonde woman. I still had absolutely no idea what to tell him. I cleared my throat again.

"Oh dear," said Wormwood, his eyes narrowing until he looked like some sort of large oily weasel. "You've brought me fuck-all, haven't you?"

"I, um," I said. "Um."

"For fuck's sake," Wormwood snapped. "Hurt him, Connie."

I don't know how something that big could possibly move that fast, but it did. The minder's massive fist went into my guts like a freight train, and then somehow I was on my hands and knees six feet away from where I'd been standing, choking for breath. My bacon roll made an explosive return to the world all over Wormwood's carpet.

"Nasty," said the minder, whose name seemed to be Connie of all things.

He wasn't kidding. I wiped snot and vomit from my mouth with the back of my hand and gagged again.

"Look, Wormwood," I gasped. "Gimme a few days and I'll find a way to…"

"No," said Wormwood, "you won't. Will he, Connie?"

"I doubt it, Mr Wormwood," said Connie.

"What you *will* do," Wormwood went on, "is exactly what I tell you to do. Do you understand me, Drake?"

I nodded, still trying to catch my breath. I didn't, not really, but that was hardly the point. One thing I did understand very clearly indeed was that I didn't want Connie to hit me again.

"Good boy," said Wormwood. "Now, we both know you ain't got a fucking chance of paying what you owe me, so you're going to work the debt off instead. That sound fair?"

Kneeling in front of him in a puddle of my own puke wasn't exactly a strong negotiating position, so I just nodded again.

"Get him up," Wormwood said.

The huge minder picked me up by the scruff of the neck, one handed, and plonked me down in the armchair opposite Wormwood. I groaned.

"Thanks, Connie," I muttered.

"It's Constantinos, actually," he said, "but don't worry about it. Connie's fine."

"Now then," said Wormwood, "I've got a situation. You're going to sort it for me."

"What sort of a situation?" I asked him.

"The sort you handle best," Wormwood said. "I need some people removing."

"People?" I repeated.

"Yeah, actual human people," he said. "I mean, if this was my own type of folk I'd sort it myself, but my boys are a bit…"

He gestured wordlessly at Connie, who was looming beside his armchair with his horns almost brushing the ceiling of the club.

"Conspicuous?" I suggested.

"Yeah, *conspicuous*. That's a good word for it," he said. "They're conspicuous, and you ain't. So you're gonna sort it for me. Summon and send something, or go shoot them in the fucking head for all I care. I don't care how you do it, but you *are* going to do it, Drake. You owe me."

"Who are we talking about, exactly?" I asked him.

Then he told me, and I started feeling ill all over again.

CHAPTER 2

"He's had you good and proper, hasn't he?" the Burned Man said. "I reckon he knew all along you weren't good for that skull."

I sighed. It was right, of course. I'd figured that much out for myself on the long, miserable trudge home from Wormwood's club. I'd never actually played cards with Wormwood himself before last night, but I went to his club often enough. He knew who I was, where I lived, who I usually played cards with and how much the stakes were, and far too much else for him to ever have thought I had any money. The only thing of value I had left was the Burned Man itself, and I knew damn well Wormwood didn't know I had that. No one did, and it was staying that way.

I mean yeah, I made money, really *good* money – when I had a job. Even in South London though, even these days, there are only so many people who might want a demon set on someone. Jobs didn't come round often, and money doesn't last forever. Let's just say I've always been better at playing Fates than I have at budgeting, and I'm shit at Fates.

No doubt about it, Wormwood had set me up to fail. I'd *thought* the little bastard was cheating last night.

"Yeah," I said. "There's not much I can do about it though, unless I want Connie rearranging my internal organs."

The Burned Man snorted. "If you welch on Wormwood, Connie will be the least of your problems."

"Yeah," I said again. "So we're going to have to do it, aren't we?"

"Looks that way," said the Burned Man. "Who is it, anyway?"

"Vincent and Danny," I said.

"Shit," it said. "That's going to be tricky. Can't he just buy them off instead?"

"Why didn't he just hire me to do the job?" I countered. "Wormwood didn't get that rich by *spending* his money."

"Fair point," it said. "Bad luck, mate."

Bad luck was an understatement. Vincent and Danny McRoth were known to every serious magician in the country, and not in a good way. They were the only people I knew of who had enough clout to even think about trying to muscle in on one of Wormwood's business interests, and recently they'd been doing a lot more than just think about it. They were based out of Edinburgh, where, if anything, the Veils are even thinner than they are in South London. It's a spooky old city is Edinburgh. The two of them had a nice little interest going in imported artefacts of power – pebbles from the shore of the Astral Sea, jewellery made of hellfire obsidian, holy relics, warpstones, various demonic body parts and fluids, all that good stuff. All the things magicians like me could use in our work. Wormwood had been cornering that market for years, and he wasn't at all pleased to suddenly find he had new business rivals on the scene.

"Their place will have wards on it a mile wide," I said. "I don't think *tricky* really covers it."

"Have faith, you miserable git," the Burned Man said. "Where there's a will there's a way, and all that. You *have* made a will, haven't you?"

"Oh piss off," I said, "this is serious."

"Yeah it is," the Burned Man agreed. "That Vincent's a nasty piece of work, we'll have to hit him fast and hard, floor him before he can get his shit together. Screamers, I think. I don't know his missus so well."

"Danny's nastier, if anything," I said. "From what I hear, she practises necromancy in her spare time. For fun."

"Oh joy," it said.

In a funny sort of way Wormwood was probably doing the world a favour by having those two bumped off, even if he *was* doing it for all the wrong reasons. I just wished he hadn't dragged me into it.

"So?" I asked it. "Any bright ideas?"

"Oh you know me, I'm full of bright ideas," it said. "You'll need to run out and get me some bits and pieces though."

"What do we need this time?"

"Two pounds of iron filings," it said, and I nodded. "Three pints of goat's blood, one vial of tincture of mercury, two live toads, and a quarter ounce of powdered manticore spines."

"Oh for fuck's sake!" I shouted at it. "Manticore spines?"

"Do you want this done properly or not?" it said. "Manticore spines, or you take your chances with something that ain't up to the job. Do you want Vicious Vincent and Danny-a-Necromancer-for-Fun living long enough to come looking for you?"

"Fine, fine," I grumbled.

"Say hi to Debbie for me," it smirked as I left the room.

Yeah, that's going to go well, I thought. Debbie, as I think I mentioned, was my sort of girlfriend. Sometimes, anyway. She was also one of the best alchemists in London, and the only one even remotely likely to let me have anything on credit. You don't need an alchemist to get hold of iron filings of course, and I had plenty of those already, a big sack of them in the bottom of my wardrobe, and goat's blood and toads are cheap. To be fair, you don't strictly need an alchemist for either of those either, but you'd be a long while waiting to catch any toads or a wild goat on Peckham High Street, know what I mean? The alternative, to head out into the bloody awful countryside with a big net or whatever the hell you'd need, didn't exactly appeal to me. The tincture of mercury wasn't going to break the bank either, but manticore spines were another matter. Even a quarter of an ounce was a quarter of an ounce more than I could afford right then.

I supposed I'd just have to hope the old Don Drake charm worked a bit better on Debbie than it had on Selina.

It didn't.

"You've got a bloody nerve," Debbie said, glaring at me through a haze of purple smoke. "Why should I?"

She was crushing something unidentifiable with a big stone pestle and mortar. All around her, mysterious things bubbled through what looked like several miles of strangely curved glass tubing and condensers and retorts and other things I didn't even know the names for, before dripping into a variety of flasks and beakers and bottles. There were Bunsen burners hissing away underneath some of the apparatus, and purple and green smoke escaping from various seemingly random valves and gaskets along the way. I had no idea what any of it was for, but the whole affair looked like some sort of mad chemistry teacher's wet dream. This was in her living room – the rest of the flat was much worse. I knew she kept the toads in the bathroom, for one thing, and the kitchen didn't even bear thinking about. The last time I'd seen the inside of her bedroom there had been a live goat in there.

"Old times' sake?" I suggested, hopefully.

"Get stuffed, Don," she said. "I don't know why I even let you in."

"Because..." I started, about to say something glib and cute, but the look on her face made me think better of it. I gave honesty a try instead. "Because you know I need your help."

"You should have thought of that the last time you stood me up to go and play cards, or because you were drunk, or out with some tart or whatever the hell you were doing," she muttered, putting the pestle down to fiddle with some of her glass tubes.

"I'm sorry Debs," I said. "Really. And I'm in deep shit if you don't help me."

"Tough," she said, and looked at me. "Who with this time?"

"Wormwood," I confessed.

She winced. "Ouch," she said.

"Yeah," I said, "it's pretty bad."

"Not that you pillock, I burned myself." She came out from behind her workbench and gave me a stern look. "I'll be back in a minute – don't touch anything."

She disappeared into the bathroom, sucking on a scalded finger. I sighed and looked around the room. Most of two walls were covered floor to ceiling with shelves full of hundreds, maybe thousands, of glass bottles, vials and jars, each one with a carefully handwritten label. She had pennyroyal oil and graveyard dirt for the hoodoos, holy water for people who liked that sort of thing, bloods and tinctures and ground this and powdered that and distilled the other in a bewildering array. She'd have some manticore spines somewhere, I knew she would. She certainly had a lot of pickled dead things in jars, most of them with far too many tentacles for my liking. At least I really hoped they were dead.

Debbie came back a minute or two later with a damp cloth wrapped around her hand and a slightly less pissed-off look on her face. She had a smudge of soot on one freckled cheek, I noticed now, and bits of some sort of dried plant caught in her auburn ponytail. I smiled at her, and she laughed and shook her head.

"You really are a bloody idiot, Don, you do know that don't you?" she said.

"Yeah," I admitted. Next to her I certainly was – Debbie was a hell of a lot cleverer than I'll ever be, I knew that much. She was also, bless her, a bit of a soft touch. "Come here, you've got a bit of something…"

I wiped the soot off her cheek with my thumb, and leaned forwards to kiss her. That, as it turned out, was exactly the wrong thing to do.

"No, I don't think so," she said. She stepped back, away from me. "I don't think that's going to happen, Don. Not anymore."

Ouch indeed. "Look," I said, feeling a bit awkward, "that last time... well, I wasn't with a woman, OK?"

"Just drunk and gambling then? Well that makes it all OK, I'm sure," she said, a bit snippily I thought. "No, I'm sorry, it's your life, you do what you want with it. Just, well, you just do it on your own from now on, OK?"

I sighed. Charm obviously wasn't my strong suit today either. I rubbed a hand over my face and sighed again.

"Look, Debs," I started, but she cut me off.

"You can have your bits and pieces," she said. "We're still... whatever we were all those years ago, before I was ever stupid enough to start going to bed with you. Friends, I suppose. Whatever you want to call it. I wouldn't want to see Wormwood eat you, OK?"

At least that was something we could agree on.

"Thanks Debs," I said. "I owe you one."

"You owe me thirty-four, by my count," she said.

In all honesty it was probably more than that, but it didn't seem like a good idea to say so just then. I stood there while she packaged up what I needed, feeling like some naughty schoolboy being told off in the headmistress's office. At least she let me have it all on tick.

"Here," she said at last as she thrust an old supermarket carrier bag into my hands. "It's all there."

I peeked into the top of the bag. It *was* all there as well, even the manticore spines.

"You're a sweetheart," I said.

"I'm an idiot," she muttered as she turned away. "Now go on, piss off before I change my mind."

I wanted to say something but I honestly couldn't think what, and now she had her back to me as she fiddled with her tubes and things. Her shoulders were trembling, I noticed. I chickened out and left.

It wasn't that far back to my place, but the whole time I kept the bag clutched tight in my hand and a wary eye on the people around me. There'd be no replacing this stuff if it got nicked now. The bag was wriggling horribly on account of the toads, which I supposed reduced the chances of anyone actually wanting to pinch it, but all the same. In that neighbourhood you never knew.

The Burned Man was waiting impatiently when I got back.

"Well?" it said. "Did you blag it with her?"

"Shut up," I muttered as I emptied the bag onto my workroom floor. "It's all here."

"Good ol' Debs," it sniggered.

"Shut up," I said again. "Just leave her out of it, OK?"

"Touchy," it said, and smirked. "Go on then, get us set up."

Getting us set up took most of the rest of the day. Summoning and sending is *hard*. By the time I had the circle laid out exactly right, it was dark outside. I stood back and admired my handiwork. It had taken an age to mix the iron filings with the goat's blood and mercury until the consistency was just right, but now the end result was piped perfectly onto the outline of the grand summoning circle that was inscribed on the floor. I had used the powdered manticore spines to draw the correct glyphs inside each point of the pentacle, and done what was necessary with the toads. I put the knife down and stretched my back until it cracked, and looked at the Burned Man.

"Ready?" I asked it.

I could see the hunger in its eyes.

"Ready," it said.

Of course, it was a fucking disaster.

CHAPTER 3

Sometimes you just can't get drunk enough. God only knew I was trying though.

There's this little trick I can do with probability. Not enough to win the lottery or beat Wormwood at Fates, more's the pity, but I'm good enough to tickle the hundred quid jackpot out of the fruit machine in the Rose and Crown when I need to. As long as I don't do it often enough to get Shirley suspicious, it's all good. It keeps me in beer money if nothing else. I'd drunk about half of it so far and I was still awake, which was a lot less good. I don't know if I even *could* have got drunk enough to forget the last few hours but I was determined to give it my best shot.

"Gis another round Shirl," I said.

"Really, Don?" she asked me. "You ought to be getting off home, duck."

I looked up at her from my position half slumped over the bar. Shirley was an absolute sweetheart, a proper old-fashioned East End matriarch. What she was doing in the haunted wilds of South London I never had found out, but she kept a nice pub.

"Come on Duchess, it's cold out there," I said, mustering what passed for a grin. It was a pretty piss-poor effort in all honesty, but considering that all I wanted to do was break down and cry it would have to do. "Gis another."

I waved a twenty at her and she sighed and pulled me a pint. She set a whisky chaser down beside it and smiled sadly.

"Penny for 'em," she said.

I shook my head. "Nah," I said. "Trust me, treacle, you don't want to know."

I didn't want to know, that's why I was in there in the first place. I can't tell you how much I didn't want to know what I had done that night. *Fucking disaster* didn't even come close to it. I drank off the top of the lager and upended the whisky into my pint glass. I was on a fucking mission to oblivion and no mistake. I gave the drink a swish around and drank.

You rely on that bloody thing too much, I told myself, thinking of the Burned Man and how it had looked at me, afterwards.

I remembered the very first time I had worked a proper job with it, and how it had laughed at me. Summoning and sending is complicated, and kind of misnamed. Summoning is just what it sounds like, making something appear before the circle so you can talk to it, ask it questions or make deals with it, whatever. Summoning and sending though, when you want to set something on someone, is a bit different. If you want your demon to savage someone in Paris, say, and you're in London, you don't actually call it to where you are and then wait around while it flies or swims or fucking hitchhikes to Paris. What you do is, you focus your Will on where your target is and you use your summoning circle to call up your demon and send it straight there, to where you want it to be. Obviously you can't *see* Paris or wherever it might be, so you use a scrying glass to see through your demon's eyes instead.

The beautiful part of that is you're in its head, and that means you can control it properly. I mean *really* control it if you want to, like you're wearing the thing. The ugly part of that is that you're in its head. Trust me, inside the head of the kind of demon you use for this sort of thing is not a nice place to be. Anyway, the first time we did this the Burned Man had laughed itself silly at me.

"Just let it be," it told me, "it knows its business."

"What if it gets loose?" I asked it.

The Burned Man had gestured at the grand summoning circle around me, at the carefully inscribed glyphs and all the expensive ingredients.

"What do you think all this shit is for?" it asked me. "It *can't* get loose, that's the whole fucking point. Just let it do its thing and it'll run off home again afterwards like a good little vorehound."

It was right, of course, but all the same I couldn't help staying with my demon just to make sure. The moment it attacked and I felt my mouth fill with hot human blood the whole thing suddenly lost its appeal.

The next time I gave the demon its head just before it attacked. The time after, I only rode it long enough to make sure it had got to the right place. Ever since then I had settled for just watching in the scrying glass to make sure the job got done. Tonight I hadn't even really done that, and look what had fucking happened.

"It's her fault," I said.

"Oh pet, it always is," Shirl laughed. "Who is she this time, and what did she do to you?"

"What?" I said, before I realized I had said that last bit out loud. The sound of her laugh went through my head like broken glass. No one should be laughing tonight. "Oh, nothing. Never mind. Gis another round Shirl."

"You really have had enough, my love," Shirl said. "Get off home with you now."

"Just a short, then," I said.

Shirl pulled a face but stuck a glass under the whisky optic for me anyway. *God, what a total fucking balls up.* I knocked back the whisky in one swallow. Too much to drink, and not nearly enough. *Nowhere fucking near enough.* Oblivion was still frustratingly out of reach. I prodded my empty pint glass across the bar.

"Don't be silly love," Shirl said.

"I want another beer," I said, a touch belligerently.

Now Shirl is lovely, she really is, but in her pub she's the absolute monarch, make no mistake about it. She's sixty if she's a day and she's still saucy-looking in a brassy sort of way, but one thing she does not take is crap off drunks.

"Alfie, c'mere a minute," she shouted up the stairs behind the bar. "I could do with a hand."

Alfie is Shirl's son. If there's a human version of Connie, he's it. It was time to go.

"No bother, Duchess, no bother," I said. "I'll be on me way then."

Shirl gave me a sweet smile.

"Mind how you go now, love," she said. "It's cold out there."

It was. The pub door swung shut behind me, and I swung gracefully into the hanging baskets as the freezing air hit me in the face and my balance decided it didn't want to work anymore. Drink is a bastard sometimes. I couldn't talk properly, I couldn't see straight and I certainly couldn't walk straight, but I was still remembering perfectly well – and that was the very thing I was trying to stop doing. I didn't want to remember anything at all, but I kept seeing his face.

The wards had been easy enough to get through in the end. The Burned Man knew its business, you had to give it that. Those manticore spines had bought me three perfectly formed screamers, and they went howling across Edinburgh and tore through Vincent and Danny's wards like they weren't even there. I'd still been watching the scrying glass then, out of curiosity if nothing else. Inside, the house was much what I would have expected – a magician's version of Debbie's flat. There was stuff absolutely everywhere, books and scrolls and crystals, swords and wands and skulls, and even an honest-to-god stuffed crocodile hanging from the ceiling of Vincent's study. I'm sorry, but I had to laugh when I saw that. I hadn't laughed since, that was for fucking sure.

I burped and staggered into the street, blinking tears out of my eyes. *Keep your shit together till you get home, Don,* I told myself. *You can break down in private later, where no one can see you.*

The Rose and Crown was my local, but despite what you might see on the telly there *isn't* a pub on every street corner

in London so it was still a good fifteen minute walk home.
That's if you're walking in a straight line, and I wasn't. It was
getting late now, well past eleven, and the pavements were
empty. I was only a couple of streets away from my office
when I heard her scream.

I almost kept walking. I know, I know, I'm a shitbag. It
was late and cold and I was blind drunk and I had more
than enough fucking woes of my own, and I almost kept
walking. But I didn't, you have to give me that much credit.
I stopped, listening, until she screamed again. It was coming
from my left, from an alley that ran between two long, low-
rise blocks of flats. I rubbed a hand over my wet eyes and
turned into the alley, stumbled off a wall and bumped into
a dustbin, and started to get angry. Angry was good. Angry
would burn the hurt away.

I had a sudden moment of doubt when it belatedly
crossed my mind that it might turn out to be half a dozen
skinheads hassling whoever she was, but thankfully it
wasn't. It was a night creature, as I had suspected, and
I could cope with those. By some miracle there was a
streetlight in the alley that actually worked and she had
at least had the sense to get under it. The night creature
was keeping outside the pool of dim yellow light, its scaly
clawed hands emerging from the patch of darkness it had
shrouded itself in and darting out at her in short, vicious
slashes. She was pressed back against the wall under the
light, her long red hair in a wild tangle around her face.
There were rips in her little black dress where the night
creature had been at her. Have I mentioned I'm a sucker
for redheads? And blondes? And, you know, attractive

women in general really.

"Oi!" I shouted. "Pack it in, you wanker!"

The night creature turned with a snarl, its long, alligator-like snout pushing out of its shroud of darkness to menace me. I glared at it.

"Do you know who I am, pissant?" I said.

It growled, and backed off a step. It knew, all right.

"We've got a deal," I said. "You don't bother me and I don't come and bother you, remember? Well you're fucking bothering me. Now piss off, or come the morning I'll summon and send something down your holes to eat the bastard lot of you."

What on Earth I thought I was going to do if it just went for my throat there and then I have no idea, and to be honest right then I didn't really care. Luckily, night creatures aren't very brave or very bright. I forked the sign of the evil eye at it with the outstretched fingers of my right hand and growled a few words of banishing under my breath. I gave it a hard stab of my Will to make my point. Wisps of smoke rose from inside the shadows around it and it hissed with pain. Pain was good. Pain was better than anger. I jabbed at it with my Will again, wanting to hurt it. It backed off again, whined, and turned and ran.

"Wow," the girl said in a shaky voice. "Just... wow."

"Are you all right love?" I asked her.

"Yeah," she said, and brushed her hair back with one hand. She was wearing a silver bracelet, I noticed, shaped like some sort of snake or something. "No, no not really."

She started to cry. I took a half step towards her before it occurred to me that someone who had just been almost raped and eaten by a demon probably didn't really want a cuddle from a drunk stranger. Apparently I was wrong. She threw herself into my arms, and started sobbing on my shoulder.

"What was that thing?" she whimpered.

"A night creature," I said. "They're nasty and they're bullies, but they're all cowards at heart really." *Well, that one was anyway.*

She pulled back a little and smiled at me, and suddenly she wasn't crying at all.

"It's like it was scared of you," she said. "It was amazing! Who *are* you?"

"My name's Don," I said. "I'm a magician."

That may have been the single most stupid-sounding thing I had ever said in my life, but I was drunk and it had been a fucking horrific night, and dear God she was cute. She pushed her hair back from her face again. She had very long nails, I noticed, painted a glossy dark red. Now that she was nice and close I could see that her bracelet was in the shape of an ouroboros, the snake eating its own tail that symbolizes eternity. She'd probably got it from one of those awful, naff new age shops in Covent Garden but it was pretty and I was drunk enough to think maybe it was a good omen for once. I could have really used one of those about then.

"Well Don," she said, "I'm Ally, and I could really, really use a drink about now."

"Yeah, me too," I said. "It's a bit late for the pub but my place is just round the corner. We could pick up a bottle from the late shop and, well, I dunno…"

Fuck it. Just *fuck* it, you know what I mean? Debs had dumped me anyway, and I didn't think I *could* sink any lower than I already had that night.

Turned out I was wrong.

"I do," she said, and winked at me. "I know exactly what we could do."

She did as well, and it was bloody great. It didn't have any right to be, trust me I know that, but it was all the same. I knew that if I closed my eyes I'd still see his ruined face but so long as I kept them open I could see Ally's eyes staring up into mine instead, willing and wanton. That and I was drunk as a lord from the pub and then the bottle of corner-shop vodka we'd killed between us before we moved from the sofa in my office to the bedroom. Her nails were as sharp as they were long and she seemed to get a great deal of pleasure out of tearing into my back with them. It hurt like hell but like I said, pain was good right then. My pain, the night creature's, even hers. I had to take that night out on someone and there she was, right there under me.

We went at it like fucking animals, rough and ugly. That's not my style normally but I had to do something to keep his face away. I don't think I'd ever done it quite *that* rough before but then I was feeling weird in general, more than even the horror and the shame and the truly monumental amount of booze could account for. I'm not sure I was completely in my right mind at the time, looking back on it.

Maybe I finished a bit quickly but she didn't seem that

bothered, and at least she'd had the good grace not to mention the patchwork of old, faded scars that covered my chest, or the fresh plaster that I had stuck over my latest wound. Afterwards I sagged onto the sweaty sheets beside her, out of breath and knackered, and wishing I still bothered to keep some tissues near the bed. My back was actually bleeding, so I could still hold out some hope that she had enjoyed herself too.

It *had* been a while, to be fair – there hadn't been anyone since the last time with Debbie, whatever she might think, and that was a good few months ago now. All the same, I had forgotten that sex could feel quite that good. I closed my eyes and groaned with a satisfaction I knew I didn't deserve. His face swam up out of the darkness in front of me, deep pools of black blood where his eyes had been. Fuck it, that well and truly pissed on the mood.

I sat up and wiped a hand over my face, coughing.

"Well," Ally said. "That's that then."

"That's what?"

She sat up beside me, the sheets pooling around her waist to bare her small, white breasts. Her nipples were a very dark pink, almost red.

"I ought to be off," she said. "I've got an early start in the morning."

I nodded vaguely, my head still full of booze and cum and shame. "You OK getting home?"

"Oh I'll be fine," she said. "You frightened all the monsters away, remember?"

I felt like telling her that no, I'd frightened *one* of them away and there were hundreds more where that one came from, but there was a mocking tone in her voice now that definitely hadn't been there earlier so I thought *fuck it*.

"Yeah," I said. "I did, didn't I?"

"If you say so," she said, and got out of bed. There was no mistaking her tone that time.

Was I that bad a shag, really? Damn it, I thought it had been pretty good all things considered. She kept her back turned to me as she put her clothes on. The only thing she had kept on in bed was that bracelet.

"Can I get your number?" I asked her. By that point I have to admit it was more out of habit than hope.

"No," she said.

"Oh," I said. "Oh well, fair enough."

"You don't need my number. You'll be seeing me again, Don, I promise. I'll let myself out."

I let her go on her own. I shouldn't have, what with the Burned Man in the next room, but she went out the right door and I heard her footsteps going down the stairs. I lay back on the bed and groaned. My head was starting to pound now, my dick was sticky and my back hurt like buggery. *White knights in stories never have these problems when they rescue the damsel in distress*, I thought, but then I was no one's idea of a white knight. Not by a long way I wasn't.

"Fucking hell," I groaned.

What had I been thinking? I didn't deserve a good time, not tonight of all nights. Maybe not ever again, after what had happened. I really *hadn't* been in my right mind. I let my eyes close, and saw it again.

My screamers had found Vincent in the kitchen. He'd

been cooking dinner, spaghetti bolognaise. There were three bowls out on the counter top, and if I'd still been watching properly, maybe I'd have noticed that in time for it to mean something, but I hadn't been. I had been thinking about Debbie, and arguing with the Burned Man about her, and barely watching the scrying glass at all by then. After all, as the Burned Man had told me enough times before, the demons knew their business.

They slaughtered Vincent before he even knew they were there. Danny put up more of a fight. She had to. She was in the sitting room watching telly while Vincent did their dinner. Dinner for three, I knew now. How the hell was I supposed to know they were grandparents? They were only in their early fifties after all. Danny had the boy on her lap when my screamers smashed the door to splinters. Wormwood had never mentioned a child, but then he wouldn't, would he? He didn't care.

I have to hand it to Danny. She might have been a recreational necromancer and an all round evil bitch, but she fought like a cornered bear for that child. By the time I really took in what was happening in the scrying glass one of the screamers was on fire and a second was maimed beyond saving.

"Stop them!" I had shouted at the Burned Man.

"No chance," it said. "It's too late. There's no stopping screamers once they've got their blood up."

When Danny finally went down I tried anyway. I plunged my Will through the scrying glass and into the mind of the last screamer. My world had washed red at once in a bloody haze of animal sensations, killing frenzy and madness.

Stop it you fucker! I thought at the screamer, but you can't talk to screamers. They're not rational – they're barely sentient in fact. A screamer is an insane killing machine, not something you can reason with, but I had to try. I knew it was hopeless but I had to try anyway.

You got them both, you're done, I thought, desperately trying to calm the blood-maddened beast that was even then trying to force me back out of its head. Leave it! Just leave it and go home!

I fought it for control. I fought it for that child's life. I saw the little boy cowering beside the fireplace, blubbering in terror. All the screamer saw was something else to kill. The room whirled crazily around me, tilting and lurching as the screamer sprang forwards. There was television glare and child wail and the stink of blood and shit and death.

I fought it for control, and I lost.

I felt the killing howl building in my chest and then the screamer threw me out with a shriek of fury and I stumbled back across my workroom with hot blood pouring from my nose and mouth, and that was that.

I knew right then that I was never going to do this again. Never. I collapsed to my knees and vomited horribly in a corner of the workroom while the Burned Man laughed at me.

"I should have been in control," I gagged. "I should have been watching them."

"You should have stayed and fucked Debbie, and done this tomorrow when your head was straight, but she wouldn't have you would she?" it said. "It's her fault."

I threw up some more. It *wasn't* Debbie's fault, of course

it wasn't, but that was better than it being *my* fault. He was five years old. He was five, and my screamer tore him to bloody rags.

Never again.

CHAPTER 4

I suppose I must have passed out at some point. When I woke up my eyes were crusted with dried tears and my bloody back was stuck to the sheet under me. My head was hammering like it was about to burst, and I felt sick to my stomach. I whimpered when I realized I hadn't dreamed it. Daylight streamed through the half-open curtains and made my eyes water.

"I'm sorry," I whispered, my voice hoarse from sobbing. "I'm so sorry."

I felt broken, there's no other word for it. The hangover was nothing new, although this felt like it was going to be a vintage one even for me. I shouldn't have brought that girl back with me last night, whatever her name was. Ally, I remembered. Ally who was far more fun than I deserved, even if she had seemed to like hurting me. I vaguely remembered I had probably hurt her, too. That hadn't been right, any of it. I felt… to be honest it had been so long since I last felt this way, I could hardly find the word for it. Guilty, that was it. I felt guilty. Hell, I *was* guilty.

Now look, let's be absolutely fucking honest here – I kill people for a living. Oh sure, I tell the world I'm a hieromancer, and I tell myself I'm a great magician and a mighty diabolist, master of the Burned Man and all that. What I am really, when you boil it right down to the gristle, is a hitman. I summon and send demons, and they kill people. I might not rip my targets' throats out with my own teeth, but then neither does a sniper. The Burned Man is my rifle, the demons are my bullets, and it's the same fucking thing in the end.

Me and the Burned Man, well, we've killed a lot of people together over the years. In my defence though, for what little it's worth, they were bad people. My clients, the sort of people who know that what I do even exists, well they're bad people too, by and large, and people like that tend to make enemies among their own kind. I've killed gangsters and terrorists and black magicians, for other gangsters and terrorists and black magicians. And sometimes for other people too, well-spoken gentlemen in Savile Row suits who I've always rather suspected might work for the government. Anyway, the point is I'd never killed an innocent as far as I knew, until last night.

He was five years old.

"I'm so sorry," I said again.

"So you should be."

I sat bolt upright, my heart thundering in my chest. The light was behind her, coming through the gap in the curtains and stabbing into my bloodshot eyes like blades. The crusty sheet had torn away from my back when I sat up, and I could feel myself bleeding all over again. *Damn, how bad did she cut me up exactly?* Not that I cared. It had been fucking brilliant, and that just made the guilt so much worse. I deserved to bleed for that thought alone.

For a moment I thought Ally had changed her mind and come back, but this wasn't Ally. She had swapped her tight leather coat for a cream linen jacket and white silk blouse and designer jeans, but the blonde's aura was as blindingly bright as it had been when I'd seen her across the road from Big Dave's café window the day before yesterday.

"It's you," I said, rather stupidly.

"It is me," she said. "Well spotted."

"I mean…" I stopped to rub my eyes, to get my shit together enough to *think* for a moment. "How the hell did you get into my bedroom?"

"The front door was open," she said. "I came in."

Bloody Ally must have left the door on the latch when she swanned off last night, I thought. *Oh that's just wonderful.*

"I'm not really… y'know, awake yet," I said. "Who the hell are you anyway?"

"I'm me," she said. "You just told me that."

"Yeah. Wait, I mean… for fuck's sake, what are you doing in my bedroom?"

She smiled and opened a handbag that looked like it was probably worth almost as much as I owed Wormwood. She took out a flat silver case and extracted a cigarette, then lit it with a slim gold lighter. She smoked those weird Russian cigarettes, I noticed, the black ones with the gold filters that cost a fortune and stank to high heaven.

"Smoking a cigarette," she said.

I massaged my temples with both hands and groaned. Now,

as I think I said before, this woman was absolutely bloody gorgeous. I mean seriously, captivatingly, I-can't-think-straight-for-looking-at you beautiful. I was a hell of a long way from being in any fit state to really appreciate her at that precise moment but I wasn't dead, you understand? I started to get that weird feeling again, like maybe I wasn't quite in my right mind. I probably wasn't, all things considered.

"What's your name?" I asked her.

"My name is Meselandrarasatrixiel," she said, almost singing the peculiar name. "Just call me Trixie, it's easier."

"Trixie, right," I said. "And you're a… what, exactly?"

"Breath of fresh air, I should think," she said, "after the couple of days you've had."

"What the hell do you know about that?"

She smiled and flicked ash on my bedroom carpet.

"Oh I know a lot of things, Don," she said.

I coughed. "Fresh air you're not," I said. "At least open the window if you're going to smoke those bloody things in here."

She turned and did as I asked, giving me a moment to admire her behind in those tight jeans. Like I said, I wasn't dead yet but I wasn't completely daft either. Even leaving the aura aside, no human woman had ever looked like that no matter how much surgery or Photoshop was involved. My first thought was *succubus*, but she was way too classy for that. Succubi tend towards streetwalker-chic at the best of times, and this Trixie looked more like a princess than a prostitute.

"Can I at least get dressed?" I asked her.

"You can do whatever you like, it's your flat," she said.

"Maybe some privacy?"

She laughed. "I want many things, Don, but seeing you naked isn't one of them," she said. "I'll wait in your office."

She closed the bedroom door behind her on her way out. I swung my legs out of bed and sat there for a moment, my head pounding and my tongue curled up against the roof of my mouth like some awful cross between a rancid mothball and a dead hamster. At least I didn't feel sick anymore, that was something. I worked my shoulders, trying to feel if my back was still bleeding. It seemed to have stopped again so I crawled into my dressing gown and dragged myself to the bathroom.

I felt a lot better for doing the shit, shower and shave routine, and by the time I'd got some clean clothes on I was actually feeling almost human again. That meant it was time to worry about why there was a total stranger in my flat. A drop-dead gorgeous total stranger with an impossible white aura, at that.

I wandered through to the office to find Trixie sitting on the sofa smoking another one of her posh cigarettes, her legs crossed and one of my clean cups balanced on her knee for an ashtray. I darted a look at the door to my workroom, but it was reassuringly still closed. Hopefully she hadn't felt the need to be too nosy while I was in the shower. To be fair, if she had, if she'd stumbled upon the Burned Man, I doubted she would still be there.

"Right," I said, "first things first. Coffee?"

"On your desk," she said.

I blinked. She had actually made coffee, which was great, but that meant she must have been in the kitchen. That wasn't so great. There were still the two dead toads left over from last night lying in the sink, after all.

"Oh," I said. "Thanks."

She shrugged. "Sit down Don," she said.

I sat in the chair behind my desk and pulled the coffee gratefully towards me. She'd got it dead right, black as tar and so strong it was almost burned. Perfect. She smiled at me as I sipped it.

"Now then," she said, "are you awake enough to listen to me yet?"

I nodded. "I think so," I said, wondering if she was going to mention the toads.

She didn't.

"Good," she said. "You messed up last night."

I almost choked on my coffee. "What?"

"You know very well what," she said. "Don't give me that innocent look, Don, it won't wash with me. I'm not Debbie. Not by a long way I'm not."

I feigned another coughing fit to give myself a moment to think. Not only did she know about last night but it seemed that she knew about Debbie too, and that was bad. That could be *really* bad, and it knocked all thoughts about what she was doing there in the first place clean out of my head.

"Debbie is a good woman," Trixie went on. "Ally is not. If you carry on like this, Don, you'll be seeing a lot more of Ally and a lot less of Debbie, do you understand me?"

"Seriously?" I said. "You're here to give me relationship advice? Maybe I like Ally."

Trixie stared at me. Her eyes were a truly astonishing shade of blue, like chips of frozen sapphire. I gazed into them, feeling strangely lost. Oh fuck me no, I wasn't in my right mind at all, was I?

What are you fucking doing to me, woman? I thought. I tried to muster my will and put a stop to it, but I was so hungover and emotionally battered I just couldn't seem to focus.

"Don Drake, drunken wanker, it says on your door," she said. "Don't make that true, Don."

I flushed. *Damn that sign,* I thought. *I really must do something about that.*

"Yeah, I know," I said, feeling ridiculously embarrassed. "I'll sort it."

"You do that," she said. "You do that soon, Don. You need to sort a lot of things, don't you?"

"I s'pose," I said, although now I wasn't even completely sure what we were talking about anymore.

She crushed her awful Russian cigarette out in the bottom of the cup and stood up. Her long, thick braid flicked over her shoulder as she tossed her head. She met my eyes again, and I could feel my head swimming.

"I won't be far away," she said.

She picked up her handbag and left me sitting there, dazed and bewildered but strangely not feeling at all hung over anymore. I heard her shoes clicking down the stairs, then the sound of the front door opening and shutting again behind her. I sighed and drank the rest of my coffee.

I really didn't feel right and I had no idea what all that had been about, but I remembered one thing from last night very clearly. I was absolutely never going to do that again.

CHAPTER 5

Noble thoughts don't pay the bills. I'd done Wormwood's job for him, that was something. Whatever happened now, at least that was sorted, but I had no idea what I was going to do for money from now on. Hieromancy wasn't likely to keep me alive on its own, that was for sure.

Trixie had left me with a lecture I didn't really understand, a flat that stank of Russian cigarettes, and a vague sense of uneasy arousal that I didn't know what to do with. Now I'm not too proud to have a wank, I'll admit that, but it wasn't really that sort of feeling. It reminded me a bit of being in primary school, and the first girl I ever fancied. Her name was Melanie and I had been absolutely obsessed with her, in a prepubescent sort of way. She made me feel funny but without a clue what to do about it, so I had spent a lot of time in my bedroom just sort of thinking about her, and feeling funny. Trixie had left me feeling a bit like that, if I'm honest about it. I sprawled on the sofa in my office with a fresh cup of coffee, and thought about Trixie, and felt ten years old all over again. At least my back had stopped hurting, that was something.

I spent several days doing that, just sort of thinking about Trixie and not doing much of anything else. When I got hungry I'd wander down to Big Dave's and eat something bacon-based, when I ran out of coffee I'd nip over the road to the shop and restock. Other than, I didn't really do a whole hell of a lot. I tell you, I really wasn't myself. I was *so* not myself, in fact, that I didn't even seem to be able to muster the enthusiasm to wonder why not.

Needless to say, I ran out of money very quickly. I was sitting on the sofa in my office, looking at my last tenner and trying to decide if it would be better spent on food or coffee, and whether it was too soon to have another crack at the fruit machine in the Rose and Crown, when the doorbell buzzed.

The noise stirred me out of a vaguely confused miasma of thoughts about blonde braids and white auras, money and fruit machines, tight jeans and bright sapphire eyes. I got up and wandered across the room to lift the handset of the intercom from its cradle.

"Don Drake," I said.

"Don baby," said a nauseatingly familiar voice, "let me in. It's Steevie."

That snapped me out of it quick enough. I winced and pushed the button. The door buzzed, and I heard the tread of footsteps on the stairs. I had just settled behind my desk when he came in. Gold Steevie sauntered into my office like he owned the place and took the chair opposite me without waiting to be asked. His minder stayed by the door, looming in a bulky leather jacket. Compared to Connie he looked like nothing special really, but I knew damn well he'd have a shooter tucked away in that coat somewhere.

Steevie crossed his legs and straightened the crease in the trousers of his thousand pound suit, the cuff of his shirt sliding back over the chunkiest gold bracelet I'd ever seen. There was a huge Rolex on his other wrist, solid eighteen carat and studded with real diamonds or I'm a monkey's uncle. No fakes for Gold Steevie, not if you knew what was good for you.

"Don baby, it's good to see you," he said.

Steevie was in his early forties, and wore his receding hair slicked straight back with enough gel to flatten a forest. His suit was dark grey silk, his shirt a pale shade of pink and open at the throat to flash a heavy gold crucifix on a chain almost as thick as his bracelet. When he smiled at me his teeth were the artificial white of television celebrities, and his every finger glittered with sovereigns and diamond signets.

"How's it going, Steevie?" I asked him.

He grinned again, shrugged expansively, and straightened his crease again. "Business, you know how it is," he said. "Ups and downs."

I nodded. I knew exactly how Steevie's business was. In the shit with the Albanian mob was how it was, since he'd lost control of the docks in a brief but bloody turf war a couple of months ago. Not that he'd ever admit that to the likes of me, of course. I was just the hired help to Steevie, not someone you had to tell the truth to. That was why I had always made it *my* business to keep up with how my regular clients were getting on. I'm a great believer in not backing the losing side, by and large, and I don't like to let these pricks pull the wool over my eyes. I wouldn't have survived long in my line of work otherwise.

"Sure," I said. "I know how it is, Steevie."

He uncrossed his legs and leaned forwards, resting his forearms on the edge of my desk.

"So, listen baby, I've got a little piece of work for you," he said. He was close enough that I could smell his expensive aftershave. "A little job, you know, what you do best."

I nodded. This wasn't going to happen, but I could hardly come straight out and tell him so. That, I knew, wouldn't be good for my health. Now luckily I've always been a bit of a showman. The punters expect it, after all. It makes them feel like they're getting a real magician for their money and not just some hired thug. Whenever Steevie or someone like him came to me with a job I always made a big show of consulting the omens, making plenty of mumbo-jumbo about whether it was auspicious to do what they wanted or not. Funnily enough, the more they were paying the more auspicious it got, by and large. Not today though.

I opened a drawer in my desk and took my cards out. They looked very old, those cards, ragged and creased and stained and a bit greasy round the edges. None of your new age shop nonsense for Don Drake, oh no. In truth those cards were all of a year old, bought after I lost my last deck somewhere one drunken night, but I'd gone to a lot of trouble to make them *look* like they'd been handed down from my wise and powerful old great granny. It's all part of the show, you understand.

"Let's see what I can do for you then," I said.

I shuffled and cut the deck, my eyes never leaving

Steevie's. He'd seen me do this enough times before to know to be patient. I cut again, palmed a card, shuffled, palmed, cut. I'm good with cards, if I do say so myself. If only Wormwood had let his customers deal the cards once in a while I'd never have got myself in this bloody situation in the first place.

"Show us the way, oh spirits of the magnificent ether," I muttered, and began to lay out the spread.

The first card was the Wheel of Fortune, reversed. Then came the Devil, then the Ten of Swords. I winced, feigning surprise. That was just about the worst spread I had managed to think up in the short amount of time I'd had to tickle the deck. I flipped the last card off the top of the deck, trusting to luck that it wasn't going to spoil things. It didn't – the cards obliged nicely and gave me my old nemesis, the Tower.

"Oh dear," I said softly.

Steevie stared down at the cards, then at the carefully arranged expression on my face.

"What?" he said.

"Steevie, this isn't good," I said. "This really isn't good."

"Bollocks," he said. "It's bullshit. I want this doing, Drake."

"I can't," I said. "Look at the cards, Steevie."

"No, you fucking look at me," he countered. "Paul's downstairs in the motor with a bag with ten grand in it. You want it or not?"

I wanted it. Of course I wanted ten grand for a few hundred quid's worth of ingredients and a day's work, who wouldn't?

I could see the boy's face, the bloody pits of his eyes staring up at me.

Steevie's driver Paul would be sitting outside the Bangladeshi grocers in Steevie's big, overly conspicuous Bentley, drawing stares the way a turd draws flies. Sitting there with ten grand in a bag. Ten grand for me, if I just said yes.

He was five years old.

"I can't," I said again. "For you Steevie, for you I can't. The cards say you'll go to Hell this time."

Steevie stared at me. Strange as it might seem, I knew the crucifix wasn't just for show. Steevie was a devout Catholic.

"You what?" he said.

"The Devil, Steevie, look for yourself," I said. "The Wheel of Fortune reversed is bad luck enough, and then the Ten of Swords and the Tower. It'll all come crashing down around you if you do this one, whoever he is. The Ten of Swords means cruelty from above, and the Devil... well, you know..."

I was bullshitting like all buggery now, obviously, but Steevie didn't know that. He tugged nervously at the cuff of his shirt and cleared his throat. I've always thought a religious gangster was a bit of a weird combination, but he was far from the only one I'd met. It made things a lot easier for me in the long run. Hell, I'd been raised Catholic myself for that matter. Look where that had got me.

"Fuck," he said. He slammed the flat of his hand down on my desk with a bang and leaned forward until his nose was almost touching mine, and bellowed in my face. "Fuck! Are you taking me for a cunt?"

"I'm sorry Steevie," I said, looking as mournful and as scared as I could. I didn't really have to fake the scared part, to be perfectly honest with you. "It's in the cards, you can see it as well as I can."

He lurched to his feet and glared at me for a moment, then his shoulders seemed to sag. "No," he said. "No, you're right. You're just looking out for me, Don, I know that."

I nodded, not quite daring to speak. Steevie might look slightly ridiculous, but I knew what he was capable of. If he'd thought for a moment that I wasn't being straight with him he'd have had no qualms at all about taking my fingers off with a pair of bolt cutters.

"I'm sorry," I said again.

Steevie shrugged, and shot a glance at his minder. "Right, well I suppose we'll just have to do it the old-fashioned way then," he said. "Cheers anyway, Don."

He reached into his jacket and for a heartstopping moment I honestly thought he was going for a gun. I felt my heart turn over in my chest as his hand came back out with his wallet in it. He peeled two fifties off his roll and tossed them on the desk in front of me.

"For your bother," he said.

It was all I could do to nod my thanks as he turned away. I didn't trust myself to speak in anything other than a whimper of fear. I hated Gold Steevie, and everyone else I knew like him. I absolutely hated them, but they were my customers. This was the other world I moved in, the world away from magic and places like Wormwood's club, and these were the sort of people I worked for. This was my life. *Was* my life, I reminded myself.

I sighed as the door closed behind Steevie and his minder, but I didn't dare move until I heard the Bentley pull away from the curb outside with a completely unnecessary squeal of tyres.

"Fucking hell," I said.

This was going to present no end of problems. Steevie had given me a few quid, out of some odd mixture of superstitious gratitude and pity I suspected, but that wouldn't happen next time. I had bluffed him once, that was something, but he wouldn't fall for it a second time unless I could rustle up an actual priest from somewhere to back me up. Funnily enough I didn't know any priests any more. There was no saying that whichever of my other customers came to me next would fall for it at all. Right then I was actually *glad* that jobs didn't come around all that often. All the same, what the bloody hell was I supposed to do? I pushed myself to my feet and went through to the workroom.

"Where the fuck have you been?" the Burned Man demanded. "I haven't seen you for days."

"Sorry," I muttered. "I've been…"

"I don't give a fuck what you've been doing," the Burned Man snarled, "I'm *hungry*. Come here you git."

I opened my shirt and knelt down in front of it, wincing as it started to feed with more than its usual ferocity. Just how many days had it been, anyway?

"I'm sorry," I said to it at last. "I've not been myself, I don't think."

It slobbered something unintelligible against my chest, a thin trickle of my blood running down the scorched ruin of its face. At last it pulled away, sated and smiling.

"Who was that cracking bint?" it asked me.

"Er," I said, feeling ridiculously embarrassed. "Which one?"

It snorted laughter hard enough to make a bubble of blood and snot pop out of its left nostril. Oh my days, but the Burned Man was revolting.

"Blondie, you pillock, the one with the weird white aura," it said. "If you're cheating on *that* you're even stupider than I thought you were."

It reached down and rubbed its tiny, burned little cock in a disgustingly suggestive way.

"Her name's Trixie," I said. "She's... Wait a minute. How the hell do you know about her?"

"Oh, she popped her head round the door one morning," it said. "About the same time you started trying to starve me to death."

I went cold all over. "She did?"

It nodded. "Yup," it said. "I offered her a bunkup but she wasn't having any of it. She just gave me this funny sort of look and shut the door again. You're a lucky little bastard, you do know that don't you?"

"No," I said slowly. "No, I don't think I am. And I don't think I want to see her again."

"Can I have her then?" the Burned Man said, but I wasn't really listening anymore.

If Trixie had been in here and seen the Burned Man, then whatever she was I could well be in a truly immense amount of shit. I turned my back on the altar and went to rummage through the old wooden chest of drawers that stood against the wall of the room, next to the door. There was an untidy pile of books and other junk on the top that I kept meaning to put away, and kept not getting around to. I rooted around in a drawer until I found the stone I was looking for, and a small artist's paintbrush as well.

Years ago people used to think a pebble with a hole in it was magic. They aren't especially, but they're nice and easy to thread on a cord or a necklace or whatever, so they make great amulets if you know what to do with them. I laid the pebble on the edge of the altar and dabbed the tip of the paintbrush in the fresh blood that was still trickling from my chest.

"Do you know–?" the Burned Man began, but I cut it off.

"Yeah," I said. "Yeah, actually I do as it happens."

I smiled grimly to myself as I used the brush to draw the necessary sigils on the pebble, muttering the word over and over again under my breath as I worked.

Fuck her, I'd had about enough of this.

It was a good job I hadn't left it any longer, as it turned out. It had just got dark that evening when she came back. I was sitting on the sofa in my office with a cup of nearly cold coffee in my hand and my new amulet lying cold and heavy against my chest on a leather thong under my shirt. She didn't ring the bell, but by then I wasn't really expecting her to.

"Hello Trixie," I said as she opened the door to my office and stepped inside.

"The door was open," she said.

"No," I said, "it wasn't."

I'd checked it not half an hour ago, for maybe the eighth time since Gold Steevie had left. I'd even set the deadlock just to be sure.

"Well," she said, and smiled at me. "No, perhaps it wasn't."

She opened her bag and took out her cigarette case.

"What do you want, Trixie?" I said.

"Nothing," she said. "Just checking in."

She lit her cigarette and blew a plume of acrid Russian smoke at the ceiling.

"Well don't," I said. "I'm a big boy, I can look after myself."

"No you can't," she said. "Are you going to invite me to sit down?"

"No," I said.

"How about a drink then?"

"No, Trixie."

"Oh dear," she sighed. "That horrible thing told you I saw it, didn't it?"

"Don't know what you're talking about," I said.

She tutted and perched on the edge of my desk. She was wearing her leather coat again, with black patent high heels. Her legs were bare, and I couldn't help wondering what exactly she had on under the coat. If anything.

Damn it, Don, stop that!

I could feel that weird, not-quite-all-there feeling trying to creep up on me again when I looked at her. I focused my Will on my amulet instead and forced myself to be strong. It was a lot, lot harder than it should have been, but whatever she was trying to do to me I managed to overpower her this time.

"I think you and I need to have a good long chat," she said.

"I don't," I said. "Go away, Trixie."

She flicked ash on the floor and gave me a long, cool look. I focused on the amulet again and gave her a subtle shove with my Will. Nothing overtly hostile like I had used on that night creature – I didn't want to provoke an open confrontation until I knew for sure what she was, and how dangerous she might be. I doubt she even consciously felt it, but it was enough to do the job. Sometimes subtlety is best. Not often, granted, but now and again.

"I'm sure you know best," she said at last. "I'll be around."

She got up and stalked out of my office without another word.

I sighed and leaned my head back against the sofa. I listened to her high heels click down the stairs, then to the very deliberate sound of the front door opening and closing behind her. Funnily enough she hadn't make a sound coming in.

The thing that really worried me was that the Burned Man obviously didn't know what she was either. I didn't always much like the Burned Man, but at least I understood it. In the same way I understood vorehounds and screamers and Wormwood and Gold Steevie and their ilk, I knew what made the Burned Man tick. I didn't understand Trixie at all, and that was starting to seriously bother me, given the sudden interest she seemed to have taken in my life. She was absolutely not human but she was obviously *something*, and I really didn't like not knowing what. I drained the cold dregs of my coffee and looked at my watch. It was only half nine. Ten minutes later I had my coat on and was halfway down the street.

Debbie opened the door in her pyjamas and a big fluffy dressing gown that had probably been pink once. I was ridiculously pleased to see her, but I could see straight away that the feeling wasn't exactly mutual.

"You've got to be taking the piss," she said.

"Debs, look…" I started, but she cut me dead.

"Don't you Debs me, you bastard," she said. "You think I haven't heard? You think *everyone* hasn't heard?"

"I–" I said.

"You *bastard!*" she shouted at me.

The flats where Debbie lived weren't in a much better area than where I lived, so some woman screaming at her bloke on the doorstep was hardly likely to draw much attention. Even so, I can't say I liked the thought of curtains twitching behind me.

"I'm so sorry," I said at last. "I didn't know. You have to believe me, I didn't know."

She glared at me, and didn't say anything. She glared at me for so long I was starting to wonder whether I ought to say something else, but just then she punched me full in the face. I was so tired and so relieved to see her and so weirded out in general that I never saw it coming. Debbie isn't a big woman but she works with her hands in noxious chemicals all day every day, and her fist was like a lump of rock. Her knuckles slammed into my nose hard enough to snap my head back and make me see stars.

"Fucksake!" I gasped, my eyes full of tears and hot blood welling out of my nose. "Debbie please, I didn't know!"

"If I thought you *had* known, I'd have thrown acid at you," she said.

She stepped back and yanked me into her flat by the lapels of my coat. The door thumped shut behind me and she thrust a tissue into my hand.

"Wipe your nose," she said. "You're making a mess."

I pressed the tissue to my face and tipped my head back, pinching the bridge of my nose until the blood stopped. It hurt like hell.

"Thanks," I muttered.

"Tell me why, Don," she said. "Tell me why the *hell* I should listen to you any more?"

I swallowed, coughed, and looked at her. She looked so fierce, so angry, and so bloody scared I didn't know whether I should hug her or hide from her. I just sighed instead.

"I've packed it in," I said.

She blinked at me. "You've packed what in, exactly?"

"Work," I said, for want of a better word for it. "The whole... you know. What I do. What I *did*, anyway."

"Oh," she said.

She sat down in her armchair with the table full of pipes and tubes and bottles behind her, and waved vaguely at the only other chair in the room. It was an old dining chair that had presumably once belonged to the table behind her, and it creaked alarmingly under my weight. I settled gratefully into it anyway.

"I had Gold Steevie round today, offering me a job," I said. "I told him no. Ten grand for a day's work and I told him no."

"Oh," she said again, and blinked. "That's the least you can do I suppose, after what happened."

I nodded. "Yeah," I said. "Yeah, I think it is. I've had... someone else round, too. This woman, Trixie. She... she *knows* things, Debs. Things she shouldn't know. I dunno who she is, but she's starting to frighten the bloody life out of me."

"Trixie?" Debbie echoed. "Stupid name. What does she

look like, this frightening Trixie?"

Gorgeous, I thought, but I knew that wouldn't be a clever thing to say. *Captivating. Otherworldly. So special I can hardly think about anything else, and that's the most frightening part.* No, that really wouldn't do either. I focused on my amulet again and forced myself to think straight.

"Blonde," I said at last. "Sort of Swedish looking. Creepy."

Debbie shrugged. "Could be anyone," she said, although I knew damn well that it really couldn't. "Anyone else?"

I knew that mentioning Ally would have been even stupider than telling her I'd spent the last however many days it had been mooning about over Trixie before I had come to my senses and done something about it.

"No," I said. "I've just been keeping my head down, to be honest."

"And not working," Debbie said.

"That's right," I said. "And not working."

She looked at me. "Don, how are you going to live?"

I leaned forward and put my head in my hands. "I have no fucking idea," I said.

CHAPTER 6

Bless her, Debbie let me stay the night. Just sitting up in her armchair, mind you, with her spare summer duvet chucked over me, but it was better than nothing. It was a hell of a lot better than going home would have been, that was for certain. I didn't *think* Trixie would come here looking for me, although I still had a nasty suspicion that she could have found me if she'd really wanted to.

When I woke up from my cold, fitful sleep, Debbie was sitting on the other chair staring at me. I winced and stretched, feeling my spine crunch unpleasantly. I'm too old to be sleeping in armchairs and that's all there is to it. Debbie was already dressed, in jeans and trainers and a big sloppy brown jumper with burn marks on the front.

"What time is it?" I asked her.

"Gone eight," she said. "There's coffee in the kitchen if you want it."

I nodded. Not so long ago she'd have brought me that coffee in bed, and then got back in with me to wish me a happy morning. I almost smiled at the thought, but in that

73

momentary little fantasy she kept turning into Trixie and that just got me scared all over again.

"Thanks," I said, hoping the rough shake in my voice just sounded like morning mouth. "Uh, can I use your bathroom?"

"You've spent enough nights here before that I don't think you have to ask to go pee," Debbie said, and I spotted the shadow of a smile on her face.

When I came back from the bathroom she'd brought my coffee through, and pinched the armchair. I sat on the rickety dining chair and sipped my drink gratefully.

"Look, thanks Debs," I said. "I mean, you didn't have to. I'd have understood if...."

"I nearly didn't," she said.

Oh. That was harsh, really. *For fuck's sake, Don, no it isn't,* I told myself. *Think yourself lucky.*

"Yeah," I said. "I'm sorry. I really, really am sorry."

"Mmmm," she said. "I've heard that somewhere before."

"That's not fair," I said. "I mean, well, maybe it is, but... oh c'mon Debs, nothing like this has ever *happened* before."

"No, I suppose not," she said. "Look, Don, I've been thinking. What I mean by that is I've been awake all night, which is your fault, but while I was awake all night I was thinking. You need to hide for a bit, don't you?"

I nodded. "Yeah," I said. "Yeah, I sort of do."

"And you're broke, aren't you?"

I still had my tenner in my pocket, and the two fifties that Gold Steevie had given me. In case you didn't know, a hundred and ten quid doesn't go very far in London these days. I nodded.

"Well," she said, "I could, you know, use a hand here.

Maybe you ought to stick around for a bit, just keep your head down and do some honest work for a change. How does that sound?"

"I'm no alchemist," I said.

"Dear God, I know that," Debbie said. "I'm not going to let you near anything that actually matters, Don. I'm sure you can grind herbs and write labels and bleed a goat though, can't you?"

I supposed I could, at that. I nodded.

"Thanks Debs," I said.

"I mean," she went on, "I can't afford to actually pay you but I'll let you sleep here, and I'll feed you and..."

"Damn," I said suddenly.

She raised an eyebrow. "I'm not a minimum wage employer you know," she said.

"No, no it's not that," I said. "Look Debs, I really appreciate it, and yeah sure I'll take you up on it, but I've just remembered something. I'll have to pop back to my office once a day, OK?"

"Are you sure that's a good idea?" she asked me.

It wasn't, but nor was forgetting to feed the Burned Man again. I think I'd only got away with it last time because it had been spending just as much time thinking about Trixie as I had. Which, now that I thought about it, was bloody odd. Oh the Burned Man could be a lecherous little bastard, that was true enough, but beyond the odd reference to "a nice bit of skirt", I'd never known it to take that much interest in any one particular woman before. There was definitely something about our Trixie that appealed to all comers.

"Can't be helped," I said. "I need to check my messages and stuff."

I'm a bit of a technophobe, as you might have gathered. My answering machine was at least twenty years old, a proper one with the little cassette tape in it. The point was I couldn't phone it and get it to read me my messages, I had to be there to listen to them. Which was pretty handy just then.

"Tell me again why you haven't got a mobile like normal people?" Debbie said.

I snorted. I hate bloody mobile phones. "I don't like being bothered by the phone when I'm at home," I said. "Why the hell would I want to be bothered by it when I'm out?"

Businessman of the year I know, but there you are.

"Well, OK," Debbie said, "but be careful."

I nodded. I'd be careful all right.

It actually went OK for a few days. I worked for Debbie during the day then nipped back to the office afterwards to give the Burned Man its feed while she was cooking our dinner. There was nothing on the answering machine, and while the Burned Man was obviously getting bored and starting to feel neglected, it wasn't anything I couldn't handle. I certainly wasn't about to tell it I wasn't in business anymore – the Burned Man loved its work far too much for it to be at all happy about that.

"Business is dead," I told it with a shrug on the fourth day. "Can't be helped. It'll pick up again, it always does."

It had grimaced at me, but nothing further came of it, and I didn't see or hear any more from Trixie. Subtlety I tell you, there's definitely a place for it now and again.

On the sixth day, I'd just finished feeding the horrible little thing when the phone rang. My heart sank, but I hurried through to the office to pick it up anyway. *Don't be Steevie, please don't be Steevie,* I thought as I reached for the handset. It wasn't Steevie. It was much worse than that.

"Don Drake," I said.

"About bloody time," said Wormwood. "Where've you been, fucking Timbuktu?"

"Um," I said, my heart starting to beat double time in my chest.

He was phoning me personally instead of getting Selina to do it, I realized, so it must be important. I remembered that Wormwood refused to talk to answering machines for some reason. He could have been calling for days for all I knew.

"I've been seeing someone," I said lamely.

Wormwood's laugh was one of the most disgusting noises I think I've ever heard, full of phlegm and malice. "So you're hip deep in cunt and I'm left wondering where the fuck you are, that's bleeding marvellous that is," he said. "Get your arse down the club, I need to talk to you."

"Um," I said again. "What, now?"

"No, a week on Tuesday, you fucking prick," Wormwood snapped. "Yes, now."

He hung up, leaving me staring stupidly at the handset. I groaned and punched Debbie's number.

"I'm, um, not going to make it back for dinner," I said.

There was an arctic pause. "Oh?" she said, at last.

"Look, I'm sorry OK," I said. "It's Wormwood. I dunno what he wants but I can't stand him up, you know that."

"You've retired," Debbie reminded me.

"I know, I know," I said. "I'll just nip over to the club and tell him that, and I'll be back before you go to bed, OK?"

"OK," Debbie sighed, and hung up.

Needless to say it wasn't that simple.

At least I still had enough money for a taxi. I got out at the end of Wormwood's alley and walked into the bar feeling no more nervous than I ever did coming here. I'd paid my debt, after all, and if he wanted another favour he was just shit out of luck, and that was all there was to it. It was only seven-ish and the bar was empty, but Connie was waiting for me at the bottom of the stairs.

"Evening Connie," I said, as nonchalantly as I could manage. "Wormwood wanted to see me."

"That's right, he did," said Connie.

The huge minder took me by the arm with a hand that went all the way around my bicep with ease. He steered me away from the stairs and through a door beside the bar that I didn't think I'd ever noticed before. There was an office on the other side of the door, and Wormwood was sitting behind a desk with a cigarette in his hand and the *Financial Times* spread out in front of him.

"Evening," he said, without looking up. "Hurt him, Connie."

"What?" I managed, before Connie belted me in the guts.

I actually felt my feet leave the ground, and the back of my head cracked painfully into the wall when I flew backwards into it. My knees collapsed under me and I sagged to the floor, retching and gasping.

"That's for missing my calls," Wormwood said in a mild voice. "And again, Connie."

This time Connie kicked me. I've had a few beatings in my time but I'd never known anything quite like that, and I'll be quite happy to never know it again. I crashed sideways into a filing cabinet this time, and lay there curled into a foetal position with both my hands clamped to my midriff. I drew an agonizing breath and wondered if anything was broken inside me.

"That's for being off cunting when I wanted you," Wormwood said. "Want another?"

I heaved in another breath and shook my head.

"No," I croaked.

"Nah, didn't think so," Wormwood said. "Get him up, Connie."

Connie yanked me to my feet and dropped me into the chair opposite Wormwood. I gagged and whimpered and tried very hard not to puke on the ornately scrolled leather top of Wormwood's desk. I had a feeling he wouldn't appreciate that very much.

"Right then, down to business," Wormwood said. "It's time to talk about your next instalment."

"Instalment?" I gaped at him. "Now look Wormwood, I did that job for you. Vincent and Danny McRoth for fucksake, that's a thirty grand job easily. An angel's skull isn't worth any more than that!"

"Two things," said Wormwood, holding up two fingers that were stained a dark, treacly brown with nicotine. "One, you fucked it up and now everyone in the business hates you on account of that kid. I'll let you off that, because I don't give a fuck. Two, and this is the important one, you're forgetting interest."

"Interest," I repeated, with a sick feeling in my stomach.

"You'll have heard of the notion I'm sure," Wormwood said. "It's like a bank loan, only I ain't no fucking bank, Drake. You've paid the interest due to date, that's all. You still owe me for that skull."

"Oh for fuck's–" I managed, before Connie's enormous arm snaked around my neck and yanked me bodily up out of the chair.

I dangled helplessly in his grip, fighting for breath as he slowly crushed my larynx in the crook of his elbow. A few more seconds of that and I'd simply be dead, no two ways about it.

"Put him down, Connie," Wormwood said.

Connie dropped me back in the chair and I heaved in a great lungful of air, not even caring that the air in the room was mostly Wormwood's recycled cigarette smoke. There were great big black patches floating in front of my eyes, and tiny points of light that made me feel faint. I breathed again, and put my head between my legs until I got myself under control.

"Little bit too much there, Connie," I heard Wormwood say.

"Sorry, Mr Wormwood," said Connie.

"Now then," Wormwood said, "pay attention, Drake."

He folded the huge salmon-pink expanse of newspaper and turned it around on the desk to show me a photograph. It was some youngish bloke in a suit, smiling smugly for the camera outside an office block. From what my watering eyes could make out of the text under the photo, he seemed to be something to do with hedge funds or some bullshit like that.

"Him?" I asked.

"Him," Wormwood agreed. "He's single, lives alone, only fucks posh whores. You won't run into any little kids on this one."

"What's he to you?" I asked.

Wormwood lurched forward over the desk towards me with a feral snarl, his rancid breath blowing hot in my face. He had far too many teeth, did Wormwood, and they were all very rotten but very sharp.

"That's my business," he hissed. "Do your fucking job."

I squirmed back into my seat to get away from him, and nodded helplessly. There really wasn't a lot else I could do. So much for remorse, and redemption's a mug's game anyway.

CHAPTER 7

I couldn't face Debbie after that. Not tonight, anyway. I'd have to go back in the morning, of course, to make nice to her and apologize again for not coming back for dinner. And to nick the stuff I'd need to do Wormwood's job, obviously. Sometimes I really am a shitbag, I know that. Honestly I do. I paid off the taxi and unlocked my door, and trudged up the stairs to my office.

Trixie was sitting in my swivel chair, her feet up on my desk and one of her awful cigarettes smouldering in her hand. She had jeans on again tonight, with high-heeled boots and a short white fur coat. I was so many shades of not in the fucking mood for her I hardly knew where to start.

"Piss off," I said, for want of anything more eloquent to say.

She laughed. "Now now, that's not very nice is it," she said. I noticed with a sudden sinking feeling that the door to my workroom was open. "I've been having a little chat with your friend in there."

I took a quick look into the workroom. The Burned Man

was still there of course, chained to the altar like it always was. Whatever Trixie might be, there was no getting it off that altar. It couldn't be done, simple as that. At least, I sincerely *hoped* it couldn't.

"Oh yeah?" I said.

"Yes," she said. "He's quite cross with you, you know."

"It's an *it*, not a *he*," I said, "and we get along just fine."

"Ah, well," she said, and tapped ash from her cigarette as she smiled at me. "You seemed to have neglected to tell him you'd retired. He's not terribly pleased about that, you know."

"I've just un-retired again," I said. "So you can bugger off now, can't you."

Trixie frowned at me. "Un-retired? I'm sorry to hear that, Don," she said, "and I'm afraid poor Debbie will be heartbroken to hear it."

Right, that was it. That was just fucking *it*. Fuck subtlety, that obviously hadn't worked for long. I glared at her, and tugged my amulet out of the open neck of my shirt. Her eyes narrowed as I lifted it up in front of her, the pebble dangling from its thin leather thong.

"Get thee gone," I said, putting my Will into the words. "Get thee gone from me and mine. I bind thee to stay away, from this moment hence."

"Oh I don't think so," she said. "You need me, Don. You need me more than you can possibly know."

"I know one thing," I said. "I know your true name. You didn't think I'd remember it did you, the state I was in, but I *never* forget a true name."

"I don't believe you," she said.

"I bind thee, Meselandrarasatrixiel," I roared at her. I yanked the amulet off my neck and held it out at arm's length in front of me, thrusting it almost into her face. I forced my Will down my arm in a hot rush and into the amulet until it quivered with power in my hand. "Get thee gone from me and mine from this moment hence!"

"Oh you swine," she said.

The sigils I had painted on the stone in my own blood flared with ruddy light as my Will flooded into them. Trixie winced like she'd just bitten into an unripe lemon.

I advanced on her, the amulet still held out in front of me.

"Go away, Meselandrarasatrixiel," I said, slowly and clearly.

"Oww," she protested. "That hurts!"

She dropped her cigarette on the floor, grabbed her handbag, and ran for the stairs. I heard the door bang shut behind her, and heaved a sigh of relief. I ground her smouldering cigarette out under the heel of my shoe before it could burn my flat down, and chanced another look into the workroom. The Burned Man was glaring savagely at me. It really, really did not look best pleased.

"Oi," it called out. "I want a little word with you."

I sighed and went in there.

"Look," I said, "I can explain."

"Explain?" it growled at me. "Explain me this, you wanker. Explain why the fuck I ever put all that time and effort into you. Explain what you're going to do to stay alive if you aren't working, and far more importantly explain how you're going to keep *me* alive. Explain to me, Drake, what the *hell* that bitch even is!"

"All right, all right," I said. "It's all crap, OK? We fucked up the last time, you know we did. I... I felt bad, afterwards. I *still* feel bad, but Wormwood's got my balls in a vice and there's nothing I can do about it. No one's retiring around here, OK?"

"And the bitch?"

"Well," I said, and pushed my hands back through my tangled hair. I needed a haircut, but then I usually did. "Well, shit, I was hoping you could tell *me* that."

"She's not human," it said at once. "Certainly not demonic. Not elemental, not fairie. Not angelic, obviously. Buggered if I know."

"*Obviously* not angelic? Why obviously? They're not extinct are they?"

I must admit if I'd had to put a bet on what she was, that was probably where I'd have put my money. But then I'm shit at gambling.

"Might as well be," the Burned Man said. "There hasn't been an angel on Earth for, oh, a good thousand years or so now. Anyway, her aura's wrong."

"Oh I dunno, it's very white and shiny," I said.

"Exactly," it said. "You've never actually seen an angel before, have you?"

"Well of course not," I said. "I'm not a thousand years old." *For all that I might feel like it, some mornings.*

"An angelic aura is sort of golden, kind of like the halos in medieval illuminations," it said. "Nothing like hers, anyway. Not at all. That whiter-than-white crap is like what you'd fake if you wanted to *look* like an angel to a particularly thick magician who's never actually seen an angel before."

"Oh," I said. "Oh well that's wonderful. So she's not an angel after all. And I suppose you haven't been thinking obsessively about her for days then, in the same way I haven't?"

"Fuck off," it muttered.

"Pardon?"

"I said fuck off," it snapped. "I don't get out much, understand? Messing with people's heads doesn't make her an angel. Look, just forget about angels. They went away. And even before they went away, they didn't have shiny white auras, or a forty a day fag habit, or an arse like that. She's not an angel, OK?"

"OK," I said, and shrugged. "So she's what?"

"This is where we came in," it said. "I don't fucking know."

"Succubus, maybe?" I said. "A particularly posh one?"

"Bollocks," it said. "Before I was bound I had more succubi than you've had runs of bad luck, and I never found one like her. Anyway, they're still demonic and she's not that."

I sighed. "Oh what the fuck does it matter?" I said. "I banished her, she's gone. Forget about her."

"Yeah," it said. "Shame though."

"What is?"

"Arse like that," it said. "It's a shame, is all."

"Oh shut up," I said. "We've got a job to do."

I explained about the mark Wormwood had given me, and the Burned Man nodded and muttered to itself for a few minutes.

"Should be easy enough," it said. "This is just some mundane business rival by the sounds of things, not a magician like Vincent and Danny were. It's no big deal in the great scheme of things."

I winced at the mention of their names, and saw the child's face all over again. *I still feel bad* had to be the understatement of the decade but the Burned Man was hardly likely to understand the concept of guilt, or offer any semblance of sympathy even if it did. I might have been used to the Burned Man, I might have understood it and even enjoyed bullshitting with it sometimes, but I never let myself forget what it really was.

"So?" I asked it. "What's the shopping list?"

"Nicking list," it corrected, "unless you want Debs putting deadly nightshade in your coffee."

I flushed with shame, but nodded. It was absolutely right, of course. There was no way I could admit to Debbie that I had just rolled over for Wormwood and gone right back into business again. I could hardly even admit it to myself if I'm honest, but there you are.

"Yeah whatever," I said. "Go on then."

It sniggered. "Iron filings, obviously, but I assume you've still got enough of them. A couple more toads, an ounce of graveyard dirt, and a pinch of powdered mandrake."

"Right," I said, nodding.

At least it wasn't anything too exotic this time. I'd spent enough time in Debbie's flat recently that I had a fair idea where she kept the graveyard dirt and the mandrake. I was confident that I could slip a couple of vials into a pocket while her back was turned. The toads were going to be the tricky part, obviously – they had to still be alive when I brought them back.

"When do you want to do it?" the Burned Man asked me.

"Soon," I said. "Wormwood hasn't got his patient head on. Tomorrow night?"

"Fine by me," it said. "Just get the stuff and we're good to go."

I nodded and wandered back into my office and glanced at the clock. It wasn't as late as I'd thought, not quite ten yet, so I picked up the phone and called Debs.

"Hi," I said when she picked up. "Look, um, did you eat yet?"

"Couldn't be bothered," she said, and the chilly tone in her voice was almost enough to make me change my mind. Almost, but not quite.

"Me either," I said. "You fancy a Ruby?"

There was a long pause, so long that I was worried she was going to say no.

"Oh go on then," she said at last. "I'll meet you at the Tandoori Spice in half an hour. You stand me up and I'll bloody poison you, Don, I swear I will."

Ruby Murray is cockney for curry, in case you didn't know, and if there was a faster way to get in Debbie's good books I hadn't found it yet. I smiled.

"I'll be there," I said.

I was as well. I was ten minutes early in fact, and I'd even changed my shirt and everything. I was making an effort, you know? I figured tomorrow's light pilfering from Debbie's flat would go a lot easier if she was stuck on the bog, to be honest. Debs loved curry, but it really didn't love her. I know, I know, I should have a word with myself sometimes, I really should. I was sitting at the bar nursing a cold bottle of Cobra when she came in.

"Hey babe," I grinned at her.

She'd dressed up too, bless her. Well, what I mean is she'd actually put a skirt on for once, but for Debbie that's the equivalent of full evening dress for anyone else.

"Mmph," she said. "Get me a red wine. A large one."

Ah, still a little on the frosty side then, I thought.

"You OK?" I asked as I paid for her drink. I still had some of the money from Gold Steevie left, but nowhere near enough to make this a big night out. She sipped her wine and looked at me over the rim of her glass.

"So what did he want?" she asked.

"Um… oh, you mean Wormwood?"

"No the sodding pope," she said. "Yes, I mean Wormwood."

"Well, you know," I said, "the usual. But like I said, I've retired and I told him so."

Debs sipped her wine again and arched an eyebrow at me.

"And how did he take that little piece of news?"

I was still having trouble standing up straight after the battering Connie had given me, and I wasn't convinced I didn't have a couple of cracked ribs at least.

"Oh, fine," I said. "You know me, I soon talked him round."

"I *do* know you, Don, that's what I'm worried about," she said, and sighed. "Are we eating then or what?"

I caught the eye of a nearby waiter and let him seat us by the window. Debbie picked up the menu and studied it with her usual indecision. *It'll be a prawn biryani*, I thought. *It's always a sodding prawn biryani; why does it take her twenty minutes to remember that every sodding time we go out to eat?* I sipped my beer, thinking of my wallet and trying to make it last, and glanced down at my own menu. I didn't really want anything. My guts still felt horrible from my little chat with Connie, and the thought of putting curry in them was making me feel a bit ill. Debbie looked up and was no doubt just about to announce that maybe she'd have the prawn biryani after all when I caught a flash of red hair out of the corner of my eye. My stomach turned over and sank like a stone all at once. *Oh no*, I thought. *Oh fates, you can't be this cruel.*

Yeah, yeah they could.

"Don baby!" she squealed. "Don, I've been looking for you *everywhere!*"

It was Ally, obviously. All of Ally, just about, spilling out of the littlest little black dress I think I'd ever seen. The look on Debbie's face could have frozen a volcano mid-eruption.

"Um," I said. "Hi. Hi Ally."

"Sweetie!" she gushed again, and leaned over to kiss me.

I half flinched, half cringed, and generally made a complete twat of myself.

"Don, aren't you going to introduce me to your charming friend," Debbie said.

My face must have been as red as Debbie's wine by then, I'm sure it must, and I wanted nothing more than to crawl under the table and hide.

"Debs, this is Ally," I said. "Ally, this is my friend Debbie."

That was exactly the wrong thing to say. I *knew* it was the wrong thing to say the moment I said it, but the moment you say something is always a moment too late. Debbie's face set like a glacier.

"Yes," she said in a strangely flat tone of voice. "I'm his friend."

Damn it, *she* had told *me* we were just friends!

"That's nice," Ally said, dismissing Debbie with barely a glance. "Look, babes, I'm *so* sorry I haven't been in touch since that night. Stuff got in the way but, hey, look, now I've found you again! This is just *so* awesome. Come and *party!*"

"Um," I said. "I'm, um…"

Something didn't feel right. I mean, she was *this* pleased to see me, really? After our previous encounter, and what we had done to each other? I was having a hard time believing that, to be perfectly honest with you.

"Don't worry about it," Debbie said. "Really, it's fine. We're just friends, after all. You go and have fun. It's fine, honestly."

I gave Debs a stricken look as Ally almost pulled me out of my chair, but she was staring down at her menu again and refusing to meet my eyes. I remembered my last night with Ally in painful detail, but suddenly all thoughts of saying no went straight out of my mind. I was getting that weird feeling again, the same feeling of not being quite in my right mind that I'd had last time I was with her.

"I've been *so* looking forward to seeing you again," Ally gushed at me. Her silver ouroboros bracelet flashed in the restaurant's lights as she waved towards the door. "Come on, let's get out of this dump and go get some drinks!"

Fucking hell but she's gorgeous, I thought.

I was vaguely aware that I might be losing my powers of reasoning, but too vaguely to really be able to do anything about it at the time.

"Where, um, where have you been hiding then?" I asked as she all but dragged me out of the restaurant and into the cold night air. "I thought you didn't want to see me again."

"Oh babes no, nothing like that," she giggled. "I want to see you again and again!"

Foggy in the head I might have been but all the same I found that a tiny bit hard to believe. Now to be fair I'm a bloke, and blokes tend to think with their dicks at the best of times, but even so I was starting to get a bit of a bad feeling about this. Something definitely didn't feel right – I mean, I'm not exactly what most women would regard as a catch. I looked back over my shoulder through the window of the restaurant. Debbie was talking to the waiter, her back turned towards the street. *Ordering her prawn biryani*, I thought with a fondness that I must admit surprised me a bit. Stood up at the last minute or not, Debs wouldn't miss out on her curry for anyone.

"So, um," I said as Ally pulled me down the pavement. "Where are you taking me then?"

"Your place," she said, and grinned at me. "Drinks and bed. Drinks *in* bed. It's party time, Don!"

God that sounded good. *I'm not thinking straight*, I told myself, but by then it was far too late.

Drinks there certainly were – well, there was booze anyway. I don't think two litres of cheap Latvian vodka from the late shop can really be dignified with the term "drinks". There was bed, too. Oh dear me yes, there was definitely that. At some point, and I can't be certain but I'm pretty sure we were well into the second bottle by then, Ally convinced me to let her tie me up. That, looking back on it, was fucking stupid of me.

You might remember what a mess she'd made of my back last time. With me stark naked and tied spread-eagled to the bed and her straddling my waist, I'll just let you imagine what she did to my chest. The worst of it was she hadn't even taken any of her clothes off yet. This wasn't exactly sex this time, at least not the way I know it. I was struggling to see where the fun in this was supposed to be, but then I've never been all that fond of the sight of my own blood. Ally certainly seemed to enjoy herself though.

"I've missed you, Don," she sighed as she ground herself back and forth on top of me, her nails gouging my chest and shoulders with each roll of her fully-dressed hips. "I'm so glad you got rid of your little friend."

"My what?" I mumbled.

Thinking about it, I'd probably drunk most of the vodka myself. Ally had kept on filling my glass up but I couldn't remember her actually drinking that much at all. I winced as she twisted my nipples between her fingers, her hips moving faster on me as I gasped in pain.

"Your friend," she said. "The mean one."

"That doesn't narrow it down," I said, trying to make a joke of it. "I've got a lot of mean friends."

She smiled. "I'm sure you have," she said.

"I'm starting to wonder if you're one of them," I said. I was starting to wonder if she was ever going to take her knickers off, actually, but that's not really the kind of thing you can say out loud on a second date.

"Now don't be like that," she said, and slapped my face. Hard.

I blinked with shock, more surprised than hurt. "Debs

didn't mind me going off with you," I said, although I knew for a fact that wasn't true. She *had* minded, for all that she didn't have any real right to. "We're just friends, she said so herself."

Ally laughed and raked her nails from my shoulders to my belly button, leaving long red welts behind them and re-opening the half-healed wound the Burned Man had left me with when I last fed it.

"That sad little thing in the restaurant?" she said. "No, not her. *She* could never keep me away from you, Don."

"Fuck me, that hurts!" I gasped.

"It's supposed to hurt," she said, "and I'm not fucking you. Not again. Once was enough, sweetie. Once is all I need."

She gave me another slap across the face that made me gasp, then grinned and hopped off me without warning, leaving me standing to attention like the last private on parade.

"Where are you going?" I demanded. "We've got unfinished business here!"

Maybe I'm slow on the uptake but I was still assuming that at *some* point we were going to have some semblance of sex. You know, like normal people. How silly of me.

"Two ticks," she said.

She bent over her handbag, giving me a view of her behind that ensured she held my full attention. She pulled something out of the bag, and kept on pulling. When she turned back to face me with six feet of rapidly uncoiling bullwhip in her hand I think the awful truth finally sank in. I have to confess I actually started to whimper. No doubt there are people who'd pay good money for this sort of thing but I assure you I'm not one of them. The fingernails had been more than kinky enough for me, ta very much.

"Oi, leave it out!" I said, trying to keep the rising panic out of my voice.

I've never gone in for stuff like this, and now suddenly the whole being tied up business was rapidly losing whatever scant appeal it might have had in the first place. Ally cracked her whip in the air over my prone and helpless body, her eyes gleaming with obvious excitement.

"You've been a bad boy, haven't you Don," she said. "A very bad boy *indeed*."

"I fucking mean it," I said, twisting against the knots that held me. "I don't want to do this, Ally. Seriously, I don't."

That was the end of the last private on parade, let me tell you. He was asleep on duty in double-quick time.

"Oh you spoilsport," Ally said. "You rotten spoilsport, I was really hoping to give that a good lick of the whip."

She flicked me with it anyway and I twisted away just in time. All the same, she laid a long red stripe down the outside of my right thigh. I howled.

"Jesus!" I shouted. "Jesus fucking Christ you bitch!"

"Potty mouth," Ally giggled, and cracked the whip again.

She was so fast I barely saw it coming, but just managed to jerk my head out of the way so that it only laid open the side of my cheek. If I hadn't moved quickly enough I seriously think she might have taken an eye out.

"I don't want to!" I yelled at her, struggling violently against the woolly winter scarves and old belts she'd used to tie me up with.

I worked my left hand free at last and flailed wildly in

the air with it, trying to keep the whip away from me. Ally giggled and snapped the length of oiled leather back into her hand.

"Oh you're no fun tonight," she giggled. "You're regretting telling your little friend to get lost now, I bet."

I was regretting all sorts of things by then, to be honest. Letting Ally tie me up was pretty much top of the list, but leaving Debs in the restaurant was running a very close second. Blokes, I told you – we think with our dicks. I fumbled lefthanded at the belt wrapped around my right wrist until it came loose, all the while watching Ally standing there laughing at me.

"What's wrong with you?" I demanded. "Why the hell can't we just sleep together like normal people."

Ally laughed. "I'm not normal people, and neither are you," she said. "Besides, I don't sleep much."

I was still untying my ankles by the time she'd finished coiling her whip back into her bag. She blew me a kiss and slipped out of the door. For some mad reason I half thought about going after her and dragging her back to bed, but I shook my head and told myself just how daft that would be. What the hell was wrong with me?

The cuts on my leg and face were really starting to hurt now. I flopped back on the sweaty sheets and groaned. It was about then that I realized I'd been so busy looking at *Ally* that I hadn't realized what I *wasn't* seeing when I looked at her. She had no aura, none at all.

Now, everything that's alive has an aura, and by something that's alive, I mean everything with any sort of conscious energy at all, demons, monsters and animals included. If it moves, if it thinks, it has an aura of some sort. The only way Ally could possibly appear *not* to have one was if she was savvy enough to know how to hide it, and therefore how to hide what she was. That meant she was either a pretty sharp witch, or something else altogether. That, now that I thought about it, might go a way towards explaining a few things. That feeling of unreality I seemed to get around her, for one.

You're regretting telling your little friend to get lost, she had said. It suddenly occurred to me that I hadn't seen Ally since the first time Trixie had visited me, and almost as soon as I banished Trixie there was Ally again. Coincidence? Maybe, but no magician worth his salt is a great believer in coincidence. I frowned. It was a worrying thought, but I soon lost track of it as the pain started to really clamour for attention over the haze of vodka and sexual frustration. Ally had torn my chest up pretty good with her nails, but that was fast fading into insignificance as the searing whip cuts on my leg and face began to burn like a mad bastard.

"Dear God," I whimpered, and forced myself up into a sitting position on the bed. "Why the hell didn't I force down a vindaloo and go home with Debs?"

I sat there waiting for the pain to subside, but it just didn't. Eventually I swallowed my pride and dragged myself in front of the Burned Man. It gawped at me for a minute, then began to laugh.

"Oh cock me silly," it snorted, "did you try to fuck a bear or something?"

"Or something," I said. "God knows what, though. Do me a favour, will you?"

"I take it this wasn't our blonde friend's doing?" it asked me.

I shook my head. Somehow I couldn't imagine Trixie really went in for sex, sexy though she might be. I just couldn't see it.

"Nah," I said. "Just a girl without an aura."

The Burned Man frowned at me. "Never a good sign," it said. "She's got something to hide, that once has, and the brains to know how to hide it. Come here then, you thick twat."

I winced and knelt down in front of it, feeling the long cut on my thigh pulling open again as I did so. I bowed my head. The Burned Man reached forwards, its chains rattling, and put a tiny blackened hand on my forehead like some awful parody of a priest giving the benediction.

"Bugger me, how much have you had to drink?" it complained. "Even your aura's ninety percent proof!"

"Just fix me," I said. "Please mate."

"Mate, he says, when he's shagging arse and I'm not," the Burned Man muttered.

I shuddered as it did its thing, feeling the long wet cuts on my thigh and face and chest slowly close up and heal over. The Burned Man wasn't just a Summoning machine, after all.

"Thanks," I said when it was done.

"You'll have bruises like you did ten rounds with a pro," it warned me, "and I'm leaving you the hangover for the morning. You earned that, you can bloody well keep it."

I nodded. I felt like shit already and I knew it was only going to get worse. The Burned Man can do some clever stuff, but only gods can create energy from nothing and it's not a god. The healing energy it used had to come from somewhere, and I'm afraid its not the charitable sort. My knees sagged and I fell forwards onto my hands, feeling utterly drained. Even my heart felt like it was beating much too slowly in my chest.

"Go to bed while you can still get there," the Burned Man said.

I nodded and crawled pathetically out of the room on my hands and knees, struggling to keep my eyelids open. By the time I dragged myself back into the bedroom my eyes were all the way closed and I was going by feel alone. I think hauling myself up off the floor and into my sweaty, bloody, crumpled bed was possibly one of the hardest things I had ever done. I fell backwards onto the pillows and passed out.

CHAPTER 8

I'd rather not dwell on the next morning. I was so pitifully hungover from all that godawful cheap vodka that it was all I could do to kneel on the bathroom floor hugging the toilet and whimpering until it was over. I finally got back on my feet and had a look at myself in the mirror over the sink. I really wasn't a pretty sight, even by my standards. The side of my face sported a yellow-edged purple bruise from temple to jaw where the Burned Man had healed Ally's whip cut, and my chest and the side of my leg were much the same. I groaned and leaned over the sink to bathe my face in cold water, wincing as my fingers touched the puffy skin of the bruise. Explaining this to Debs was going to take a truly masterful work of bullshit, I thought.

It didn't though. She just shook her head disgustedly when she opened the door to me a couple of hours later, and ushered me inside.

"I got mugged," I muttered.

"What a shame," she said. "Those mandrake roots still

need grinding, the ones you were going to do before you left yesterday."

"Right, OK," I said.

So, it's like that then. I supposed that's what I got for introducing her as *my friend*, although what the hell else I was supposed to have said I really didn't know. *My girlfriend?* Well, not according to her she wasn't, so I was buggered if I knew.

"What was your curry like?" I asked as I set to with the pestle and mortar.

"Lonely," she said.

Oh for fuck's sake!

"Look, I'm sorry OK?" I said. "I thought... well, and you did say..."

"Yes," Debs said. "I did."

I sighed and gave it up as a bad job. If she wanted to be pissed off that was fine with me. Whatever, yeah? At least she'd let me in, and conveniently it was cold enough in her flat to give me a reason to keep my coat on. I had the Burned Man's shopping list in the back of my mind, and I just needed the chance to grab what I needed and get out of there. I looked at her, leaning over one of her enormous handwritten recipe books with her beautiful auburn hair hanging in her eyes just so, and sighed again. If she just hadn't been so damn cute, if she hadn't made me feel so... I don't know. So much of a *shit* all the time, I supposed. The hell with it, it wasn't me who'd called things off.

Handily enough she already had me powdering mandrake so it was easy enough to swipe a pinch or two of that, and

I spotted the graveyard dirt on a shelf nearby in a neat little row of half-ounce vials. Two of those sneaked into my coat pocket while Debbie had her back turned for a moment. That only left one more thing I needed.

"How're the toads?" I asked after a while, breaking the chilly silence.

"What?" Debs said, giving me the sort of look you might give a puppy that had just crapped on the carpet. "How do you think they are? Warty, croaky, ugly and living in my bath, same as always."

I nodded. It was a good job the bathroom in Debbie's flat had a separate shower cubicle, that's all I can say. The bathtub hadn't been usable on account of toads for as long as I'd known her.

"Sure," I said. "Just wondering."

"Don," she said, and pushed the hair back from her eyes with an irritated sweep of her hand, "if the health of my toads is your idea of smalltalk while we work then I think I'd rather you just kept quiet, if it's all the same to you."

I flushed. "Whatever," I said.

I had to admit, now that I'd thought it through with a clear head, that there was a tiny flaw in my plan. The grand scheme had originally been to swipe what I needed from Debbie's place this morning while she was on the bog having a discussion with last night's curry. Of course, I had expected to be spending the night there at that point. As things had sadly worked out I'd turned up so late this morning that ship had already sailed. The other fundamental problem with my plan, now that I thought about it, was that the toads and the toilet were in the same room.

"Bugger," I muttered to myself.

"What?" Debbie snapped.

"Um," I said, thinking fast. "Nothing. I just, um, caught my thumb with the pestle."

"Well don't," she said. "No one wants your thumbnail in their mandrake."

"No, no, I suppose they wouldn't," I said. "I'm just going to the bathroom to give it a wash, OK?"

Debbie shrugged in a way that said she didn't give a rat's arse what I did. I slipped past her and down the short corridor that led to her bedroom, one hand stuffed in my coat pocket to stop the vials of graveyard dirt clinking together. The bathroom door was on the left, and I closed and hastily bolted it behind me. I looked into the bath, and the toads looked back at me. One of them croaked reproachfully.

"Shhhhh," I told it.

The phone was ringing when I got home. I was in a bit of a rush so I let the machine pick it up.

"You bastard!" Debbie's voice shrieked out of the speaker. "Pick up! You must be home by now, fucking pick up the fucking phone!"

I wasn't in the mood. It wasn't that long a walk home from her place, but any walk is basically too long when you've got a pair of live toads stuffed under your coat and they really don't want to be there. I finally dumped them in the sink and tossed my coat on the kitchen floor. I thought maybe I'd just burn it, later.

"You went out my fucking bathroom window, didn't you?" Debbie shouted out of my answer machine.

I pulled my soggy shirt off as well and dropped it on top of the coat. Toads aren't entirely pleasant, all things considered. I went back through to the office to take my bollocking like a man.

"I had.. to kick... the *fucking* door in!"

I had to smile despite myself. Debbie always started getting short of breath when she'd really got her yelling head on.

"You stole... my fucking... *toads!*"

Damn. I'd been holding out some sort of half-hearted hope that she wouldn't realize she was short two toads, but needless to say she had. Sooner or later she'd notice a couple of vials of graveyard dirt had walked too, not that it really mattered now. There was only one thing I could possibly want with live toads, and she knew damn well what it was.

"If I *ever* see your lying, thieving, ugly fucking face again I'll..."

I reached across the desk and hit the mute button. I didn't want to hear it any more. *That's that, then,* I thought. I sank onto the sofa and sighed. Debbie knew I was going back into business, even after what had happened last time. After everything I'd said to her, and all the promises I had made. She was never going to speak to me again and that was that.

"Damn you, Wormwood," I whispered.

"Oi," the Burned Man shouted from the workroom. "Is that toads I can hear now the screaming has stopped?"

"Yeah."

I heard it cackle. "The boy done good," it said.

"No," I said. "No, he really didn't."

I sighed again, and leaned forward to bury my head in my hands. The amulet I had made swung from its leather cord around my neck. It felt heavy as a millstone, weighed down with my guilt. For a moment I half considered taking it off and letting Trixie come back but I wasn't sure that was really the answer. I still didn't even know what she was, for one thing, and while she might have been full of advice, I hadn't understood half of it. Not only that, but while I was prepared to admit it was technically possible that she really had been keeping Ally away from me somehow, I was still far from sure that she had my best interests at heart herself. *Oh what the bloody hell am I going to do?*

"Oi," the Burned Man called again. "Are we doing this or not?"

We were doing it. It's not like I had any choice, is it? I'd burnt my last bridge with Debbie for good and all now, whether I did it or not. If I didn't I'd have Wormwood to face. And Connie, of course. Let us not forget dear, sweet Connie and his fists like cannonballs.

"Yeah, we're doing it," I said.

I got up and went to weigh out the iron filings and round up the toads. This job was nowhere near as complicated as the last one had been, and we were good to go by about six o'clock. I squatted on my heels in the circle and fixed the Burned Man with a hard stare.

"This time," I said, "there aren't going to be any screwups, OK? I'm going in with it, and I'm riding it all the way."

"You don't really want to do that, do you?" the Burned Man said.

"I want to do that a *hell* of a lot more than I want a repeat of what happened last time," I told it. "We've got one mark, that's who we've got to kill, and it's damn well going to be the *only* person we kill this time."

The Burned Man shrugged.

"Suit yourself," it said. "I don't suppose you want to use a vorehound then."

I grimaced. "Not if I can help it," I said. "I hate wearing quadrupeds, I keep getting my legs in a muddle."

"Well you can't have a screamer, not with just graveyard dirt and mandrake," it said. "I did the shopping list for a vorehound. Throw in the last of that goat's blood and I could probably rustle up a talonwraith, I suppose."

"Oh that'll be a barrel of fun," I muttered.

"For fuck's sake, it's a talonwraith or four-legged Fido, mate," the Burned Man snapped. "There are limits, you know."

"Yeah OK, OK," I said, "a talonwraith it is then."

I had to admit the goat's blood was a bit past its best by then, congealed and clotted into rancid lumps, but I did my best to work it into the mix. Fuck it, it would just have to do. I got myself set up with the scrying glass while the Burned Man did its thing.

"Ready?" it asked me after a while. "One grumpy talonwraith, on its way."

I focused my Will on the glass, gazing into it until the smooth black surface resolved into an image of an empty hallway seen through the wraith's eyes. There was a thick, plush carpet on the floor, and a few widely-spaced doors with little brass numbers on them.

Flat 702, I reminded myself.

The image in the glass moved slowly as the talonwraith took a step forwards, pulling itself out of the wall opposite the doors. I plunged my Will through the glass and into the wraith's mind before it had a chance to orientate itself.

I may have mentioned this before, but inside the mind of the kind of demon you use for this sort of thing is not a nice place to be. Doubly so, if the demon in question is a talonwraith. Now a vorehound is basically just a nasty demonic animal, and at the other end of the spectrum a screamer is something like a rabid, psychotic axe murderer hopped up on PCP. Neither of them are anything you can have a conversation with, to put it mildly. A talonwraith though, now those are different. They might not be as savage as screamers, but talonwraiths *think*.

I shuddered as I settled into the wraith's head.

You don't need to come and watch, little diabolist, it hissed in its mind. *I have my instructions.*

I'm not here to watch, I told it. *I'll be driving.*

Oh will you now?

It tried to throw me out there and then, but I'd been expecting that. I dug my Will into its horrible black little brain and squeezed. Hard.

Yes, I told it. *Yes I will.*

It called up a stream of images in our newly shared mind, scenes of horror and madness. I wrestled with it as it dragged me through its treasured memories of murder and rape and torture, concentration camps and famine and plague. I opened the dark door in my own memory and brought forth the child's face, the horror where his eyes had been, and threw it back at the wraith. Whatever atrocities it might have seen and done, they weren't anything to do with me. The child was. That was personal, and that made it so much worse than anything the wraith showed me could ever possibly be.

I'm not impressed, I snarled at it. *Now pipe down, you fucker.*

I felt a furious rush of malice and hatred, but I thought I had it under control now. The emotional charge that image carried for me had been enough to break the wraith's concentration. I lifted one of its hands into view in front of its face. Talonwraiths are invisible to the human eye, but of course now I was seeing through its own eyes and it could see itself perfectly well. It stood at least seven feet tall, and its skeletally thin hand was enormous. Flaky grey skin was stretched taut over the prominent bones, and each of its three fingers was tipped with a filthy two foot long claw. When I lowered its hands back to its sides, the tips of those terrible claws brushed the carpet underfoot.

Stop masturbating and get on with it, you pitiful sack of meat, the talonwraith sneered at me. *Your jealousy disgusts me.*

I snorted and walked it through the front door of 702. The wraith passed through the wood-veneered steel door as though it wasn't there, and stepped smoothly into a spacious entrance hall. I could hear music playing from somewhere, something classical that I didn't know. I followed the sound.

You get off on this, don't you? the wraith thought. *Have you ever summoned a succubus just to fuck her? I bet you have. You're that sort, aren't you? You're all about the control you can't get any other way.*

Shut up, I told it.

You have, haven't you? I thought so.

I told you to shut up.

I slipped through another door and the music got louder.

The room was starkly white and enormous and virtually empty, one of those minimalist places that very rich people seem to like so much. It's almost like he was saying *I don't need all this space because I don't actually like stuff, but I can afford to have it anyway so fuck you*. The far wall was all glass, commanding a magnificent seventh-floor view of the City of London. It was dark outside now, and the thousands of lights glittered like stars.

Look at the wealth he has, that you will never have, the talonwraith thought. *You want to be him so much that you have to kill him, is that the way of it? There's a name for that sort of illness, I think. You want to be him almost as much as you want to be me.*

I ignored it. The mark was sitting in a black leather and chrome armchair, staring at his multi-million pound view. There was a low glass table beside the chair, with a tumbler of whisky on it. I took a step towards him.

Next time you want a succubus, you could summon her and me together and wear me to fuck her in, have you ever thought of that? I'm sure you must have thought of doing that, you oily little pervert. Or isn't that enough? Why not wear a vorehound, that's got a cock too. Even a succubus probably wouldn't like that much. You'd prefer it that way, wouldn't you? If she really didn't like it. Raping her, wearing a hound…

Will you shut the fuck up! I snarled at it.

Why should I? You're raping me right now. It's no different. You're inside me, using me, and I never said you could. It's the same thing. Do you like that? I think you do.

I gritted teeth I couldn't feel anymore, back in my workroom, and ignored it. I drove the talonwraith forward while it continued to rant obscenities at me. I made it circle the chair, trusting in its invisibility, until I could see the mark's face. I had to be sure I had the right bloke.

It was him all right, the man from the photograph in Wormwood's paper, his eyes open and staring out of the window. I raised the wraith's hands and was about to drive those awful talons into the mark's chest when I noticed the blue tinge to his lips.

There wasn't a scratch on him but he was quite, quite dead.

I pushed myself free of the talonwraith and opened my eyes with a shudder of relief. I was glad to see the back of it, obviously, but more than that I was strangely relieved that I hadn't had to do the job after all. In a way I felt like maybe I hadn't betrayed Debbie quite so badly, this way. Yeah OK, I'd still lied to her and stolen from her, but at least I hadn't killed anyone else.

"Well?" the Burned Man said. "All done?"

"Yeah," I said. "Send it home."

"How was it?"

"About as charming as they usually are," I said. "Horrible bloody things."

"But what?"

I looked at it, and realized it could tell something was up.

"It's done," I said, "but I didn't do it. Someone beat me to him."

"You what?" it asked.

"He was dead when I got there," I said. "Blue around the lips, not breathing. Like he'd had a heart attack or something but, I dunno, I mean this bloke was only in his thirties and he looked pretty healthy to me."

"Apart from being dead, you mean?" The Burned Man snorted. "Waste of time and toads then, we needn't have bothered."

"Mmmm," I said. "It's a hell of a handy coincidence, him just deciding to die like that. I'm not a great believer in coincidence, as it goes."

"Me neither," it said. "Still, job done. Dead's dead, at the end of the day, and that's what his nibs wanted."

"There is that, I suppose," I said.

I balled my fists in the small of my back and stretched until my spine cracked satisfyingly. Fuck, that felt good. I half turned, stretching my arms out over my head to pop the stiffness out of my shoulders, and spotted something out of place.

"What's that?" I said.

"What's what?"

"That," I said, pointing.

There was something on top of the chest of drawers. I hadn't noticed it before, busy wallowing in my own misery as I had been, but now I'd relaxed a bit it had caught my eye. I walked over and picked up the small white stone from the top of the drawers. It wasn't much bigger than a kid's marble and had been tucked away behind a corner of one of the books that littered the surface. It wasn't anything to look at, just a plain little pebble, but I knew it wasn't mine.

"Did you put that there?" I asked.

The Burned Man lifted its arms and rattled its tiny chains sarcastically. "What do you think?"

"Course you didn't, sorry," I said. "No one else has been in here though, except…"

"Blondie," said the Burned Man.

I nodded. "Did she maybe sneak this onto there?"

"I haven't got a clue," it confessed. "I, you know... wasn't paying that much attention."

You were looking at her arse not her hands, I thought, but I could hardly blame it in all honesty. I sighed and held the stone up where the Burned Man could see it.

"Any idea what this is?"

It shrugged. "Could be anything," it said. "Could be a lucky charm, could be a hexstone. It could just be a fucking rock."

"Could it," I began, with a sinking feeling of growing certainty, "perhaps be a way of spying on us?"

The Burned Man's ugly little face twisted into a grimace. "I suppose it could," it said.

"In which case someone might have known exactly who we were going after tonight, mightn't someone, if they had been listening to us in here."

"They might," it admitted. "Fuck."

I opened the window and flung the stone out of it.

"That's put a stop to it, whatever it was," I said.

"What'd be the point, though?" the Burned Man asked. "I mean, even if it *was* her who left that there and you haven't just forgotten you had it, even if she *was* spying on us for whatever reason, why the hell would she want to do your job for you?"

"No idea," I said, and patted the amulet through my shirt. "With a bit of luck I won't get the chance to ask her, either."

"Shame though," the Burned Man said. "Arse like that."

I shook my head and left it to its sordid little fantasies.

I needed to check in with Wormwood, to let him know

the job was done. I hadn't bothered last time, what with everything, and anyway I had figured he would just know. That was when he'd started in with all that crap about owing him interest. I wasn't falling for that one again.

I decided to have a good hot shower to wash the filthy taint of the talonwraith out of my system then pop down to Big Dave's for a bit of dinner. I could wander over to the club later on and give Wormwood the happy news in person.

CHAPTER 9

I never got there.

I don't have a lot of luck in life but right then I was actually feeling pretty good about myself, all things considered. I sauntered up the road with a belly full of Big Dave's meat and bacon pie, my amulet riding comfortingly against my chest. My bruises were horrible but I hadn't had to kill that bloke after all, Wormwood was paid off for real this time, and Trixie couldn't get near me anymore. I was even starting to let myself think that I could probably talk Debbie back round in a week or two. Admittedly I was running out of money so fast I hadn't wanted to shell out for a taxi, but all the same things were, as far as they get for me, going relatively well. I was halfway to the club when it all went to shit in a sack.

I don't even really know how it happened. I was crossing a deserted backstreet when a white van pulled out from the forecourt of one of those grotty tyre-and-exhaust places you get all over the place round this part of town. The van stopped dead in front of me so hard I almost walked straight into the side of it.

"Oi, watch it mate!" I shouted, then something hit me very hard in the back of the head and that was all she wrote for a while.

It's all a bit confused after that. I sort of came to at one point, lying on the dirty metal floor in the back of the van with my hands tied behind my back. There was an angry looking black woman crouched beside me, wearing jeans and a red hooded top. Something silver glinted around her left wrist. The van was moving, bouncing over the pothole-ridden streets. Somewhere in the distance I could hear a siren.

"You don't get to touch her again," she said. "I don't like it when you touch her."

She drove something sharp into my shoulder, through my coat.

"Sorry," I said. "Who…"

I passed out again.

The second time I woke up I was somewhere else, and the black woman was cutting my clothes off with a Stanley knife. I was sitting in what felt like a cheap folding garden chair, my wrists tightly tied to the plastic armrests. From what I could see, we were in an underground car park of some sort. The van was standing a dozen yards away with the back doors open.

"What…" I started.

She slapped me across the face with her free hand as the knife sliced my shirt open. I felt her hand close around my amulet.

"No," said another female voice, from somewhere behind

me. "I think we'd better let him keep that."

"You don't *touch* her," the black woman hissed in my face.

I heard footsteps behind me, the sound of heavy boots on concrete, then another needle went into my arm and it all went black again.

The third time I woke up I felt horrible. I was lying on my side on the ground, with cold damp concrete against my bare skin. I was stark bollock naked except for the amulet, which was still hanging round my neck on its leather cord. My wrists were tied in front of my body with a length of thick, greasy blue nylon rope. I looked down and saw that that they had used the same stuff to lash my ankles together as well. I was cold, and my head was pounding like I had that morning's five-star hangover all over again. Whatever they'd been injecting me with obviously wasn't gentle on the comedown.

I looked around as best I could. The van was still there, although the lawn chair had been taken away. There was a car parked over there now too, a big black one. For one heartstopping moment I thought it was Gold Steevie's Bentley, that he'd rumbled me and I was about to lose some fingers, but it wasn't. This was some American job that I didn't recognize. I shivered, and coughed up bile onto the concrete.

"He's awake," said a woman's voice.

It sounded like the one I'd heard before, the one who'd told the black woman to let me keep the amulet. She walked into my field of view, the heels of her heavy motorcycle boots scuffing on the concrete. She was very tall, and looked like she might be worryingly muscular under her faded jeans and black leather bomber jacket. Her pale blonde hair was cut severely short, clippered round the sides and back like an army haircut. She looked me over like I was a side of meat, her grey eyes showing no hint of emotion.

"Well," she said, "you're nothing special are you."

It wasn't a question. I shivered in the cold again, feeling overly self-conscious about my current shrivelled state.

"I'm not exactly at my best at the moment," I admitted.

"I don't think you have a best," she said. "What do you think, Meg?"

The black woman jumped down from the back of the van and sauntered over, her white Nikes almost silent on the hard ground.

"I think," she said, "that I want to hurt him."

"Well…" the tall woman said again.

"*Can* I hurt him, Tess?"

"Yes," she said.

"Now hang on a minute," I said, only to be cut off by Meg's foot connecting with my face at high speed.

My head snapped back into the concrete and I saw stars for a moment.

"Do we have your attention now, Mr Drake?" asked Tess, looming over me with her large hands on her hips. She was wearing some sort of silver bracelet, I noticed. "Your undivided attention?"

"To be fair, you had that already," I said. "I don't get kidnapped very often."

"Pity," said Meg, and kicked me again.

Her foot slammed into my stomach this time, bringing me up sharply into a sitting position with my bound hands clasped to my guts.

"For fucksake!" I gasped. "Who the fuck even are you?"

"I'm sorry, we haven't been introduced have we?" said Tess. "I'm Tess, this is Meg."

"Yeah, I got that much," I muttered.

"Of course, you already know our sister."

She pointed towards the big black American car. The back door opened just then and a high-heeled shoe emerged on the end of a long, nylon-clad leg. The leg was followed by a flash of short black skirt, which was followed by Ally.

"Oh shit," I said.

"Shut up," Meg snapped, and kicked me once again.

Ally stalked towards me, her high heels clicking on the concrete.

"Don, sweetie," she said. "How did you enjoy last night?"

"I didn't," I snapped. "You know fucking well I didn't, you mad bitch. I don't know why the bloody hell I left Debbie to go off with you."

"Ah, well to be fair you didn't have a lot of choice, sweetie," she said. She wound a lock of her red hair around her little finger and smiled at me. "Not a lot of choice at all."

I'd been right then – she *had* been doing something to my head. I was fucking sure she had.

"Don't look at her like that," Meg snarled. "Don't *look* at her!"

She stamped on my left knee, and I howled.

"Oh don't be such a baby," Ally said. "From the look of you today, I'd say you heal suspiciously quickly."

"I can hurt him faster than *anything* can heal," Tess assured her.

"Why do you want to hurt me at all?" I protested.

"Why darling, it's what we do," Ally said. "My sister Meg gets very jealous when I've been with a man, I'm afraid, and Tess, well… Tess just enjoys hurting people like you."

"People like me how?" I said.

"Oh come on sweetie, don't play innocent with me," Ally said. "I know what you did. We *all* know what you did."

"That little boy," said Tess.

"That poor child," said Meg.

"That was an accident," I protested, wondering how in the world they could *possibly* know about that. "I'm sorry!"

"He's sorry," Tess said in a low, flat voice.

Ally pouted. "He was so sorry he got blind drunk, took me home and fucked me," she said. "That's how sorry he was. Going to bed with me was a bad idea, I'm afraid. Once I've had you, sweetie, I've *got* you. I'm in your head and you're mine now, whenever I want you. You didn't have any choice but to come with me last night and you know it. I *own* you now."

"You set me up from the start, didn't you?" I said. "That night creature attacking you, everything. It was all a fit-up, wasn't it?"

"Oh yes," said Ally. "Dear me, did you only just work that out? Are you so used to total strangers leaping into your bed that you didn't stop to think that perhaps it was a *teensy* little bit unlikely?"

I had to admit she had a point there. I mean I had wondered, but whatever spell she had put me under had left me too foggy to really join the dots until now.

"Well…" I started.

Tess grabbed my hair with one hand and yanked my head up, and slammed the inside of her other forearm into my throat. I choked and gagged, and Meg landed a solid kick to my guts.

"You're no fun tonight, sweetie," Ally said. "I liked you better when you put up a bit of a fight."

"I tied your hands in front of you for a reason," Tess said. "You're supposed to at least *try* to defend yourself."

"It's more fun that way," Meg said. "You try, and we show you that you can't."

"Like this," said Tess, and booted me in the face.

Pain and brilliant white light exploded in front of my eyes. I rolled helplessly across the concrete, skinning my elbows and knees in a largely pathetic attempt to get away from them. Tess had a point of course, but with my ankles tied how they were I was stuck on my knees at best. I struggled up into a kneeling position and raised my bound hands in front of me, and just about managed to fend off the next kick Meg sent towards my face.

"That's the idea," Tess said encouragingly. "That's much better."

"Yes, much better," said Meg, and deftly hooked a roundhouse kick around my guard and into the side of my head.

I crashed sideways into the concrete, seeing stars all over again. This was bad, I knew it was. The two of them were knocking lumps out of me and showing no sign of stopping, but I'd been beaten up enough times before for that not to be the end of the world. I hate to admit it but it was Ally I was really scared of. She was somewhere behind me where

I couldn't see her, and I was getting increasingly worried about what she might be doing back there. Those fears were all too soon justified when her bullwhip cracked violently over my head.

"Oh, fuck me," I whimpered.

"Oh no, sweetie, I don't think so," she said. "Not again. You're really not that good."

The whip lashed down my back in a searing flash of pain. I shrieked. I know, I'm not proud of it, but for fuck's sake have *you* ever been bullwhipped? No, I didn't think so. The force of the blow threw me to my face on the concrete, and it was all I could do to roll desperately sideways before she struck again. The whip cracked against the concrete where I had been sprawled, and I heard Tess laugh.

"There," she said, "he's starting to get the hang of it now."

I whimpered and spat, feeling hot blood trickling down my back. I struggled onto my knees, my bound hands held defensively in front of me as they started to circle. I was trying to keep all three of them in sight at once but it was hopeless. Ally with her whip was the most terrifying, but every time I swivelled on my torn and bleeding knees to keep my eyes on her, one of the others would blindside me with a kick or a punch. Meg's feet were quicker, I soon decided, but Tess punched like a professional boxer.

Bruised and bleeding, I sobbed as Meg knocked me off my knees yet again with a kick I never even saw. I fell heavily onto my side and Ally's whip flicked over my head, then lashed down to open a long red gash across my left shoulder.

"Please!" I screamed.

"Please, he says," Tess said. "Please don't hurt me. Please

don't kill any more children. Please, Don, please."

"Please *us*," Meg snarled.

"Please *me*," Ally chuckled.

The whip hit me again, and I screamed until my throat was raw.

"I'm bored. I'm going to get my knives out of the van," Tess said. "Back in a tick."

"No!" I sobbed. "No knives!"

"She's good with those knives," Meg assured me. "Really good. Have you ever seen one of your own bones?"

She yanked me up by the hair and kicked me in the kidneys so hard I actually pissed myself a bit.

"You dirty boy," Ally laughed, and cracked her whip so close to my head that she sliced my right ear open.

I threw myself sideways as hard as I could, blood from my torn ear streaming in the air like a ragged red banner as the whip lashed after me again. I don't know if it was the pain or the humiliation or the sheer fucking terror that made me do it, but right then I was desperate enough to clutch at any straw I could think of, however unlikely it might seem. I reached up to my throat with my bound hands and yanked the amulet off over my head. I grunted as I hurled it as far away from myself as I could. I heard it bounce off the concrete and skitter away into the distance. It was no wonder Tess hadn't wanted to take it off me, all things considered.

"Meselandrarasatrixiel, I undo thy bindings," I screamed. "Trixie, *help!*"

"You worthless little fucker," Tess snarled, jumping down from the back of the van with a glittering blade in each hand. "She won't come for you."

But she did. Mother of all that's merciful, she came. I didn't know how or why or from where, but right then I couldn't have cared less. All I knew was I could suddenly smell Russian tobacco. I dragged myself up onto my knees and gaped.

Trixie stalked out of the shadows on glossy black low-heeled boots, her long leather coat open over jeans and a tight brown jumper and the glow of her unnatural white aura. She had one of her black cigarettes in one hand, and a sword in the other.

"Now we're talking," she said.

"You just wait a minute," Ally started.

Trixie smiled. "I don't think so." She took a drag on her cigarette and dropped it to the concrete. Ally, Meg and Tess stared at her as though they had forgotten me altogether. Trixie ground the cigarette out under her foot and took a two-handed grip on her sword. The long silver blade burst into roaring flame. "Come and dance."

Tess sprang like a leopard, her knives flashing in the air. Trixie sidestepped and brought her burning blade up and around almost too fast to follow, leaving a glowing afterimage of fire in the air behind it. Tess howled and spun away, both her knives gone and smouldering blackened cuts across her arms and eyes. Meg charged in after her as Ally cracked her whip savagely at Trixie's face.

Trixie's sword struck again and sliced cleanly through Ally's whip. Meg was in midair by then with a flying kick hurtling towards Trixie's head. Somehow Trixie twisted away at the last instant, the movement so lithe and graceful she appeared almost boneless. She spun her sword into a reverse grip and drove the point between Meg's shoulderblades.

Meg howled like a banshee and disintegrated. Her whole body crumbled to charred and broken pieces as Trixie's burning blade exploded out of her chest. Trixie turned on one heel and brought the sword back up into a guard position in front of her, her eyes flashing arctic blue in the gloom. Tess was crawling helplessly on her hands and knees, burned and blinded.

Ally stood with her hands on her hips and faced Trixie down. She had discarded the end of the severed whip, but there was no hint of fear on her face. I had a nasty feeling that she was by far the most dangerous of the three.

I really do need to be more careful who I go out with in future, I thought.

"I never liked you," Ally said. "You do know that, don't you?"

Trixie snorted laughter. "You're not supposed to *like* me, dear. This is what I'm for."

"Fuck what you're for," Ally snapped. "I'm not having it. He's ours."

She held her hands up in front of her face, and those long red nails that I was so intimately acquainted with began to grow. Ally grinned. Her nails extended, the nail varnish sloughing off as they became steel claws a good two feet long. It was uncomfortably reminiscent of the talonwraith, but so much worse. I had been to bed with her, after all.

"You're not the only one who can play with swords," Ally said as she slashed the air in front of her.

"Oh, I don't play," Trixie said.

She hadn't moved a muscle, I realized. Her flaming blade was still held perfectly upright in both hands in front of her, making her look like some medieval illumination of a knight of the Round Table or something. Now I know absolutely fuck all about sword fighting, but I've seen bare-knuckle prizefights. The blokes who jump around and punch the air and beat their chests are all well and good, but it's the coldeyed bugger who just stands there and waits to kill the other one that you want to bet on. Trixie was like that, right then.

Ally dropped into a crouch and started to circle, snarling as she whipped her claws back and forth through the air. Trixie held her sword steady, just moving her feet when she had to in order to keep Ally in front of her. I hardly dared breathe.

"You deluded bitch," Ally spat. "Do you really think you can make good now?"

Trixie ignored her. Her sword didn't move.

"It's too late by far," Ally snarled.

She struck high with her right hand, claws slicing towards Trixie's head. Trixie turned her wrists and her sword knocked Ally's talons away, the hilt moving maybe three inches in total from its position in front of her sternum. Ally hissed and took a step backwards, and I realized I had the privilege of watching a master swordswoman at work.

"Be quiet," Trixie said.

"I won't," Ally said. "Why the fuck should I?"

Trixie said nothing, tracking Ally with her cold blue eyes.

"You're pathetic, you know that?" Ally went on.

"Ridiculous. You're not fooling anyone except yourself and maybe this idiot here, and I'm not even sure about him."

Still Trixie didn't speak, but I could see a hard line of irritation along her jaw. Something caught my eye, moving. I glanced quickly sideways and saw Tess crawling towards one of her knives.

"Tess is still alive!" I yelled.

Trixie's attention flickered for a split second, and Ally sprang at her with both hands extended. The flaming sword cut high then low as Trixie stepped back and pivoted on her right heel, slashing through the claws then turning into Ally's leap and sweeping the blade across her exposed side in a long downwards cut. Ally screamed and rolled, slamming into the side of the van, her torso opened and on fire. Trixie kept moving, her other foot stepping out behind her, turning the move into a graceful figure of eight with her sword now extended at waist height. It took Tess in the side of the neck as she was rising with her knife in hand. Her head spun away into the darkness, trailing char and ashes. Trixie came back to her guard position with her blazing sword held upright before her, facing Ally once more. The whole sequence of movement had taken perhaps half a second.

"Fucking hell!" I gasped.

"Shhhhh now," Trixie said.

I watched in horror as Ally slowly got up. The whole left side of her body was sliced open, but instead of blood, slow drops of molten gold flame dripped from the hideous wound. The claws on her left hand had been sheared off by Trixie's burning sword, leaving twisted stumps of semi-molten metal. She raised the blades of her right hand in front of her face in a form of salute, and bowed from the waist.

"Next time, bitch," she said.

CHAPTER 10

I have no idea what happened after that.

The next thing I knew I was waking up in my own bed, somehow still alive. My wounds had closed and my bruises healed, and from what I could see of myself when I peeked under the sheets, I had no more than some faint white scars to show for any of it. If the Burned Man had healed me that thoroughly I'd have been pretty much in a coma, I knew, but I felt fine. Well, I say that but *fine* might be stretching it a bit. I was shitscared for one thing, and my head was again full of more questions than answers. Who the hell Ally and her sadistic sisters really were, for one thing. And then there was Trixie. The whole question of Trixie was another thing altogether.

I have to confess, I had pretty much already admitted defeat when I called her. I hadn't been remotely sure that she would come at all, or whether she would even be on my side if she did. As it turned out she had been, but I was left with even more questions about who and what the hell she was. Magic knights with burning swords don't cross your path every day, after all, and that was without all her other various weird quirks.

"Well that was fun," I muttered as I dragged myself out of bed.

According to my bedside alarm it was ten o'clock in the morning. I made myself take a shower, then slipped on a dressing gown and went to speak to the Burned Man.

It listened quietly while I told it the story, I suppose I have to give it that much credit. It waited until I'd finished until it started to all but cry with laughter.

"Ally, Meg and Tess? Are you fucking kidding me?" it snorted. "Just how stupid are you?"

I sighed. I knew that look it had on its face, like I was some schoolboy who was the only one in the class who hadn't read the homework before the test.

"Enlighten me," I said through gritted teeth.

"I believe it was Virgil who first recorded their names," it said. "Aleto the Unresting, Megaera the Jealous and Tisiphone the Avenger. The three Furies. Ally, Meg and Tess. Ring any bells, you thick twat?"

I stared at it. The *Furies?* Seriously?

"You're having me on," I said.

It shrugged. "It's no skin off my cock if you believe me or not," it said. "Can you perhaps think of anything you might have done recently to bring the Furies down on you?"

I saw his face again, and grimaced. *That little boy. That poor child.*

"Shit," I said.

"Shit, you say," said the Burned Man, "but that's not the half of it, is it?"

"Isn't it?"

"At least the Furies won't kill you," it said. "They never do. Oh sure, they'll torment you relentlessly and persecute you until they drive you to madness and suicide, but they never actually kill a victim themselves."

"That's a huge fucking consolation," I said.

"Well cling to it then, and look at what you could have won," the Burned Man said, "because you've probably made it a shitload worse now, haven't you?"

"Have I?"

"You un-bound Blondie," it said. "You begged her for help, and what's even worse than that is she actually came and helped you. And we still don't even know what the *fuck* she is!"

"She saved me from those three bitches," I said. "That'll do for me."

"Oh will it now?" the Burned Man scoffed. "You don't think there's even the tiniest chance she might want something in return?"

"Oh," I said. I coughed. "I, um, I suppose she might. What, though?"

"How the fuck do I know?" it snapped at me. "But listen, she comes to you out of the blue for no apparent reason, she sees me but doesn't run a mile, she puts up with being banished, accepts being un-banished again when you feel like it because you need her help, she turns out to be hard enough to get rid of the Furies for you and then heals you of a kicking that I'd have had to put you under for a week to sort out... Whatever she wants, it's not going to be to borrow a fucking fiver is it, you understand me?"

I groaned, and put my head in my hands. "I was desperate," I said. "I wasn't thinking straight. I mean, seriously, what the hell else could I have done?"

"Been a man?" it suggested. "Put up with it? Had enough of a fucking clue to realize who they were, and enough education to know that they weren't going to kill you? I've invested a *lot* of time in you, Drake, and right now I'm seriously starting to wonder why." "Oh shut up," I snapped at it. "I was hurt and scared, OK? You can't expect me to remember my Greek myths when I'm being bullwhipped, for pity's sake."

"I expect a fucking lot more than I'm getting at the moment, I know that much," the Burned Man grumbled. "Come here and feed me if nothing else, you useless cunt."

I sighed and knelt in front of it, opening my dressing gown to bare my chest. It sank its teeth savagely into the meat beside my left nipple and started to suckle. I winced. I ought to be used to it by now, I knew I should, but it still hurt like hell.

"You know your problem, Drake?" it asked me when it had drunk its fill.

"No, but I dare say you're going to tell me," I said.

"You've got no ambition, you know that? No vision."

"Oh yeah?"

"Yeah. For fuck's sake, I put the power of Hell at your fingertips and what do you do with it? You rent it out to cheap scum like Gold Steevie."

"He pays well," I said.

He *paid* well, anyway. I didn't do that anymore, whatever the Burned Man might think. *I was ready to do it for Wormwood though*, a little voice said in the back of my head. *What's the real difference at the end of the day?*

"He's pathetic," the Burned Man snapped. "A nasty, cheap little local gangster is all he is. You could *own* him, Drake, if you put your mind to it. Him and all his ridiculous little friends and enemies."

"Jesus, are you mental?" I said. "They've got *guns*. Not to mention blowtorches and bolt cutters and who-the-fuck-knows-what-else that they like to use on people. I'm not getting on the wrong side of them."

"Pitiful," it said. "You're just pitiful, you really are. Guns? You've got *demons!* Queer Steevie, that other twat – the Russian one – that greasy Albanian cunt, fuck the lot of them. If you only put your mind to it you could *own* London, don't you realize that?"

"I'm not a gangster," I said. "I don't want that."

No, I'm not a gangster, I thought. *I'm a hired killer, because that's such a whole lot better. What's the bloody difference?*

I knew I was right though, I *didn't* want that. I hated Steevie and the Russian and all of them, but I worked for them just the same. Sure there were the other gents too, the ones I'd always suspected were something to do with the government, but they didn't come around that often. Anyway, I was hardly likely to get one of them to admit who they were, or to land myself a regular job with GCHQ or MI6 whoever the hell they were. So what *did* I want? Me and Debbie all cosy in a little cottage in the country somewhere with roses around the door? It was a bit late for that, if so.

The Burned Man looked at me like I was something it had just stepped in.

"The time's coming, Drake, when I'm going to lose patience with you," it said.

I met its stare, but inside I started to feel cold. As I think I said, on my own I'm really not that great at magic. The Burned Man was pretty much all I had.

"Don't be like that," I said. "We'll sort it out, we always do."

"Mmmm," it said. "Don't we, though. We sort it out one minor emergency to another, but nothing ever moves forward with you, does it? We're still here in this shitty little flat in shitty South London, working for the sort of arsewipes who ought to be kissing your handmade shoes in Monte Carlo by now. You are, on balance, probably the shittiest waste of space I've ever belonged to."

"Oh do fucking tell," I shouted at it. "I suppose you ruled the world in 9,000 BC or something, so high and mighty you got yourself chained to a fucking piece of wood!"

It growled at me.

It growled, and the sound filled the room like there was a whole herd of rabid grizzly bears in there with me. It had never done that before. Now I'm sorry, I know it's only nine inches tall and chained up as well, but that growl frightened the fucking life out of me. It was the fastest way to remind me that the Burned Man was only the fetish of the demon it represented. Right then I could feel the full malice of the real thing blazing behind its tiny eyes, and honest to God I almost wet myself. *That*, if you hadn't quite got the idea yet, is what the Burned Man was really like.

"Sorry," I said. "I'm sorry, I shouldn't have said that."

"You listen to me, you dogsucking little puke," the Burned Man said. "You are going to make a fucking choice, and you are going to make it very soon. You're going to man up and make something of yourself and make me proud, or you and I are going to part company."

Now, perhaps I ought to explain something. I haven't always owned the Burned Man, obviously, and I haven't always been this much of a shit either. It doesn't take a genius to work out that maybe there's a connection there. It started liked this.

Debbie and I were at university together. She was reading chemistry and I was sort of drifting between various arts courses, not really doing a whole hell of a lot. We were dating but it wasn't anything meaningful, just the usual sort of student relationship that you take terribly seriously at the time but always know deep down isn't going to last past graduation. Anyway this was in the late Eighties, about the time the third Indiana Jones film came out, and me and my mate Jim and a handful of other academic layabouts went to the flicks and then naturally got all enthusiastic about taking an archaeology course. That's when I first met Professor Davidson, and that was when everything in my life suddenly started to get very weird.

To my intense disappointment, and that of my fellow layabouts, Professor Davidson was not Indiana Jones. He was a proper professor, right down to the tweed three-piece suit and half moon glasses. That and he was about a hundred years old, to our undergraduate eyes. Jim was the first one to drop out, two days in. Three weeks later I was the only one of our little crowd still on the course.

I don't know if it was Debbie urging me to take something

seriously and stick with it for more than half a term for once, or if it was Davidson himself, but something kept me turning up lecture after lecture. Now these were the late Eighties as I said, those hazy student years of Jack Daniels and Guns N' Roses, of Thatcher and Reagan and the Lockerbie bombing and the end of the Cold War. The world was changing all around us and like everyone else in my circle of friends I was looking for a way to make sense of it all.

Sense for Debbie came from the ordered relationship between agent and reagent, in atomic weights and the periodic table. For me, it was provided by occultists like Crowley and Gardner, by Israel Regardie and Franz Bardon and Austin Osman Spare. The university library had a surprisingly well stocked selection of what they liked to call "esoteric" books, and I devoured them all. I locked myself away in my student digs and studied like I had never studied for an actual course subject before. I was learning magic, real proper magic, and I discovered I was good at it. I mean OK, nothing ever really *happened*, as such, but all the same I felt I was making real progress. I was in touch with my Will, and I trained myself to see auras. Debbie scoffed, of course, until I dug out a couple of volumes on medieval alchemy and showed them to her. She was fascinated from that moment on, and we grew even closer.

It was about then that the professor's class size really began to dwindle and I found I got more tutorial time with him than I had ever had before. He might have been a fossil himself but he struck me as a genuinely nice guy, and we got on fairly well. If I'm honest about it, I suppose I was still looking for some sort of father figure in those days. My own dad had been a total shitbag of an alcoholic who had battered my poor old mum black and blue on a regular basis. The only good thing he had ever done for our family was to die of a heart attack when I was ten years old. Life had got a bit more tolerable after he was gone.

It wasn't long before our one-to-one time in Davidson's office turned into me going to the pub with him and chatting over a pint instead. It was about then that I discovered just how bad his drinking problem was.

We had gone for a quick lunchtime pint one day in lieu of my scheduled half hour tutorial, but that was three hours ago and it was now the middle of the afternoon. He had been supposed to be taking a freshman class at one o'clock, but he assured me his researcher could handle it without him.

"I'm fucking the librarian," he announced, very loudly. He had one of those overly educated accents which somehow made him sound even more dissolute, like some awful cross between Brian Blessed and Uncle Monty, if you've ever seen that film. Still, he seemed harmless enough. He wasn't the same sort of drunk as my dad had been, that was something. "Sandra, Sheila, whatever her name is."

"Are you, sir?" I asked politely.

I was still sipping the end of my second bottle of lager. He'd had six pints of bitter and at least five whiskies and about fifteen cigarettes by then, and I was starting to feel a bit scared of him. I knew it was just bad childhood memories, though. I still had a lot of them, in those days. Davidson was OK.

"Anyway, doesn't matter," he said, leaning unsteadily

across the table between us. "Point is, she's worried about you, Drake. Asked me to have a word, and all that."

"Worried about me how, sir?"

"All those books you've been taking out," he said. "So-called magic. Aleister Crowley, all that crap."

I sighed. *Of course, he's a scientist. An old, pickled one maybe, but a scientist all the same. Of course he doesn't approve.*

Of course he didn't, but not at all for the reasons that I had been expecting.

"It's all bollocks," he said. "It's a load of watered down, mistranslated and mangled shit, mixed with wishful thinking and makebelieve. You're doing it all bloody wrong, boy."

"She, um, told you that, sir?"

"Who? What, oh, you mean Sandra? Sheila, whoever she is? God no, she wouldn't know a hex from a handbag." He snorted with laughter and drained his pint. "God bless her, I'm fucking her you know. Well, I haven't been capable for years, between you and me, but you know what I mean."

He waggled his tongue disgustingly at me, and informed me that it was my round. I suppressed a shudder but went to the bar anyway to get him yet another pint. Student funds being what they were, I got myself a lime and soda. I wasn't much of a drinker in those days anyway, for obvious reasons. I'd spent my whole life determined not to turn into my old man.

I ought to have just left him to it, I knew I should, but he'd caught my attention by then. I'd heard a lot of slurring and bluster and innuendo from him, but I'd also heard *you're doing it wrong* and that had caught my attention more than

I really cared to admit even to myself. There was something here I didn't quite understand yet, but it was more than a little bit interesting. It was certainly worth turning a blind eye to his drunkenness to hear what else he might have to say. I took the drinks back to our table and sat staring expectantly at him.

"Aren't we supposed to be going over your... your last paper or something?" he asked me. "I, um, I can't quite remember."

"You were talking about my books," I reminded him. "About magic, and what you think I'm doing wrong."

"Oh God yes, hopeless," he said. He swallowed half his pint in one go, and glared at me with bloodshot eyes. "Bloody hopeless."

"In what way, sir?" I prompted when it looked like he wasn't going to say anything else.

"What? Oh, yes. Well it doesn't work, does it?"

"Well," I said, feeling defensive and embarrassed all at once. "Well, I feel I'm making some good progress actually."

"Towards what, a better understanding of your navel? Bullshit!"

"Well..." I said, preparing to defend the occult mysteries that I, at all of twenty years of age, was sure I was on the brink of mastering.

"What have you ever actually summoned?" Davidson interrupted me.

"Summoned?" I echoed, wondering if I'd heard him right. "Well, I've studied the Goetia of course, and Bardon's theories of evocation, but obviously they shouldn't be taken literally, so..."

Davidson was in the middle of gulping his beer, and my statement made him laugh so hard he almost choked on it. A vile mixture of beer and snot trickled out of his nostrils. He wiped it away with a nicotine-stained finger and grinned at me.

"Come back to my rooms with me," he said. "There's someone I want you to meet."

Now drunk or not I was fairly sure he wasn't going to try and stick his hand down my trousers like Jim's rowing coach had to him last term, however much he reminded me of Uncle Monty out of whatever that film was called. Besides, with the state he was in I was even more sure I could just knock him on his arse and leg it if he did. I nodded.

"All right," I said.

He led me somewhat unsteadily out of the pub, resting one hand on my arm for support. It was a long, slightly uncomfortable walk back to his flat, what with him having to stop and cough and wheeze or talk incoherent bollocks every ten minutes or so, but we got there in the end. I remember hoping nobody I knew had seen me with him. He shut the door behind us, and grinned at me.

"Come through," he said, gesturing to a door at the end of the hall. "Come into my study, and I'll explain everything."

"Thank you," I said politely. "Who are we meeting, again?"

"What," he said. "What, not who. It."

He opened the door, and I gaped in astonishment. The study was filled with all manner of occult paraphernalia, things I never would have believed he owned if I hadn't seen them with my own eyes. At the far end of the room there was a huge piece of ancient-looking wood standing on a pair of trestles, and on top of it was some sort of hideous statue bound with tiny chains.

"Come here and feed me you useless old cunt!" it screamed.

I woke with a start, my head on my desk. Dreaming of poor old Davidson after all these years had left a sour taste in my mouth. He had been a wreck of a man towards the end. *Is that where I'm heading?* I couldn't help but ask myself the question, for all that I didn't really want to know the answer. I reached for the phone before I had a chance to change my mind. She picked up on the fifth ring.

"Debs, it's me," I said.

She hung up so hard the bang made my ear hurt. I winced and redialled.

"Don't..." I said, and she hung up again.

"I didn't do it!" I shouted the third time, before she had a chance to react. There was deathly silence, but at least she hadn't hung up on me again. Yet. "It's Wormwood, he's gouging me, I haven't got any choice but I didn't do it, honest to God I didn't. It was some rich bloke, no one else, but he was already dead so I didn't..."

"Get fucked, Don," she interrupted me. "You lied to me, you stole from me, and you're probably still lying to me now. Just get fucked, and don't call again."

She hung up. I dialled again, and her machine picked up. I gave it up for a bad job.

"Fucking hell," I muttered.

I went through to the kitchen to put the kettle on, and was just stirring boiling water onto cheap instant coffee when the phone rang. I ran back into the office and all but dived across the desk in my haste to pick it up.

"Debs?" I said.

"No," said Wormwood. "It ain't."

"Oh," I said. "Oh, it's you."

"Yeah, it's me, you cretin. Thought I'd give you a bell, seeing as you haven't bothered calling me. Again."

"Sorry," I said. "I was going to come over last night but, um..."

"Never mind," he said. "That was some good work yesterday, Drake. Heart attack, nice one. No complications. How did you manage that then?"

"I, um," I said, thinking frantically. I'd had nothing to do with it after all, and only a vague suspicion of what might have actually happened. "Um, you know. Professional secret."

Wormwood snorted.

"Ponce," he said. "Whatever, that's that out of the way and all to the good. Now then, I've got another little job for you."

"What?" I said. "We're square now, yeah? We are *fucking* square."

"No we ain't," said Wormwood. "Remember that interest I told you about? It went up. A lot."

I stared at the phone in my hand. He had to be kidding me, surely? Except I knew that Wormwood had no sense of humour whatsoever. I could already picture Connie kicking in the door of my office with a bonebreaking sledgehammer in his enormous hands. No, Wormwood didn't do kidding, not one little bit.

"What now?" I sighed.

"Don't take that snotty tone with me, you prick, this one's in your interest as much as mine," he said. "There's a bit of a problem with that Scottish job."

"What? That's done with."

"No," he said. "Apparently it ain't. Turns out that pair of bastards had some insurance. Dig out your laptop, I'll mail you the details."

"Right. Right, OK. I, um, look. Look, it's going to be a problem if you want me to, um, you know, do another thing."

"For fuck's sake Drake, no one's tapping your bloody phone," Wormwood snapped. "Out with it."

I wasn't so sure about that, after the probably-government work I had done in the past, but fuck it. They already knew more than enough about my business to bury me forever if they wanted to.

"My source has dried up," I said, thinking of Debbie with a sick feeling in my stomach. "I can't get any ingredients at the moment."

"Don't worry about that," Wormwood said. "Like I said, this is in both our interests. I can get you anything you want, within reason. Just let me know what you need and I'll put it on your tab."

I winced. Wormwood's idea of compound interest was scary enough as it was without him adding fresh debts to the running total, but I didn't really have a lot of choice. I had been going to Debbie for so long I didn't even know any other alchemists any more.

"Right," I said. "Well, um, so you'll email me?"

"Already have," said Wormwood. "Now bugger off and think it through, and let me know when you've figured out what you need. And Drake, don't fuck about on this one, understand? This is what you might call a little bit urgent."

He hung up. I dropped the phone back onto its cradle and shoved my fingers through my hair with a sigh of despair. This was just never going to go away, was it? Wormwood pretty much owned my arse now, as far as I could see. I've known loan sharks, and how they operate, but I honestly never thought I'd end up letting myself get sucked into a situation like this.

"Fucking hell," I muttered as I opened the bottom drawer of my desk and dug out my elderly laptop.

I hated the thing. Me and technology don't really get on, as you might have gathered. Oh I can work it, but all the same I hate it and everything it stands for. Every time I turn the bloody thing on I long for the good old days of the Rolodex and the newspaper clipping. I mean, I was a kid in the Seventies when "the future" was going to be all flying atomic cars and holidays on the moon. What did we get instead? The internet, bag of shit that it is. Give me my flying car any day. I sighed and opened my emails.

Wormwood had written to me, true to his word. I read his email, then I read it again. I gaped. This was a fucking disaster, and one that I wasn't at all sure I knew how to survive.

CHAPTER 11

Wellington Phoenix was a stone cold killer. He'd been in the business a hell of a lot longer than I had, and his reputation was sheer bloody poison. He must be over seventy by now but I still nearly shat myself when I saw his name in Wormwood's email. He was a physically huge man, a Nigerian with a big, booming voice and a pedigree that went back to before I was even born. I had met him once, maybe fifteen years ago, at the first professional gathering I had plucked up the courage to attend.

I had still been finding my feet then, working with the Burned Man and trying to figure out what I could do with the new-found power at my disposal. Phoenix had been the de facto star of that gathering, looming over everyone. He had been wearing a Savile Row suit, I remembered, and it had strained over his six foot eight, twenty-two stone bulk. He had been the keynote speaker. I remembered his speech as well. The things he hinted at had made my blood run cold.

The thing you have to understand is this. I was suddenly powerful then, as I saw it, with the newly acquired Burned

Man in my possession. Wellington Phoenix was much, much more powerful than me all by himself. He loomed, he boomed, and he frightened the fucking life out of me. He was also, according to Wormwood, Vincent and Danny's insurance policy.

Wormwood's sources had discovered that Danny had made a pact on their behalf some years ago. Just before they started in on Wormwood's business interests, funnily enough. Anyway, there was a lot of legalese but the gist of it was that if anything untoward should happen to them, then Wellington Phoenix would come down on whoever did it like fifty tons of napalm. That would be me then, and after me it would be Wormwood.

"Fuck me, that's going to be a problem," the Burned Man said when I explained the situation to it.

I nodded. "Innit just," I said. "Any bright ideas?"

"Oh you know me, I'm usually full of bright ideas," it said. "Not right now, though."

"What?"

"This is Wellington motherfucking Phoenix," the Burned Man spat. "You do grasp that, yes?"

I glared at it. Of all the times for it to show a yellow streak, this wasn't the right one.

"You put the power of Hell at my fingertips, remember?" I said. "And what do I do with it? Right now I hurl the whole fucking lot of it at Wellington fucking Phoenix. How's that suit you for ambition? Fuck what it costs, Wormwood's sorting the ingredients. I'll have that debate with him later. What can we get? What have you got that can take care of this?"

The Burned Man paused for a moment, and looked at me. "Cost no object?" it said.

I shrugged. "If Phoenix toasts me he'll be going after Wormwood next, so I'm guessing not."

"Well," it said slowly. "There are… things. I mean, it can be done, yeah? Anything can be done, for a price."

There was something about the look on its ugly burned little face that I really didn't like.

"Hang on a minute," I said. "You're trying to pull the wool over my eyes, I know you are. What sort of a price are we talking about?"

"How many people are you prepared to kill?" it asked me.

"No," I said at once. "No, fuck that. I'm talking about artefacts here, not fucking human sacrifice. Bones, toads, quicksilver and gold, a bit of demon blood maybe. Not… not that."

It shrugged. "Well that's you bollocksed then," it said. "That's you and your fucking lack of ambition again, that is. Do you honestly think Wellington Phoenix has those sort of scruples? You've got no idea what he can get his hands on."

No, no I probably haven't. "That's not the point," I said. "I don't care what he's got. You see, I know what he *hasn't* got. He hasn't got *you*."

The Burned Man basked in the praise. It was nothing if not proud, after all.

"It's true, that," it said.

"Now, what can you get me *without* having to kill anyone?"

"Nothing that can face what Phoenix will bring to the party," it said.

I gritted my teeth in frustration. "Isn't there *anything* you can do?"

The Burned Man looked thoughtful for a moment. "That depends," it said. "Are you feeling brave?"

Not particularly. "I'll just have to be. What have you got in mind?"

"I..." it said, and started to cough.

"You what?"

It opened its mouth again, and coughed again, until it was almost choking. "Bugger!" it shouted.

I frowned. "What the hell's wrong with you?" I asked it. "You were about to tell me your grand plan. Come on, out with it."

"I can't do that," it said, and coughed again.

"What do you mean, you can't do that?" I said. "You can't tell me your own plan?"

"I... can't... say..." the Burned Man gasped between coughing fits. "There are limits to what I can do, bound and chained to your sodding altar."

I gave it a sharp look. The Burned Man never said anything it didn't mean, and it usually didn't say anything useful at all unless you asked it a direct question.

"What?" I said. "That sounded like a hint."

"There was a settlement on the Thames, where London stands now, long before the Romans came," the Burned Man said. "I was bound before even then, bound by a magic you can't even begin to imagine, you little puke. So if there are things I can't say it's not because *you're* clever, you understand me?"

I nodded slowly. "You can't say, and it's because of someone, but not me," I said. "So I have to guess?"

The Burned Man shrugged, and rattled its iron chains.

"You tell me," it said.

"So," I began, "if there's a limit to what you can do while you're bound, there might be less of a limit if you *weren't* bound – is that what you're getting at?"

"I couldn't possibly comment on idle speculation," the Burned Man said. "I could tell you a little story, I suppose, if you're bored. Just to pass the time, you understand."

I shrugged. This was getting obtuse, even for the Burned Man, but like I say, it never said anything without a reason. I had the distinct impression it was trying to get around something here, to slip through some loophole only it knew about.

"Go on then," I said. "*Jackanory* time."

"Back then," it said, "in Tir Na Nog, before the waters made this land an island, there was an antler druid called Oisin who had the gift of summoning. Oisin had the words of binding, and the working of iron, and the power to take his pick of the archdemons of Hell to enslave to do his bidding on Earth. Oisin chose me and bound me into this fetish to serve him. On *Earth*. Do you see?"

I frowned at it. "You're saying this Oisin bound you on Earth," I said, "but maybe you're *not* bound somewhere else, is that it?"

The Burned Man shrugged. "Is it?" it asked, and coughed again. "If a man asked a direct fucking question maybe I could answer it."

"Is there somewhere where you're not bound?" I asked it.

"Yes," it said.

Well fuck me sideways, that's a nasty thought. "So," I said, thinking out loud, "if we were there, and I could get Phoenix there as well, could you get rid of him for me?"

The Burned Man nodded. "I could," it said.

"Forever?" I asked. "I don't mean send him to Spain for a week's bloody holiday, I mean smash him into atoms so he'll never bother anyone again, yeah?"

"Yup," it said.

"So," I said, "where is this place where you're not bound?"

"Hell," it said.

Now I'm sorry, but I didn't exactly leap at the opportunity to go to Hell. Not just any Hell either, but a Hell in which the Burned Man wasn't nine inches tall and chained up. I could still remember that growl. To say I smelled a rat was an understatement – I was practically gagging on the stink of it.

I was sitting at my desk, staring glumly out of the window. It was mid-afternoon by now and it was pouring outside, the rain streaking down the glass like tears. *They'll be my bloody tears if I'm not careful,* I thought. *I need a second opinion on this shit before I do anything rash.*

"Meselandrarasatrixiel," I said out loud. "Trixie, if you can hear me, I'd really like to talk to you."

I almost regretted throwing away what I was still assuming had been her spying stone, but then I remembered that I hadn't had it with me when I called her the last time either. I had just screamed her name, and she had come. I'd been so bloody glad to see her that I hadn't really given that a lot of thought at the time. Having your hide flayed off by a Fury can be distracting like that, but now that I *did* give it some thought I found the idea a bit worrying. I mean, I can't summon squat without the Burned Man, but she had heard me anyway. *Was she watching me somehow, even without her little stone? Is she still watching me now?*

"Trixie, I really do need some advice," I said.

A siren whooped in the distance. The wind was really getting up out there, making the rain lash furiously against my window. Cars hissed past on the busy road below, throwing fantails of dirty water across the pavement. I sighed. *I guess not.*

"And I wanted to say thank you for last night, obviously," I said, as an afterthought. "It was really good of you to, you know, to come and rescue me like you did."

My front door banged in the wind, and I heard footsteps on the stairs. I didn't know whether to be pleased or really, really worried when the acrid smell of Russian tobacco wafted into the room a moment before Trixie did.

"You're welcome," she said. "Someone's got to look after you, you're hopeless at it."

"And you should be soaking wet, and you're not," I said. "That was careless of you."

"Oh bother being wet," she said. "I think we're a bit past you needing to think I actually came in from outside, aren't we?"

I sighed and looked at her. *A magic knight who fights Furies with a burning sword probably doesn't arrive on the bus, does she?* She certainly didn't look like she'd ever travelled on a bus in her life. In a Rolls Royce maybe, but never on public transport. She was wearing her long leather coat open over a dark skirt and jacket today, with black high-heeled shoes and a white silk blouse. She picked up a dirty coffee cup

I'd left lying around and casually flicked her cigarette ash into it.

"I suppose we are," I said.

"Good," she said, and settled on the sofa. She crossed her legs and smiled at me, the cup cradled in one hand. "Now, I believe you said you wanted to talk to me."

I nodded. I did, but should I, that was the question. *You don't think there's even the tiniest chance she might want something in return,* the Burned Man had said, but then the Burned Man wanted me to go to Hell, for fuck's sake. I still wasn't convinced I could trust Trixie, but I was getting less and less sure I could trust the Burned Man either. Whatever, I wasn't having this chat with her in here with only a cheap wooden door between us and the Burned Man's prying ears.

"Fancy a decent coffee?" I asked her. "Big Dave's will still be open."

I shot a meaningful look at the door to my workroom, and she nodded. "I'd love one," she said.

It was almost worth all the pain and grief of the last few days just to see the look on Big Dave's face when I walked in with Trixie at my side. He remembered her all right, and no mistake.

"Rosie?" he asked in open astonishment.

I winked at him. "Two coffees, there's a good lad," I said.

Trixie sat down at a table in the corner by the window, as far out of Dave's hearing as she could get. Luckily there was no one else in there at that time in the afternoon.

I sat down opposite her and waited while Dave brought the coffees over.

"So," she said, when he was safely out of the way, "what

is it you wanted to talk to me about?"

I sighed. "I, um, I don't even know where to start to be honest," I said.

"At the beginning," she said. "That's usually the best place."

So I told her some of it. As little as I could get away with and still make sense, admittedly, but I told her about Wormwood and Connie, and Vincent and Danny, and Wellington Phoenix and most of all about the Burned Man's plan.

Trixie went white.

"No," she said as soon as I'd finished. "No you can't, you *mustn't*. No, Don, absolutely not!"

I have to admit that was a bit more of a reaction than I'd been expecting. "Why not?"

"It's a trap," she said at once. "A trick, to get you where that horrible thing wants you."

The aroma of rodent was back and this time it was strong enough to drown out the smell of Dave's stale bacon, but now I wasn't even sure where it was coming from. *One of them is bullshitting me, that's for sure*, I thought. *Maybe even both of them.*

"Why would it want me in Hell?"

"It doesn't, particularly. It just wants to be free," Trixie said. "Above all else, *anything* else, it wants that."

"It's never said," I pointed out.

She shook her head. "It wouldn't," she said. "It *can't*, thankfully, or some idiot would no doubt have freed it long before now. Whoever this Oisin was knew what he was doing, I'll give him that much, for all that he should never have done it in the first place. The fetish can't talk about freedom, it can't ask to be free, and it can never know the ritual needed to free it. But its real self can. It wants you in Hell so it can learn the words that will set it free."

"I'm confused," I said. "For one thing, if it's free in Hell where it actually lives it's not really bound anyway, so I don't see its problem."

"Where does Wormwood live?" Trixie asked.

"What? I dunno, Mayfair somewhere I think. He's minted. What's that got to do with anything?"

"Not in Hell, then. Funny that, when it's supposed to be such a nice place. Why do you think there are so many nasty little things wandering around this part of London, where the Veils are thin enough for them to slip through?"

"You mean they'd rather be here?"

Trixie nodded slowly, like she was addressing a simpleton. I was starting to feel like a simpleton, to be honest. None of this was in the grimoires. "Indeed they would," she said. "Even demons don't want to be in Hell, Don."

"So why are they? I mean like you said, Wormwood isn't."

"Mostly because they can't get out," she said. "The Veils are there for a reason, after all. They can only get out in places where the Veils have worn very thin, and even then, only the little ones can squeeze through the gaps. Things like Wormwood's minder, and those night creatures of yours. Nothing much."

Connie's nothing much? She had a point though, I supposed. He was a huge, hulking brute of a monster, but as far as I knew he was no more magic than the slab of granite he so closely resembled. "Wormwood's not a little one," I said.

Trixie's mouth twisted in distaste. "No, he isn't," she said.

"Wormwood is more powerful than you give him credit for, actually. We should think ourselves lucky he's one of the more anthropomorphic ones, and a child of Mammon at that. He's more interested in making money than laying waste to the land. The Burned Man isn't."

I screwed my eyes tight shut and pinched the bridge of my nose, trying to make myself think. "So how the hell is Wormwood here then?"

"Some fool of a magician summoned him and messed it up, and he got loose," she said. "That was a very long time ago though, and it doesn't matter now. The point is that while the Burned Man is bound to that fetish in your study, it's in a fixed place on Earth and can't be summoned anywhere else by anyone else, so it can never get free the same way Wormwood did. It needs you to say the words of the ritual to destroy its link to the fetish."

"But I don't *know* the sodding words," I said. "I never knew they even existed until just now."

"No," she said, "but it thinks Wellington Phoenix does. It just wants you to get Phoenix into Hell so it can torture the ritual out of him, teach it to you, and make you say the words when you get back. Then it just has to wait for some idiot to try to summon it, which knowing what you diabolists are like probably won't take very long in the great scheme of things. As soon as someone does that it will simply destroy them, however powerful they think they are, and then we're all in terribly big trouble."

"Wait, what? You mean the trap's not even for me, I'm the fucking *bait*?"

"You are," she said, and nodded. "It's been waiting a very,

very long time for an owner like you, Don."

"Like me how?"

"Someone so unlucky and so stupid they get themselves into a fix with someone powerful and learned enough to actually know the ritual. To get into a fix so bad that it can convince them the only solution is to lure the other person to Hell so it can get its hands on them," she said. "Like you in *that* way, Don."

"Oh," I said. I sneaked a look at Dave out of the corner of my eye. He was still gawping, but somehow all the fun had just gone out of that. I was feeling a little bit crushed right then, all things considered. I supposed it did explain what the Burned Man might have been doing with Davidson before me, although as far as I knew the only monster he had ever got in trouble with was the demon alcohol. "I, um, well... Shit. What the fuck *do* I do, then?"

"The main thing is that you do not, under any circumstances, go through with the Burned Man's plan," Trixie said.

I glared at her. "The *main* thing is that I don't get torn to pieces by whatever horror show Wellington Phoenix is going to send after me," I snapped. "That's the *main thing* right now, as far as I'm concerned."

"Oh Don," she said, and smiled at me. She reached out and put her hand on mine. "As if I'd let that happen."

I turned my hand over to hold hers, feeling a sudden strange mixture of gratitude and hope. Also I have to admit I was really hoping Dave was still staring at us. He'd be sick with envy, and that put all the fun straight back into it.

"Can you *stop* it from happening?" I asked her. "Phoenix

is seriously heavy. I mean, he's stronger without the Burned Man than I am with it."

"No he isn't," she said, "he's just prepared to use different methods, that's all."

"All the same," I said. "It won't just be..."

I coughed. It had suddenly occurred to me that I wasn't sure exactly how much of my business Trixie knew about. I had glossed over as many of the details as I could when I was telling her my story, and I really didn't want her knowing more than she had to.

"It won't just be vorehounds or a couple of talonwraiths, no," she said. "Or Furies, for that matter. It might even be something I'll actually work up a sweat over, but no more than that."

She was certainly confident, I had to give her that. Proud might be another word for it. *The Burned Man is proud too*, a little voice in my head reminded me. *You still don't even know what she is.*

"Trixie," I said, "can I ask you something?"

I was still holding her hand, I realized, and I really, really didn't want to let go. She didn't seem to mind.

"You can ask," she said. "I can't promise that I'll answer."

I looked up and met her piercing blue gaze.

"What are you?"

She laughed, and slipped her hand out of mine. She picked up her cup and drained her coffee. I was starting to think she wasn't going to tell me when she leaned forwards on her elbows, her hands curled around the empty cup, and smiled at me again.

"You know what I am," she said, her voice strangely gentle.

I blinked at her. "I do?"

"Yes," she said. "You knew straight away, I know you did. In your heart, you knew."

I swallowed. There hasn't been an angel on Earth for, oh, a good thousand years or so now, the Burned Man had told me. Forget about angels. Even before they went away, they didn't have shiny white auras, or a forty a day fag habit, or an arse like that. She's not an angel.

I had taken the Burned Man at its word. All the same, that *had* been the first thing that crossed my mind. How in the world could she know that?

"What about your aura?"

"What about it?" she asked, her voice turning cold.

"If you're saying what I think you're saying, it shouldn't be white like that," I said. "It should be golden, like a halo in an old painting, and it isn't. It's... wrong."

Trixie's jaw clenched in sudden fury. The cup exploded between her hands.

"Never say that again," she hissed. "Never!"

She dropped the shards of broken pottery on the table and ran out of the café. The door slammed shut behind her.

Big Dave snorted with laughter. "You've still got your way with the ladies then, Rosie."

Haven't I just. I hurried after her.

To my relief she hadn't done one of her disappearing tricks this time. She was outside the grocers, just standing there in the pouring rain.

"Trixie," I called, hurrying over to her. "Look, I'm sorry, OK?"

She turned to face me. She didn't look angry any more.

She looked upset instead and somehow that was so much worse. It was raining pretty hard as I said, but all the same I was sure there were tears on her cheeks. Damn but it was cold out there. I reached for her hand.

"Don't," she said.

"I'm sorry," I said again, letting my hand fall uselessly to my side. "I don't understand, but I won't, um, I won't say anything like that again. I promise."

She nodded, but didn't move. "All right," she said.

"Shall we go back in?" I suggested as freezing rain trickled through my hair and down the back of my collar.

She shook her head. "Tell me about your fall," she said.

"Um," I said. "I mean, I know what you're getting at but that's a story for over a beer or ten, you know what I mean? Not for when we're standing on the pavement in a downpour."

"So let's have a beer or ten then," she said.

CHAPTER 12

We made it to the Rose and Crown in record time, both of us hunched down into our coats in companionable silence as the cold rain beat down on us. I ducked under the bedraggled hanging baskets and held the door open for her.

"Thank you," Trixie said as I followed her into the dimly lit burrow of beery smelling warmth. "Buy a girl a drink?"

Well that was awkward, and something that I must admit I hadn't even thought of until then.

"I, um, I haven't got any money," I confessed, feeling about six inches tall.

"Oh," she said.

She opened her handbag and pulled out a fat roll of twenty pound notes, wrapped up in a rubber band the way they came from the bank sometimes. I was just starting to hope she might slip me a couple when she pressed the whole lot into my hand.

"I don't mind paying," she said, "but ladies don't go to the bar. Gin and tonic please. I'll find us a table."

I gaped at her, then at the roll of probably three grand or

so that she had just given me, and then back at her again as she settled down at a corner table close to the log-effect gas fire in its implausible faux-Georgian surround. I shook my head in astonishment.

There were a few people in already who I knew by sight, if not to speak to. I exchanged nods and pats on the shoulder as I made my way to the bar. "Hello Duchess," I said.

Shirley looked up and grinned at me. "Don, how are you duck?" she said. "Pint?"

"Yeah, and a gin and tonic," I said, nodding vaguely in Trixie's direction. I thought about the fat wad in my pocket. "And a couple of whisky chasers."

Shirley glanced in the direction I'd indicated, and gave me a look somewhere between approval and flat out astonishment.

"Well duck," she said, "assuming that's not being paid for, I'm impressed."

I shrugged. "She's a friend," I said.

"I wish I had a gentleman friend who looked half that good," Shirl laughed, and went to sort the drinks.

I just about managed to carry the four mismatched glasses over to the table, and sat down opposite Trixie. I grinned at her. "So, how do you like the local?" I asked her.

"It has a certain sort of charm," Trixie said.

I knew what she meant. The Rose and Crown was one of those places where you could buy anything from a van load of Polish cigarettes to a stolen Maserati without anyone batting an eyelid. Most of the regulars were what were affectionately termed "characters" in the local parlance, which was a sort of friendly euphemism for "hardened criminals".

"This is nice," I said as I sipped my pint.

Trixie lifted her gin and tonic and looked at me over the glass.

"Tell me about your fall," she said again.

I sighed. *There really isn't any such thing as a free drink, is there?*

I started to talk.

Davidson had knelt down in front of the hideous living statue and carefully unbuttoned his tweed waistcoat and wrinkled check shirt. I winced as the thing lunged at him with a snarl, its mouth stretching wide to display a row of glistening wet, needle-like teeth just before they plunged into the old man's pale, horribly scarred chest.

"Bloody hell!" I gasped, torn between horror and fascination. "What even is that?"

"Don, my dear boy," Davidson said, "this is the Burned Man."

The awful little thing pulled its head back from Davidson's chest and stared at me, obviously only just noticing I was there.

"What's that little pissant doing in here?" it demanded.

"This is Donald Drake, one of my most promising students," Davidson said. "I thought you might like to meet him."

"What the fuck for?"

"He's a seeker," Davidson said. "A misguided one perhaps, but a seeker after truth all the same. The first I've found in a long time. There hasn't been anyone remotely worthy since Macintosh, and I'm not getting any younger."

"You're nearly dead," the Burned Man said, with no trace

of emotion, "and that Macintosser boy was a worthless piece of snot and you know it. Is this one going to be any better?"

"Um," I said, shifting from foot to foot and seriously considering just doing a runner right there and then. I'm still not completely sure to this day what kept me there in the cluttered, squalid little room, watching that monstrosity drink my professor's blood. "Better at what?"

"Magic," the Burned Man hissed. "What can you do, boy?"

"Um..." I said.

I looked at it, then. I mean, I really *looked* at it. One of the things I had learned by then was the seeing of auras, and right then I saw this vile little thing in all its appalling glory. It was only about nine inches tall and it was chained to the table it stood on as well, but its aura was an immense cloud of poisonous black malice that made me want to piss myself. I could tell that this, whatever it was, was one hell of a lot more than it seemed.

"Well?"

"I can see you," I said. "I know what you are."

It snorted. "Oh yeah? What the fuck am I then, you cocky little cunt?"

"You're a devil," I said. "Or whatever you want to call yourself. You're *evil*."

Oh, the moral assurance of being twenty years old! The Burned Man threw back its head and hooted with laughter.

"You're more fun than poor old Davidson, I'll give you that much," it said. "At least you've got a sense of humour."

"I'm not joking," I said. "I can see it."

"What the fuck can you see?" it shot back. "Some colours

in the air? Whoopee-fucking-doo for you. What do you actually *understand*? What do you *want*, boy? Why are you here?"

"I..." I said, and stopped.

This was the important question, I knew. I had no real idea what I was actually talking to, but I knew damn well I would probably never have another chance like this. Davidson was kneeling there in front of it in a sort of stupor, but he had obviously brought me here for a reason.

"I want to know," I said at last. "I want knowledge. Understanding."

"Read a book," it snapped.

"I've read all the fucking books," I snapped right back at it, feeling like I was getting the measure of it now. "I want more than that."

"But not from me," it said. "I'm *evil* apparently, whatever the fuck that means. What *does* it mean, boy?"

"It means..." I started. "It means, you know, it means *evil*. How hard can it be?"

"Very," it said. "It can be very hard indeed. Define it."

"The extreme of immorality," I said.

"Dictionary definition, bullshit," it said. "Think for yourself. What does it *mean*?"

"Wilfully doing the things that are wrong," I said.

"Who defines what's wrong?"

"I... for who?" I said. I had been a university student for long enough by then to spot a trick question when I heard one. "The law does, for most people."

"That's legality, not morality," it said. "Very different thing, a lot of the time. Who defines morality?"

"The church?" I ventured.

"Which one?"

Now that was a good question, I had to give it that. "Well every religion has its rules," I said, "but they don't all agree with each other."

"So who's right?"

"What? How the hell do I know?" I said. "I mean, if you're Jewish or Muslim then you can eat beef but you can't eat pork. If you're a Hindu it's the other way around, you know what I mean? How do I know which is right?"

"You don't," it said, "any more than I do. All we can do is hope for the best. You want to learn, fine. Just don't give me any moralistic bullshit with nothing to back it up, you understand me? If there's things you won't do then there we are, but we'll cross those bridges when we come to them. Deal?"

I stared at it. *If I want to learn?* I didn't really understand exactly what was being offered to me here, but it was obviously a hell of a lot more than I was going to get out of any of the books I'd been able to get my hands on so far. Davidson seemed to come back to life about then, and he turned and grinned at me with blood running down his white, hairless old man's chest.

"Do it," he said. "What have you got to lose?"

I nodded.

"Deal," I said.

Trixie nodded. "So what happened?" she asked.

We were about five drinks and chasers in by then, and I was fast coming to the humbling realization that she was going to drink me under the table if the night went on long enough. She was every bit as sober as she'd been when we first walked into the pub, whereas I really wasn't. Five pints and whiskies wasn't all that much for me, relatively speaking, but I'd done them in fairly quick succession and I hadn't had a lot to eat that day. Anyway, all excuses aside, I have to admit I was starting to feel quite pissed.

"Stuff happened," I said. "Why are you so interested anyway? I feel like we're comparing notes here, but you haven't said a word about yourself."

"About myself?" Trixie said. "What do you mean?"

"Well OK, don't flip out on me again, yeah? I mean, Shirl's a sweetheart and all that but she gets upset about broken glasses, you understand?"

Trixie nodded and put her glass carefully back down on the table.

"Tell me about your fall, you said," I reminded her. "Funny way of putting it, if you ask me."

"I don't understand," Trixie said.

I looked at her. She was sitting opposite me, fingering her cigarette case and obviously wondering how much longer she had to wait before she could nip outside for a fag without being impolite. She'd had at least three thousand quid in her handbag for no apparent reason. She wasn't just beautiful, but sexy as well. She was a stone cold killer, and she was obviously proud of it. Her aura was wrong, whether she wanted it mentioned or not. She was, if anything the Burned Man had told me was true, not quite right as angels go. To put it mildly. And I had a nasty suspicion I might know why.

I necked my whisky and took one hell of a chance.

"You tell me about *your* fall."

She gave me a look that made Debbie's coldest glare seem warm and cosy by comparison.

"What," she said slowly, her hands curling into fists on the table top, "is that supposed to mean?"

I shrugged. "Tell me," I said again, "or my story's over."

Trixie glared at me for a moment, then looked sharply away. She dashed a hand across her eyes, staring into the fire.

"That's a story for another drink or ten," she said quietly.

"Fine, I'll get them in," I said.

"Fine," she snapped back. "I'm going for a smoke."

I went to the bar and caught Shirley's eye.

"Same again pet," I said. "One for yourself, if you like."

"Thank you darling," she said as I gave her another twenty off Trixie's roll. "She's gone, you know."

"She's just having a fag," I said. "She'll be back in a minute."

Shirley gave me a dubious look, but did our round all the same and took a double vodka and tonic for herself.

"Cheers, duck," she said.

I carried the drinks back to our table and sat down. Trixie kept me waiting so long I started to think that maybe she had left after all, until she eventually came back inside and sat down across the table from me. Her shockingly blue eyes looked red and raw around the edges, as though she had been crying.

"Right," she said, before I had a chance to speak. "You get one thing straight. I am *not* a fallen angel, do you understand me? Don't you *ever* say that I am."

"Um, OK," I said. "So, um..."

"Look," she interrupted me, "I haven't fallen and that's that. I just... slipped a bit, that's all."

"OK, OK," I said, holding my hands up defensively in front of me. "So what does *slipped a bit* mean, exactly?"

"Nothing that matters to you," she said. "I've been following the Furies for so long it's no wonder I've picked up a few Earthly habits. It doesn't matter, the Furies are the important thing. To start with I thought you were just another unfortunate who'd attracted their vengeance, but the more I saw of you the more I realized you were a little bit different from most other mortals. And when I saw that you had the fetish of the Burned Man, well, obviously that changed everything."

"Did it?" I asked her. "Why's that then?"

"Well," she said, sipping her gin and tonic, "my superiors have been trying to keep an eye on that for a long time now, as I'm sure you'll understand, but... anyway that's way above my pay grade, as you might say. I'm more concerned about you, Don, and about the Furies. I'm sort of, well, assigned to them I suppose. It's my job to keep them under control and away from innocent people. Ultimately, I'm here to destroy them. Vengeance belongs to Heaven, after all, not to them. But now I know you've got the Burned Man, I've got a professional duty to keep you on the straight and narrow path. The wrong sort of person could do terrible things with the Burned Man in their possession, after all. I can't have you turning into that sort of person, Don."

I never liked you, Ally had said to her, I remembered, and Trixie had said you're not supposed to, or something like that. It sounded almost plausible. Almost. I supposed that spending however many years following Ally and her sisters around could cause anyone to slip a bit, even an angel. All the same I couldn't help wondering whether she might have had some help somewhere along the way. The concept of a fallen angel was hardly new, and I suspected there might be some of them out there who had done a damn sight more than just slip. If one of those had been getting to her... well, wasn't that a nasty thought?

That, and something else was still bothering me.

"What about that bloke though?" I said. "The rich guy Wormwood sent me after. He was dead when I got there, and I'm not buying natural causes."

"Oh dear me no, he was healthy as a horse," Trixie said. "I killed him."

I stared at her. I mean, I had sort of wondered, but why on Earth would she? And now I knew what she was, it seemed even less likely. I wondered again about what sort of company she might be keeping. She had said it in such a straightforward, matter-of-fact sort of way, too.

"*You* killed him?" I echoed, trying to keep my voice down. That sort of talk was a bit much even for the Rose and Crown. "Why the fuck would you do that?"

"I told you, Don, I'm looking after you," she said. She finished her gin and tonic and picked up her whisky chaser, and smiled at me over the rim of the glass. "I can't have you going around killing people – it's not good for your soul."

"The ends always justify the means," the Burned Man said. "That is, if you're the type who feels the need to be justified at all. I don't see the point, personally, but there you go. I know a lot of people seem to feel this inexplicable need to think they're in the right, whatever that is."

I was in Davidson's study, alone with the Burned Man. The professor was passed out on the sofa in the other room, an empty bottle of scotch cradled in his arms. The Burned Man had been teaching me for a little over a year now, and it had been a long time since Davidson had last been sober enough to attend one of its lessons. Not that it mattered. I still liked the old chap, don't get me wrong, but he was getting harder and harder to talk to as he sank further into alcoholism. It was a shame, but in a funny sort of way the Burned Man itself was starting to replace him, to fill that father figure void in my life. Maybe that's going too far, but it was certainly my mentor now. It had become increasingly obvious that the Burned Man had given Davidson up for dead, or as good as dead anyway. It seemed I was its new owner-in-waiting.

There was a strict succession process, it had explained to me some time ago. Apparently it couldn't be stolen, or sold, or passed on through any means other than mutual consent. I had no idea what would happen otherwise, but it was very clear on this point. Davidson had to give it to me as a gift, and I had to accept it. Whether the Burned Man itself got any say in this process wasn't clear, but I had a suspicion that nothing much ever happened to it that it didn't want to. It had long since become obvious to me that it absolutely ruled Davidson, heart and mind.

"Doesn't everyone need to think they're doing the right thing?" I asked it.

"No," it said. "Trust me boy, no they don't. I know *you* do,

I know you that well by now, but there's plenty out there that're happy enough to do something just because they can, you understand me?"

I nodded. I'd grown up on a tough estate and been to a pretty rough comprehensive before I escaped to university, and I was well enough acquainted with bullies and petty thugs to know exactly what it meant.

"Yeah, I suppose," I said. "I know what bullies are like."

"Right," it said. "Now, take those little oiks you're thinking of and imagine them with magic on their side. Imagine the local bully with a pet demon on a leash instead of his pitbull or Rottweiler or whatever sort of furry shark they go in for these days. You starting to get the picture yet?"

I nodded slowly. It wasn't a pretty thought, but then this wasn't a pretty world. The Burned Man had taught me that much already.

"Yeah," I said again.

"Right," it said, nodding. "so if you're not going to be one of them then you'll be up against them, you understand me? And that means you'll have to do some stuff. Stuff you might not be all that keen on at first, but it'll need doing just the same. People like that, you don't want them around you. You don't want them around your friends or your family either, do you?"

"Well no, of course not," I said. "I don't see why they would be, though."

It snorted. "You're going to be a magician, yeah? A diabolist, at that. Scenes like that, well, they attract people like them. Anything a bit out of the ordinary attracts its own version of people like that, doesn't matter what it is. Everything's a pissing contest to these pricks, you understand?"

I nodded slowly. I knew it was right. I remembered Jim telling me how a couple of the rowing team had started using steroids last term, and how they'd beaten one of the other lads black and blue when he threatened to grass them up to the coach. Same sort of thing, I supposed.

"So what am I supposed to do to get rid of them?" I asked. "I have to sink to their level, is that what you're saying?"

"No, no, no," the Burned Man shook its head in obvious irritation. "You're thinking about this all the wrong way. Fuck levels, and who's better than who, yeah? Just *fuck* it. It ain't about being *better*, whatever that means. It's about winning. It's about coming out alive. You do what you've got to do, you understand me? Because trust me boy, when some cunt's coming down on you with a pack of vorehounds you don't stop to worry about whether it's morally fucking OK to gut a few toads, yeah? You worry about keeping your head stuck on your shoulders. You beat that bastard off, then you do whatever you need to do to cook up something worse to send after him so he doesn't ever do it again. Because next time, those vorehounds might be going to your mum's house instead of yours. Are you starting to understand me yet?"

I nodded slowly, wondering what on Earth a vorehound was. "So it's dog eat dog," I said.

"Fucking right it is," the Burned Man said. "You're getting it, my boy, I do believe you're finally getting it. Now you get in the kitchen and sort that fucking toad or you aren't learning anything more from me."

I went into Davidson's squalid kitchen and did what I was

told. I summoned my first real, actual demon that night. It was only a sprite, and looking back on it, well, big fucking deal, but right then it was the absolute pinnacle of my magical career. The Burned Man had beamed at me with an almost fatherly pride as I teased the tiny, spiteful little faerie out of the ether and into my summoning circle. I watched it pace the boundaries of the salt circle with my heart full of wonder.

"What can it do?" I asked.

"Fuck all," the Burned Man said. It looked at the expression on my face and hooted with laughter. "This is just an exercise, lad. Sprites are virtually useless, but that's not the point is it? The point is it's *here*, and it's here because you told it to be. It's here because you can *make* it be here. It's the same principles whatever you want to summon, it's just a matter of scale from here on in. Scale, and ingredients, and the sheer fucking balls to do it. You remember the Four Powers of the Sphinx that I taught you?"

I nodded. "To know, to will, to dare, and to keep silent," I said.

"Yup," it said. "Well now you know, and you've proved you've got the Will. Keeping silent's fucking optional at this point, to be honest. All the rest comes down to *dare*."

"And you dared," Trixie said.

I nodded. "Yeah, I did," I said. "I dared for England, and look where that got me. Excuse me a minute, I'm going to the bog."

I got up and wandered across the pub to the gents. I was feeling a tad unsteady on my feet, but it must have been about nine o'clock by then and I wasn't the only one so I didn't feel the need to apologize to anyone I might have bumped into on my way across the bar. That's another thing about the Rose and Crown, it's a serious drinkers' pub.

I let the toilet door swing shut behind me and stood at the urinal with my forehead resting comfortably against the cold tiled wall. I wasn't quite sure what Trixie had made of my story so far but one thing was really beginning to strike me – she and the Burned Man seemed to be on the same wavelength about certain things. The Burned Man had always said you did whatever you had to do to achieve the goal, and Trixie was obviously of the same mind about that. *I killed him.* Just like that. I really wasn't sure if that was a good thing or not. I was just zipping up when the cubicle door banged open behind me.

"Hello sweetie."

I lurched around just in time to see a flash of red hair and steel claws as Ally caught me by the throat and slammed me up against the wall. Her talons sank into the plaster either side of my neck, pinning me to the wall with my feet flailing helplessly a good six inches off the floor.

"...the fuck?" I choked.

"Oh don't play that innocent game with me, you shit," Ally snarled.

She was a lot less pretty up close than I remembered. Her clawless left hand balled into a fist and smashed into my guts. I yelped, and she hit me again. My heels kicked against the wall behind me as she stuck a painful jab into my solar plexus.

"Pack it in, you bitch," I gasped.

"That's for Meg," she snarled, and hit me again. "And that's for Tess."

At least the Furies won't kill you, I remembered the Burned Man telling me. *They never do.* I gagged as Ally hit me again, and prayed it was right.

"Trixie's… right… out there!" I gasped

Ally nodded. "Yes," she said. "She's right out there, in this nasty little dive full of all your cheap criminal friends. Are you going to go crying to your pretty girlfriend to come and save you this time, sweetie? You want Mummy to come into the loo and look after you?"

I spat bile on the floor and had to admit she had a point. I mean, I could, sure, and I had no doubt Trixie would kick her arse again if I did, but… shit. I mean *shit*, I just couldn't, could I? A man has to have some pride, after all.

"Fucking bitch," I groaned.

"Oh yeah, I'm the fucking bitch to end all fucking bitches," Ally said. "That's the whole point of me, *sweetie*."

Her knee cracked up and caught me square in the bollocks, and I blacked out for a moment. She let go of my neck and I hit the floor like a sack of meat. She kicked me in the ribs, and then the side of the head. That time I saw stars for real, and everything went dark.

When I came round Alfie was bent over me with a wet towel in his hand and a concerned look on his flat-nosed boxer's face.

"You all right Don?" he asked me.

"What?" I mumbled.

"Your bird got worried about you and asked Ma to get me to come and check on you," he said.

"Shit, yeah... shit Alf, I must've slipped over. Banged me head, you know what I mean?"

Alfie nodded. "Yeah," he said. "Enough beers with whisky chasers can make this floor slippery like that," he said. "Come on, up with you then, you daft prick."

He hauled me up to my feet and I took a moment, leaning against the wall with one hand pressed to my crotch in a deeply undignified manner. "Jesus, I must've caught my balls on the radiator or something on the way down," I muttered by way of explanation.

"That's a shame," Alfie said, "what with a bird like that waiting for you and everything."

I shrugged. "I'll be fine," I said, and forced a grin. "Nothing another beer won't fix."

I let Alfie help me back out of the gents. I couldn't help but blush when I got a round of applause from the lads at the bar. Trixie didn't look any too pleased but at least she was still sitting at our table, waiting for me. I hobbled to the bar.

"Same again, Duchess," I said, to a further smattering of clapping and catcalls.

I caught Shirl glancing over at Trixie for her consent before she nodded and took my money. Women, huh?

"Go careful this time, duck," Shirl said.

I took the drinks back to our table.

"Well?" Trixie demanded. "What was all that about? I was starting to think you'd passed out in there."

"Ally," I said, and necked my whisky chaser straight down. "She jumped me in the bogs and kicked a few lumps out of me. I thought you were keeping her away from me?"

Trixie frowned. "I thought so too," she admitted. "She shouldn't be able to get within a mile of you when I'm around."

"Well she got a lot closer to me than that just now," I said, "and it bleedin' hurt."

"I'm not at all happy about that," Trixie said, as though that helped anything. "Why in the world didn't you call me?"

I blushed all over again. "It's... it's not like I don't appreciate it, Trixie," I said. "But, well, this is my local, you know? People know me here. And anyway, well..."

I tailed off helplessly, and sighed.

"You think you deserve it," Trixie finished for me. "Don't you?"

I leaned my elbows on the table and put my head in my hands. "I *do* deserve it," I said. "He was five fucking years old, Trixie."

"I know," she said quietly.

I looked up at her through a dull haze of booze and guilt. "You don't."

"Of course I do," she said. "It's my job to know."

"That job," I went on, lowering my voice until I was sure no one else could hear us. "Vincent and Danny, the ones who had Wellington Phoenix as their insurance. They had... they had a grandson. A little boy, Trixie. I didn't know, I swear I didn't. He was five years old. I sent screamers. They... He..."

I realized I was crying, and I couldn't stop. Trixie gave me a moment then reached out and took my hands in hers, gently pulling them away from my face and holding them tight. I could feel the hot tears running down my cheeks.

"I forgive you," she said.

I stared into her bright blue eyes through a haze of tears. I was drunk and sore, my balls ached and the side of my head felt like there was an egg growing out of it, but I suddenly felt better somehow. I don't know, maybe it was just something she could do. I mean, I'm afraid I don't know much more about angels than anyone else does. The Burned Man had touched on them briefly in its early teachings but according to it there supposedly hadn't been one on Earth in a thousand years so it had never expected me to need to know much about them.

"Thank you," I whispered.

They say confession's good for the soul, but it seemed forgiveness was a hell of a lot better. What little was left of the Catholic in me could relate to that, anyway. She squeezed my hands and smiled.

"Like I said before," she said, "I'm looking out for you."

I coughed with embarrassment, and gently took my hands out of hers. She was looking out for me. She had killed that bloke so I didn't have to, because she was looking out for me. And she was talking about doing the same thing to Wellington Phoenix.

"I'm sorry," I said, still sniffling a bit. "Sorry, I shouldn't… I mean, this is my fucking mess, Trixie. I don't want… I don't want it to be my fault, you know?"

"Pardon? Sorry, Don, you've lost me."

"Your fall," I said. "I don't want that to be my fault too. OK, so you've just slipped a bit, I get that, really I do, but… but now you're killing people Trixie. For my benefit, at that. That… that can't be doing you any good, can it?"

"You don't understand," she said. "Bless you for thinking

of me, but it's all right. I'm here to do a thing, and I *will* do it. Other things that may need doing along the way don't matter, so long as the overall objective is met. I have to destroy the Furies. The next step towards that is to get them away from you, and if that means I have to make you be a good boy, then so be it. I'm a soldier, Don, and the Furies are my war. Nothing else matters."

The ends always justify the means, the Burned Man had said. I couldn't help thinking that an "ends justify the means" policy might lead to some pretty questionable means, but was that really my problem? After all, if I couldn't follow the Burned Man's plan then I had no hope of standing up to Phoenix on my own. Why not just let her take care of it for me? *Do I want to be responsible for the fall of an angel?* I didn't, but then I didn't want to be dead either, and that was looking like it was pretty much the only other option right then.

"Thank you," I said quietly. "But... well, you've already killed two of them, haven't you?"

"Oh good grief, no," Trixie said. "If it was that easy I'd have finished this task and gone home three thousand years ago. I'm afraid Megaera and Tisiphone aren't dead, I've just kicked them out of this plane of existence for a little while. As soon as they've had a chance to lick their wounds and spin themselves some new bodies they'll be back. We have danced this dance many times before."

"Oh," I said. "So... how *do* you kill them?"

"I don't," Trixie said. "I fight them."

"So what's the point if you can't stop them?"

"I'm *trying* to stop them, that's the point," Trixie said, and

I could hear the brittle edge of anger creeping into her voice now. "That's the task I was given, and I'm doing it. I'll do *anything* to achieve it, do you understand me?"

I nodded. "Yes," I said. "Yes, I think I do."

Poor Trixie. Like Sisyphus pushing his rock uphill for all eternity, Trixie had been doomed to battle the Furies forever. I couldn't help thinking that someone up there really didn't want her going home.

"Good," she said. "So, you'll forget this nonsense the Burned Man told you and let me take care of Wellington Phoenix for you?"

I nodded. "Yes," I said. "Thank you, Trixie."

I got stuck into my pint and let her tell me her plan. I mean, how much more harm could it do?

CHAPTER 13

Ever heard the expression "famous last words"? I ought to know better, I really did.

Trixie walked me home, and, yeah, I do know it should have been the other way around, trust me I do. She left me standing at my front door, staring at my sign. *Don Drake, drunken wanker.* No, I didn't get a kiss goodnight.

I stumbled up the stairs and into my office, feeling worn out and sore and dizzy and so, so relieved. Trixie had forgiven me. That, above all else, had made me feel better. I'd told her my story, or some of it anyway, and she'd promised to get rid of Wellington Phoenix for me. That was great, don't get me wrong, but the main thing was that she had forgiven me. I felt like a ten ton weight had been lifted off my shoulders. It felt wonderful, and that wonderful feeling lasted all of ten seconds.

"Oi," the Burned Man shouted from the workroom. "Where the buggering hell have you been?"

"Out," I shouted back, feeling like a rebellious teenager talking back to my dad.

"Get in here," it ordered me. "Now."

I went. So much for rebellion. I hadn't been much good at that when I'd actually been a teenager, come to think of it. The Burned Man rattled its chains and glared at me.

"She's gone," I said, before it could ask.

"Good," it said. "Now, what about my plan? Are you ready for a little trip down under?"

I shook my head. "No, not going to happen," I said. "I've got a better plan."

"Blondie has, you mean," it said, "and I very much doubt it's better for *you*. You can't trust her, you dickhead. Having a nice arse doesn't make her on your side, you do realize that don't you?"

I shook my head slowly. The Burned Man was obviously doing its very best to forget the week or so we had both lost to Trixie. Apparently it was only me who had ever been infatuated with her, according to its version of events. Still, I supposed I was more than a bit guilty of having a selective memory myself sometimes. If I was completely honest with myself, I had only given Trixie the edited highlights of my early days with Davidson and the Burned Man.

"Never mind that," I said, "we're doing it my way and that's that. Or is there something you'd like to explain?"

The Burned Man coughed, and gave me a vicious look. *It can't talk about freedom*, I reminded myself. *Good.* "No," it muttered.

"Right," I said. "I'm going to bed then. We'll get it sorted in the morning. Phoenix has got a long flight over here and I expect he'll want to get up to Edinburgh and see what's what for himself before he does anything else. I think it'll keep that long. Start working on a doppelganger, will you?"

"A doppelganger?" it said. "Of who?"

"Me, of course," I said.

I left it to chew on that, and went to bed.

By the time I wandered back into the workroom the next morning the Burned Man was virtually gnawing its chains with frustration.

"What the fuck is the doppelganger for?" it demanded, before I could even open my mouth.

"Good morning to you too," I said.

"Fuck the morning, tell me," it said.

I shrugged. "Isn't it obvious? We use the doppelganger to lure Phoenix and his horrors to somewhere else, somewhere Trixie is waiting for them. She gets busy on them while I hide out here with you and a couple of something nasty to keep me safe. She comes and lets us know when they're all dead, simple as that really."

"Simple as that," the Burned Man echoed. The look of disappointment on its ugly little face would have been heartbreaking if I hadn't known what it was, and what it had tried to get me to do. "Well, I've got the pattern prepared. You'll need to get some stuff for it, and then whatever else we need for your idea of something nasty."

"Screamers," I said at once. "Three of them, if you can manage it."

The Burned Man spat at me. "I can manage whatever the fuck you can dare to ask for, you little prick," it reminded me. "What are you willing to pay for, more to the point?"

"Yeah, sorry, course you can," I said. I was pissed off at it, but winding it up wasn't a good plan all the same. "Three screamers then, that ought to be enough bodyguard for anyone. I'll tap Wormwood up for the ingredients."

I phoned the club, and Connie picked up. I gave him the shopping list. Two hours later my doorbell rang. I was half expecting to see Connie standing there himself with a basket of goodies in his huge hand, but then of course he was a tad conspicuous to be seen on the street in the daylight. Even in South London. It was that waitress I liked instead, the one with the cute tail. Oh, she had it tucked down the back of her jeans where it didn't show, obviously, but it was her all the same. She had a suitcase in her hand.

"Mr Drake?" she asked me.

"That's me," I said.

"Hi, I'm Tasha. I've got a delivery for you."

I looked over her shoulder to where Wormwood's black Rolls Royce was pulled up at the kerb outside. The registration plate was *WW 1*, I noticed. And he called *me* a ponce, the cheeky git. The tinted front window rolled down and Connie nodded at me from the driver's seat. How he'd got his bulk wedged in there I had no idea. I nodded back.

"Great, thanks," I said. "Tell Connie I said hi."

She smiled and passed me the big grey Samsonite. "I will," she said.

I watched her as she wiggled back to the car and slid into the back seat. She was still very cute even without the tail on show, but she was no Trixie.

Whoa there, I told myself. *Don't you start that, Don.* Trixie was... well, she was Trixie. However gorgeous she might be, I knew I was on a hiding to nothing with *that* sort of thinking. I sighed and lugged the suitcase back up the stairs to my office. I was missing Debbie, that was all it was. I wondered whether it was too soon to try phoning her again, and decided that it almost certainly was.

"The goody bag's here," I called out to the Burned Man.

I hauled the Samsonite into my workroom and popped it open to be greeted by the reproachful croaks of several large toads. There were other things in there too – three large flasks of goat's blood, several vials of tincture of mercury, and a full ounce of powdered manticore spines. It was everything I'd asked for to summon the screamers, and the other things I needed as well. There was modelling clay and a big lump of soft black wax for the poppet, and a police-issue mobile DNA sampling kit. Say what you like about Wormwood, the man was connected.

"You know what to do with this shit?" I asked the Burned Man, pointing at the DNA kit.

"I'm old, not out of touch," it said. "Of course I do. Get the bit and bobs out and shut that lid before the fucking toads escape or you'll be chasing them round the flat all day."

I did as it told me. "So I make a poppet of myself, yes?" I asked it as I fingered the modelling clay.

"Just make something with two arms and two legs and that pinsized head of yours," it said. "This isn't sculpture, it's symbolism. Then go piss in that bottle there, clip your nails into it, and give me a good hawk of spit on top. We'll run that little lot through the DNA sampler and I'll use the results to–"

The doorbell rang.

"It's OK, that'll be Trixie," I said.

"Oh wonderful," the Burned Man muttered, its voice heavy with sarcasm. "I've missed her."

I heard footsteps on the stairs, and the door banged shut behind her. I knew perfectly well she had only rung the doorbell as a courtesy.

"In here," I called out.

She marched into the room looking nothing like herself at all. She had her hair pulled back into a severe ponytail for one thing, and she was wearing black combat trousers with unflattering army boots and a bulky leather jacket. The jacket was half unzipped to reveal what I could only assume was some sort of body armour underneath. It looked like it was made from articulated plates of thick matt-black plastic.

"Show me your war face, soldier," the Burned Man sniggered.

"Shut up," I told it. "You OK, Trixie?"

She nodded briskly. "Fine," she said. "I'm expecting to work today, that's all."

"Where's your sword?" I asked her.

"Right here," she said, and patted her thigh. "One dimension over. I shift it through when I need it."

"That's a neat trick," I said, impressed.

I suppose things like that shouldn't still have surprised me, knowing what I did about her, but that was seriously cool. I wondered if she'd teach me how to do it. Probably not, thinking about it.

"How are we getting on?" she asked, ignoring my comment.

"*I* have been working on the pattern all night," the Burned Man said. "I'll get you your doppelganger as soon as numbnuts here makes the poppet and produces some

DNA for me to work with. Fuck knows what you two have
been doing."

"Shut up," I said again.

I picked up the modelling clay and the wax and got to
work, kneading one roughly into the other with my thumbs.
The wax had to come from candles used in a genuine Black
Mass, I knew that much. Wormwood really did know all the
beautiful people.

Doppelgangers are fairly simple things, spirit-wise, once
you find one that fits your pattern. The trick is in how you
make use of them. Contrary to popular belief, they *don't* just
happen to look like you. That, like so much occult folklore,
is sadly straight out bullshit. What you have to do, to put it
simply, is make a rough likeness of yourself or the person
you want to impersonate, using the clay and wax poppet.
Then you imbue the poppet with what used to be called the
essence of the person, or what we'd now call their DNA. Nail
clippings, hair, urine, that sort of thing. It's all fairly standard
Vodou stuff, but these days you can greatly enhance the
effectiveness by using the concentration of sampled DNA.
Then, and only then, you summon the doppelganger with
the correct pattern into the poppet and animate it, and away
you go. Simple.

"How long is this going to take?" Trixie asked.

"Five minutes to finish this," I said as I rolled out a leg
between my palms and attached it to the poppet's body. "It
doesn't have to be a work of art, exactly. Couple of minutes
to, um, produce some DNA. Dunno about the sampler."

"Not long," said the Burned Man. "I assume you're taking
it somewhere with you, when it's done?"

Trixie nodded. "Yes," she said. "A good way away from here. If you do it right, Phoenix will follow this version of Don and not the real one."

"Why would he?" I asked. "Sorry, I know you explained this to me last night but I was a bit pissed, to be honest with you. What makes the fake me a stronger draw than the real me?"

"Well nothing, normally," she said. "I'll have to knock you out, I'm afraid. Once you're unconscious, the doppelganger will feel much more like you than you do, if you see what I mean."

I nodded, but I had to admit I was feeling a bit dubious about the whole plan in the cold light of day. Phoenix would be hunting me by my aura, from the traces of me he would have picked up from Vincent and Danny's house. It's a bugger, but whatever you summon has little traces of you on it, and they tend to get left behind like fingerprints wherever the demon goes. It can't be helped, and thankfully it takes a very strong magician to be able to read traces like that. Unfortunately Wellington Phoenix was that strong, and then some. All the same though, the thought that a doppelganger could be made to be more *me* than I was myself made me feel more than a little bit uncomfortable.

Of course, there was always the off-chance that Phoenix was *so* strong he managed to detect the other trace at the house as well, the tiny essence of the Burned Man. I wasn't planning on telling Trixie about that part; she had enough to worry about, after all. If Phoenix managed to do that, if he sent something to follow that secondary trace to my office, well that's what the three screamers were for. There wouldn't be any getting past them. At least, I sincerely hoped there wouldn't be.

"Right, how's that?" I said, holding up the finished poppet for the Burned Man's inspection.

Truth be told, it was a pretty crappy rendition of a human figure that could have been anyone, but the Burned Man nodded happily.

"That'll do," it said. "Like I said, this is just the symbolism. The important bit is your DNA. Now go fill that bottle for me, there's a good lad."

I picked up the bottle and headed towards the bathroom. I paused at the door and glanced back briefly, to see Trixie and the Burned Man glaring at each other like two strange cats in a box. I sighed and went to do the necessary.

I came back a few minutes later with a bottle half full of my piss, nail clippings, and spit. Magic is such a glamorous lifestyle it's a wonder more people don't take it up.

"Here you go," I said.

I put the bottle down on the altar in front of the Burned Man, and it nodded approvingly. I won't bore you with the rest of it, but we ran my "produce" through the sampler and imbued the poppet with the output, and the Burned Man did its thing and summoned the doppelganger into the poppet while Trixie stood over it and did... something. I have no idea what but her dodgy white aura flared even brighter than usual as she wove her own magic into the Burned Man's mix.

I stood well back out of the way, personally. This was all new ground for me. The poppet glazed white with charred ash and fell to bits, and then there I was, standing in front of me in the middle of the circle.

"Bloody hell," I said.

"Bloody hell," said the doppelganger.

The doppelganger looked like me. No, I'm sorry, that's nowhere near good enough. The doppelganger *was* me. It didn't just look like me, standing there in an exact copy of the clothes I was wearing, it even had my very own personal, patented expression of slightly confused pissed off-ness on its face. It also needed a haircut as badly as I did. Damn, this was one of the weirdest things I'd ever experienced in a life that had been pretty much full of weird experiences.

"The fuck," I said, staring at the doppelganger.

"The fuck," the doppelganger said, staring at me.

In Germanic lore, seeing one's own doppelganger is said to be an omen of death. If the way my heart was hammering in my chest was anything to go by, I could well believe it. I honestly felt like I might just have a heart attack right there and then.

"This isn't fucking right, Trixie," I said.

So did the doppelganger.

"It's *me!*" We both said that at the same time, too.

"Ah," said Trixie. "Oh dear."

"You know what, Blondie," the Burned Man said, "I think we might just have fucked something up here."

Trixie shook her head. "No, it has to be good," she said. "Anything less than this good and it won't fool Phoenix for a minute. He'll just have to adjust."

"Will I fuck as like," we said, my doppelganger and I. "I don't like this!"

"You don't have to like it, either of you," Trixie said, "you just have to do it. Come here, Don."

Predictably, we both took a step towards her.

"Not you," she said to the doppelganger. "You wait here a minute. You, you come with me."

She led me out of the workroom and into my office and made me sit down on the sofa. She shut the door firmly behind her.

"Trixie, this... this is weird," I said.

"I know," she said, and patted me gently on the shoulder. "It's only for a little while. I just need a convincing decoy for Phoenix and his horrors. We talked about this last night."

"Yeah I know but... but that's not a fucking decoy, is it? That's actually me."

"Of course it is," she said. "It wouldn't work otherwise. Phoenix isn't stupid."

"You did something, I know you did," I said. "I saw you do it. That's not just a copy of me, it's *me*, isn't it?"

Trixie cleared her throat and started to speak very quietly. "Don," she said, "you have to trust me here. I gave the Burned Man a hand, that's all. To make it work better."

"Bullshit," I whispered back. "What happened to the doppelganger? Because that isn't it. They aren't *that* good. A doppelganger might look like me, but that bloke in there thinks what I'm thinking and says what I say, at exactly the same time. He's an actual different version of me, isn't he? Where did you get that version of me from, Trixie?"

"One dimension over, maybe," she snapped. "What do you care?"

I stared at her. "What do I care, seriously? What don't you understand here? That's *me*, Trixie."

"Nonsense," she said. "Look Don, I'm good, but I'm just one soldier. I have my limits, and I don't know exactly what Phoenix is bringing to the fight. You have to understand, I'm going to be busy today. Very busy, if what I've heard about the terrible Wellington Phoenix is right. I'm afraid I won't be able to come and help you if anything nasty finds you, and I probably wouldn't be able to protect you if you were with me either. It's safer this way. If a Don Drake has to die today, do you want it to be you or the doppelganger?"

"Well..." I started. "Well, shit, I mean... I mean, no, I'm not buying it. We're *both* Don Drake, aren't we?"

"Which set of eyes do you see through?" Trixie asked me. "Yours, or his? Whose memories do you have? Whose life have you lived? He isn't you, Don. He's *a* you maybe, but he isn't *you*."

I shook my head. "Does that make it OK?"

"Does it have to?" she countered. "It makes it him not you, that's all. I can make it the other way around if you'd prefer, but it's one or the other I'm afraid."

I looked at Trixie and again I found myself wondering just who her friends were, and about what sort of company she was keeping these days. The ends always justify the means, I remembered the Burned Man telling me. That is, if you're the type who feels the need to be justified at all.

I always had been that type, if truth be told, but then it was dog eat dog out there after all. I didn't like it, though. I could almost feel the ground shifting under my feet, the moral quicksand getting ready to swallow me up if I slipped another inch. A diabolist walks a bloody fine line at the best of times, and I couldn't help feeling like I was about to fall off mine for good and all.

"Where are you taking him?" I asked her.

"I've got an empty warehouse by the canal," she said. "Plenty of room for a fight, plenty of privacy. I'll let Phoenix come after us there. Don't worry, you'll be safe here."

"Don't let me fall, Trixie," I whispered. "Not all the way, anyway."

She squeezed my shoulder and smiled at me. "I've got you," she said. "Just sit tight Don, I've got you."

She smiled at me, and her beautiful blue eyes seemed to fill my world. That whole lost week came rushing back on me, the infatuation, the stupor, the sheer *adoration* of her. Whatever she had been doing to me then, she was suddenly doing it again in a big way. I was barely aware of her pushing my sleeve up, and when the needle sank into the vein in my arm I groaned with something like release. It was only when the warm, heavy grey blankets descended over my brain that I realized she had shot me full of pharmaceutical grade heroin.

CHAPTER 14

I suppose there was always a chance that it might have gone to plan, but of course it bloody didn't.

When the Burned Man was training me, back in my university days, I'd spent a week mashed out of my brain on heroin. It had insisted. My Crowley phase, it had called it. It told me every young seeker inevitably went through a period of infatuation with Aleister Crowley and his drug fiend methods, and it was determined to get me into and out of that phase as fast as possible to get it over and done with. It had worked, to be fair. I'd never been so fucking ill in my life, and to be honest if that was the junkie lifestyle then you could keep it. Maybe it was preemptive aversion therapy or maybe the Burned Man had just been taking the piss for its own amusement, I never did find out. Either way, it put me off drugs for life.

The world tilted hideously around me as I opened my eyes. There was a vile taste of vinegar acid in the back of my throat and I wanted to throw up. But at the same time, damn, I felt good. I had no idea how long I'd been nodding, but the euphoric warm blanket feeling of the smack was still wrapped around me so it couldn't have been more than a couple of hours. I could hear church bells, somewhere in the distance. A little part of me was telling me that no actually I couldn't, the only thing you ever heard around here were police sirens, but the euphoria drowned it out. I stumbled up off the sofa and into the warm bath of the air in my flat, watching the colours dance at the corners of my vision. There was something… something I was supposed to do. I blundered into the edge of my desk and knocked the telephone onto the floor where it began to buzz like a giant, overturned bumble bee. I could almost see its hairy little telephone-bee legs waving helplessly in the air. That, at the time, struck me as hilarious.

"Oi, are you alive out there?" the Burned Man shouted from the workroom.

I wobbled on my heels, turned, and swam slowly across the office to the workroom door. The Burned Man was swaying back and forth on its altar, leaving traces of muted colour in the air behind it. I smiled at it. I felt so warm, so cosy and comfortable and happy that even the sight of the Burned Man couldn't spoil it.

"Hey little buddy," I said. I sat down on the floor and smiled at it some more. "Hey there."

"Oh for fuck's sake," the Burned Man said. "It's Crowley time again, innit?"

I felt my chin sag down against my chest. I was comfy, but I knew I'd be even more comfy if I curled up on the floor. I wondered why I hadn't thought of that before. There was something, though. I had no idea what, but I knew I was supposed to be doing... something.

"Hey," I said again. "Hey man, you know what?"

"Oh do tell," it said.

"We gotta... do something. Y'know?"

"I know you asked for three screamers," the Burned Man said, "but I can't see you're in any fucking state to do anything about it now."

"Crowley time..." I said.

I dragged myself back up onto my hands and knees, then pushed myself up into a sort of unsteady crouch. Gnosis was one thing, but doing magic while smacked out of your head was quite another. I grabbed hold of the edge of the altar and pulled myself up until my eyes were level with the Burned Man's.

"Seriously?" it asked me.

I nodded, trying to look as serious as I could. "This is important," I said. "I need... I need those fucking screamers. Protection. That's all. I just need them to... you know. Sit there and look hard and shit. Fucking whatever, man. Gimme."

"Can you even focus?" the Burned Man said. "When I put you through this I controlled your dosage to keep you at least sort of functional. Fuck only knows how much Blondie gave you."

"I'm good," I lied. "I can fucking do this."

It took me about a thousand years to mix the iron filings with the goat's blood and mercury for the circle. I kept nodding out, and only the Burned Man shouting abuse at me kept me going at all. When it came to drawing the glyphs I found myself entering some weird sort of Zen state where each manticore spine seemed about a hundred miles long, and moving it the millimetre or so into the right position took every ounce of my concentration. I could feel the Burned Man losing patience with me.

"Toads," it said. "Don't forget the fucking toads, dickhead. Summoning doesn't run on wishful thinking."

That was tricky, I have to admit. The toads kept looking at me, and every time they did I burst out laughing and then had to sit down and cry for a bit. I'm really not cut out for drugs.

We got there in the end, though. Well, I say we, but the Burned Man did ninety percent of it to be honest. Eventually I sank into the deep, warm embrace of the sofa with three half-controlled screamers pacing the office around me, and giggled.

"Good fucking deal," I said.

"Just shut up and try to stay awake," the Burned Man called from the workroom. "You're fucked if one of Phoenix's minions shows up while you're on the nod."

"Screamers," I said. "I got fucking screamers, man."

I reached out to pet one, and it snarled savagely at me and bounded across the room to take up a sentry position behind the desk. I nodded out again.

I woke up sitting at my desk, sweating profusely and with no memory of how I had got there. I was pretty much straight again by then, and the comedown was making its presence felt in a big way. The three screamers in the room with me weren't helping, for all that they were mine. Screamers aren't sane, not even a little bit, and the effort of keeping them under control was giving me a migraine. How the fuck I had been doing it in a heroin dream was a total mystery to me. I guess the Burned Man's Crowley phase training had finally paid off.

As it turned out, they weren't worth the bother. When the door to my office suddenly flew open the screamers reared up as one in a mass of claws and hatred. The door slammed back against the wall and a man walked in. It wasn't Wellington Phoenix. This was a short, nondescript looking bloke wearing a grey suit and carrying a tool box. My screamers went for him like a hurricane of howling fury.

I watched in disbelief as the air split open in front of the little man in a great vertical gash of darkness. An enormous mass of black tentacles burst into the room through the rent in the air and grabbed my screamers, three or four to each one. They yanked hard, bulging with muscle and dripping slime on the floor, and dragged the screamers back through the hole in the air and out of sight. The hole closed with a wet sucking sound and that was the end of that. So much for my protection.

"Good evening," said the man. His voice was very soft.

I glanced out of the window, and realized that it was. Somehow I had nodded most of the day away.

"Who the fuck are you?" I said.

I was trying to sound tough but it came out in a pathetic little croak of sheer terror. I had absolutely no idea what had just taken my screamers away but it was obviously a whole hell of a lot nastier than anything I had ever messed with. I guess that was what Phoenix's methods could buy you. The fact that this creep was even here at all was enough to tell me just how strong Phoenix must be, strong enough to have detected the miniscule secondary traces at Vincent and Danny's house and followed them back here to the Burned Man. Trixie was out there somewhere, right now, trying to fight him. The thought made my blood run cold.

"They call me Lavender," he said. "Please, don't get up."

I realized that I couldn't anyway. Something was holding me tight to my chair, and I couldn't move a muscle below my neck. Lavender looked at me, his smooth, bland face completely expressionless. He switched the office light on and put his tool box down on my desk with a dull thud.

"What happened to my screamers?" I said.

"My employer has provided for my protection," he said.

He took a small, shiny disk out of his jacket pocket and turned it so that it caught the light. There were glyphs of some sort engraved on the metal.

"Talisman," I muttered.

The man nodded. "Yes. This will keep you sitting still, and if I need to use it to bring the devourer back again, I can," he said. "Now, that was the last question that you will ask me. They call me Lavender. I ask questions, and people answer them. Do you understand me?"

I nodded and swallowed in a dry throat. "Yeah," I said. I had a horrible feeling I knew exactly where this was going.

"You are Don Drake," he said.

I didn't really see any point in denying it, so I just nodded again.

"Interesting," he said. "My employer sent me to follow a minor lead, to find your accomplice. And yet here you are. Interesting indeed." He put the talisman down on the desk and opened up the toolbox. He took something out and held it up where I could see it. "Do you know what this is?"

"It's a power drill," I said.

He nodded, his face still completely expressionless. "Yes, this is a drill. This is a drill in the same way that a Bugatti is a car. This is a work of art, Mr Drake. A cordless twenty volt work of art. Do you know what I'm going to do with it?"

"I can probably guess," I said.

"No, I doubt that you can," he said. "I doubt that quite a bit. What I'm going to do, Don, if I may call you Don, is ask you a question. That question will be 'who hired you to kill the McRoths?' You can choose to answer that question, and I'll put the drill away again. If you choose not to answer the question, or if you choose to answer it unsatisfactorily, I will drill a hole through your left kneecap. Don't worry, it's not as bad as it sounds, although obviously it will hurt a great deal. I imagine it will hurt a lot more than you have ever been hurt before, in fact, but with the proper care and medical attention you'll heal, in time. You'll even walk again, do you understand me?"

I just stared at him, horrified.

"I will then ask you the question again," he said, and took something else out of his box. It looked like a lump of white putty. "If you choose not to answer the question, or if you choose to answer it unsatisfactorily, I will roll a thin tube of this and insert it into the hole in your kneecap. That will be quite uncomfortable, not to mention messy, but don't worry. I've done it before. This is C-4 explosive, by the way. I will then attach a detonator to the explosive, and ask the question again. If you again choose not to answer the question, or if you choose to answer it unsatisfactorily, I will blow your leg apart. I fully expect you to pass out before you really feel that, but rest assured once we reach that stage you will *not* ever walk again. Are you following me so far?"

I think I'd actually lost the power of speech by then, but I managed to nod again.

"I have a blowtorch with me too. I will use a tourniquet and the blowtorch to seal and cauterize your leg so you don't bleed to death. I will then give you an injection of adrenaline to bring you back to consciousness. You *will* feel it then, believe me. I will then ask you the question again. If you continue to disappoint my employer and me, I will repeat the procedure on your other leg.

"I very much doubt you will have the endurance to continue further, but, to be clear, let me explain that after your right leg I will begin again with your left wrist, and then your right wrist, and then your elbows.

"Only one subject has ever made me go so far, a military gentleman, and it chastens me to admit that he did not survive the explosive removal of the right upper arm. Of course, I can't take credit for the process, I'm afraid. It is a derivative of what the IRA used to call a six pack, although they simply used a handgun. I like to think I have refined the technique in my own way, that's all. Still, gratifying though that is, I'm sure it's all academic to you at this point. Now, shall we begin?"

He held the drill over my left knee and switched it on. There was no expression on his face whatsoever, but his dead eyes seemed to have come to life for the first time. He was going to enjoy this, I could tell. The drill screamed an inch above my kneecap.

"Who hired you to kill the McRoths?"

I broke.

You really want to try and tell me you wouldn't have?

"Wormwood," I sobbed. "It was Wormwood, he made me do it."

Lavender nodded slowly, and switched the drill off.

"Interesting," he said. "The archdemon Wormwood, I see."

"Yes!" I said. "Yes, that's right, it was Wormwood, he–"

"Oh dear," Lavender interrupted. "I'm afraid that sounds an awful lot like an unsatisfactory answer. I don't believe you. In fact I don't believe that an archdemon would need the help of a rather seedy diabolist to kill anyone. I will ask you one more time, and then I'm going to start hurting you. Who hired you to kill the McRoths?"

I stared at Lavender. Every instinct I had told me his aura should be a writhing black horror of horns and flames, but it wasn't. It was the same dull, fuzzy blue as yours or mine or the woman at the post office's. He wasn't a demon and he wasn't a monster. He was just a man, and that was probably the most terrifying thing of all.

"Wormwood!" I shouted at him. "It was Wormwood, I swear it was! That's how he works, he's all about money and threats and influence and what he can buy with them, not–"

"Your answer," said Lavender, "is unsatisfactory."

He turned the drill on again.

"Help!" I shrieked.

The Burned Man was no use to me now, I knew that much. Trixie couldn't help me either. She had *told* me she wouldn't be able to help me while she was busy with Phoenix and his horrors, but I was pretty much past the point of rational thought by then.

"Trixie please for the love of God fucking help me!"

"I'm afraid she is unable to just at the moment," a man's voice said from somewhere in the gloomy corner of the office. He had the poshest voice I think I've ever heard. "But *I* can. For a price, of course."

Lavender whirled round, the drill held out in his hand like a gun. I still couldn't move, but I twisted my neck around as much as I could until I could see the man who'd spoken. He was very tall and almost impossibly handsome. He stepped out of shadows that shouldn't have been there and I saw he was wearing an expensive looking grey woollen overcoat over a dark suit with a crisp white shirt. His tie was done in a Windsor knot and his black hair was slicked straight back in a way that reminded me of Gold Steevie, but that was where the resemblance ended. I was scared of Steevie because of what he could do, but he was still faintly ridiculous for all of that. I was suddenly scared of this man simply because of what he was. His aura was the same blinding, brilliant white lie as Trixie's own. I realized my suspicions about the company she was keeping had been right.

"Who the hell are you?" demanded Lavender, a note of alarm creeping into his voice.

"I'll pay," I gasped.

I mean fuck it, at that point I'd have given whoever this bloke was just about anything to get me away from Lavender. I already knew *what* he was, and I'm sorry but I just didn't care any more.

Lavender was inching towards the desk where the talisman was lying next to his box of tricks. The stranger looked at him, his eyes narrowing slightly as he studied Lavender's aura.

"Oh, you're only human," he said. "How very boring."

He reached into his coat and pulled out the largest handgun I'd ever seen. Lavender made a lunge for the talisman, but he was far too slow. The gun roared. The muzzle flash was a sheet of deafening flame in the sudden, unnatural darkness that had come over my office. The bullet took Lavender full in the face and blew his brains out through the back of his head.

"Desert Eagle .50 calibre," the man said as he calmly blew smoke from the barrel of the monstrous pistol. "I do *so* love modern things."

"Who the hell are you?" I repeated Lavender's question like an idiot, feeling more than a bit in shock. I'd never seen a man shot through the head before, after all.

"I am a friend of the one you call Trixie," he said, confirming my worst fears. "She said you might need an eye keeping on you tonight. You may call me Adam."

"You're a fallen angel," I said. "A proper one, I mean. Aren't you?"

"Oh yes," said Adam.

"And Trixie asked you to help me?"

"Yes," he said again. "For a price, of course, which you have agreed to pay."

That, now that I thought about it, might just be about to bite me in the arse.

"Which is?"

"Leave her alone," he said. "She has her own path to follow, and it's none of your concern where it leads her. Do you understand me, Donald Drake? Her decisions are hers and hers alone to make."

"She's a big girl," I said, "I'm sure she can think for herself."

"She's little more than a child, relatively speaking," Adam said, "but she's *our* child. Nobody needs a white knight in this day and age."

I was fully aware I was no one's idea of a white knight. Not by a long way I wasn't. I nodded.

"Deal," I said.

Adam had long since taken his shadows with him and disappeared by the time Trixie eventually came back. She limped into my office with blood trickling down her cheek from a long cut under her left eye. Her jacket was gone, and her black body armour was cracked open in two places. Her combat trousers were torn and ragged and dirty. There was a long burn down her bare right arm, and she was obviously favouring her right leg. She held two feet of broken sword in her hand.

"Now that," she said with a grin of satisfaction, "that was a *fight!*"

"Yeah," I said. "There's a lot of it about today."

Trixie's eyes widened as she took in the crimson and grey splatter all over the wall of my office, and then the corpse lying in a pool of blood on the floor on the other side of the desk.

"Ah," she said. "Are you all right?"

"Yeah," I said. "Actually, no. I'm half dead from heroin

comedown, and I've been paralyzed with borrowed magic. There's a dead body on my office floor, brains and bits of head all up my wall, and apparently you're mates with a fallen angel. I am a pretty long way from fucking *all right* as it goes, Trixie."

"Yes, well," she said. She tossed the broken sword onto the sofa and limped towards me. "I can fix one of those things, anyway."

She picked up Lavender's talisman from the desk and rubbed her thumb over it, and I sagged weakly in the chair as the paralysis lifted.

"Careful with that," I said. "He used it to summon something fucking ghastly. It ate my screamers without breaking stride."

Trixie nodded. "A devourer," she said. "Yes, I recognize the glyph for it here. They're nasty things. I should know, I've killed three of them already today."

Three of them? Her grin of savage triumph made me shiver. *I'm just a soldier*, she had said. Yeah, right. I was starting to think she was more like a one-woman panzer division, personally.

"What about your mate Adam then?" I asked her. "What the bloody hell is that all about?"

"Well by the looks of things it was about you not getting tortured to death," Trixie said. She surveyed the room again, her gaze lingering pointedly on Lavender's toolbox. "Do you have a problem with that, Don?"

"Well, not as such, but... shit Trixie, where's the *other* Don? The doppelganger?"

Trixie sighed and sank into the chair opposite mine with a

wince. The corpse at her feet didn't seem to be bothering her, but I couldn't help noticing that her injuries definitely were.

"I did tell you I had my limits," she said. "With three devourers to worry about, I'm afraid... well, there it is. That was the whole point of the exercise, after all. I knew I'd never be able to keep you safe and fight at the same time."

I put my head in my hands and groaned. *It was just a doppelganger*, I told myself. *That's all it was. A very, very convincing doppelganger. Go with that, Don, and don't look back. Don't ever look back.*

"What did you do with Phoenix?" I asked her.

"Ah," she said again. "I'm afraid he decided not to join us."

"What?" I sat bolt upright and stared at her. "You mean he's still out there somewhere? Where is he?"

"I have no idea," Trixie admitted. She looked down at the body by her feet, and smiled. "But I know someone who will."

I followed her gaze, my guts turning over in a sick knot. I was feeling like death warmed up from the heroin comedown, and the sight of that ruined corpse wasn't doing anything to help settle my stomach. What was worse, I had a horrible feeling that I knew where she was going with this.

"Trixie..." I started.

"Yes?"

She has her own path to follow. I sighed and shook my head. "Nothing."

She shrugged. "Now then," she said, "we might need your nasty little friend's help with this, I think."

I was pretty sure I knew with what, but I was going to make her say it anyway.

"With what, exactly?" I asked her.

"With talking to him," she said, prodding the body with her boot. "He must know where Phoenix is staying, or at least how to contact him."

"That's necromancy, Trixie," I said.

"It's getting the job done," she snapped. "I'm tired, Don. I'm tired and I'm hurt and I'm not finished for the day yet, and I do *not* need you lecturing me right now!"

I flinched as she glared at me, her bright blue eyes glittering in the dim light. *Her decisions are hers and hers alone to make.* I sighed and nodded. Maybe Adam was right, at that.

"Sorry," I muttered. "Do you want a plaster or something? For your face, I mean."

She shook her head. "I heal fast," she said. "Don't worry about it. Just help me get this into the other room."

I took Lavender by the feet. I'd help her if I had to, but there was no way I was holding the other end. It didn't seem to bother her from what I could tell, but then she was a soldier after all. I was sure she had made enough corpses of her own over the years. Between us we lugged the body into my workroom, Trixie almost dragging her bad leg as she went.

"You bring me the sweetest gifts, Trixie darling," the Burned Man sniggered as we dumped the body in the middle of the circle.

"Don't waste my time, I'm not in the mood," she said. "Now, help me get it talking."

"Are you fucking serious?" it asked.

"She is," I said. "Word to the wise, Burned Man. Don't piss her off right now, OK?"

The Burned Man took a proper look at her then, obviously noticing her wounds and the expression on her face for the first time. It nodded. I was beginning to suspect that the Burned Man might be a bit of a coward at heart.

"Sorry, it can't be done," it said. "Well I mean it *can*, obviously, but you'd need some serious kit to make this work. Stuff you haven't got any more. Chatting to a bloke with half a head is a bit beyond toads and mercury, if you know what I mean. If only some pillock hadn't gambled away his warpstone, but there we are."

"Just cast the circle and let me take care of the rest of it," Trixie said. "Don, you'll have to do the talking I'm afraid. Just get him to tell us where Phoenix is."

"What are you–" I started, and gaped as Trixie stepped into the circle with the body.

She crouched down with a grimace of obvious pain and pressed the fingertips of her right hand to Lavender's chest, over his heart. She nodded at the Burned Man. I watched in horrified fascination as the Burned Man cast its circle around Trixie and the corpse together. Trixie shuddered and rocked on the balls of her feet, her back arching and her mouth opening wide in a silent scream. She shot to her feet and stared at me.

"You," she said.

I'd have known that soft voice anywhere, and it wasn't hers. I swallowed. This wasn't like what mediums do, not by a long shot. This was more like a Vodou possession. I'd seen that once, seen the cool old hoodoo man from Wormwood's club when Baron Samedi had been riding him. That refined, debonair old man had downed a bottle of pepper-spiced rum like it was water and run amok, whooping and shouting obscenities like he'd had a devil inside him. Which I suppose he had done, in a manner of speaking. In the same way Trixie had now.

I didn't like this one little bit.

"Yeah, me," I said.

Trixie looked at me with Lavender's flat, dead eyes.

"What do you want?" she demanded, in Lavender's voice.

"Now this," said the Burned Man, "this is some fucked up shit."

I had to agree with it. I dreaded to think where Trixie had learned how to do this, but I'd have bet good money that her mate Adam might have had something to do with it.

"Phoenix," I said. "I want Wellington Phoenix. Where is he?"

"Why?" Lavender said. "If you think you can cut a deal with him, you are sadly mistaken. Once he takes a contract, he is relentless. Utterly."

This was going to be a bit of a gamble, I knew. I looked from Trixie to the corpse on the floor and back again, and rolled the dice.

"I don't want to fucking deal with that prick," I said. "I want to kill him."

Lavender sprayed sudden, unexpected laughter through Trixie's lips. "You?" he snorted. "You think *you* can take Phoenix?"

I shook my head. "God no, not me," I said. "Her."

Lavender paused then, as though considering the host body he wore for the first time.

"Interesting," he said after a moment. "What is she, exactly?"

The Burned Man pricked its ears up at that, I noticed. I still hadn't told it about Trixie, and I must admit I hadn't been planning to either.

"Powerful enough to have killed three devourers before dinner is what she is," I said. "I think she can take down Phoenix."

"Why should I help you?" Lavender said. "I'm dead anyway, it's no use to me."

"You're dead because Phoenix got you killed today," I said. "Are you seriously going to tell me you don't want to get him back for that?"

"His death won't give me back my life, or bring me any pleasure," Lavender said. "I choose not to answer your question."

Simple revenge wasn't going to do it then, and I knew there was no point trying to appeal to his better nature as he quite obviously didn't have one. *Think, Drake. What* does *he want?* Bring me any pleasure, he'd said. One thing I had learned about Lavender in the short and unpleasant time we'd known each other was that he loved his work. If there was one thing this vile little man wanted it was someone to hurt.

"Tell me where he is," I said, "and once he's dead I'll bind his shade to yours and send it down to you in Hell for you to torture for all eternity."

Lavender licked Trixie's lips and stared at me. "Can you do that?"

I pointed at the altar.

"That is the fetish of the Burned Man," I said. "You don't want to *know* what I can do, down in Hell."

Lavender nodded slowly. After a moment, he gave me the address of the apartment Phoenix was renting in South Kensington. Trixie got rid of him sharpish after that. When it was done, and the Burned Man had closed the circle, she just stood there with a slightly sick expression on her face. She kept rubbing her bare arms with her hands as though trying to brush off something nasty.

"What a revolting individual," she said. "*Can* you do that, by the way? Make someone suffer more, in Hell?"

I shrugged. "Buggered if I know," I said. "Doubt it."

Trixie blinked at me, as though she was struggling to grasp the concept of a bluff.

"Pity," she said.

CHAPTER 15

There had been quite a lot of debate about whether I was going to Phoenix's apartment with Trixie or not. When I say "debate" obviously I mean a standup row, which we'd had in my workroom whilst watching a pair of hastily summoned vorehounds eating Lavender's corpse. It wasn't the nicest evening I've ever spent with an attractive woman, all in all.

I won in the end, somehow. Now I'm no Sir Galahad, I think we're all pretty clear about that by now, but that wasn't the point. The cut on her face and the burn on her arm might have healed over already, but she was clearly still hurting for all that she was trying to hide it. Add to that the fact that this whole mess was of my own making, and on top of *that* I still didn't even completely understand why she was helping me at all. The Furies were her main interest, not Wellington Phoenix. He was nothing to do with her at all, and everything to do with me. She was only doing this to help me out, and it had already got her hurt. I didn't feel like I had any choice, not if I wanted to be able to face myself in the mirror the next morning.

Something was bothering me though – I wasn't sure I was really buying her whole line about keeping me on the straight and narrow. It had sounded a lot more plausible yesterday when I was pissed than it did now, to be perfectly honest. Fair enough, she didn't want me going so far off the deep end that I did something really stupid like release the Burned Man, but all that business about controlling the Furies by making me behave smelled more than a bit fishy to me now that I'd had time to think about it. That damage was well and truly done, as far as I could see. Whatever her reasons were though, she had forgiven me and no way was I going to let her face Wellington Phoenix on her own.

"I still say you shouldn't be coming with me," she said, as the taxi drove us over the bridge and into the foreign country that was North Of The River.

"And I'm still coming anyway," I said.

Trixie pulled a face and huddled into the spare coat I had lent her. There wasn't time to fanny about with changes of clothes now. Still, I could hardly let her walk around the moneyed avenues of South Ken in her ragged fatigues and broken body armour, not even at two in the morning. People would stare, don't you know, and whatever would the neighbours say, darling?

We eventually pulled up two streets away from Phoenix's building. I had decided it would be safer to do the last little bit on foot. There was no way of knowing exactly how this was going to go down, after all, and if the Old Bill ended up shoving their noses in, then the last thing I wanted was some smartarse of a cabbie remembering dropping two people off at the front door just beforehand. I paid the driver and we stepped out into a fine South Kensington night. It's a funny thing, but somehow even the weather always seems better in the posh parts of the city. We had walked maybe half the distance when I realized just how badly hurt Trixie still was.

"You're limping like a pirate with a peg leg," I said, offering her my arm.

"It's nothing," she said, but I could tell she was gritting her teeth. "The last devourer broke my femur, I think."

I stared at her. *She's walking into battle on a broken thigh bone, seriously?* "Are you in any shape to do this? Tell me honestly now, Trixie."

"Honestly? No, not really," she said, "but we haven't got any choice."

"We could–" I started.

"Do you want to go to sleep and wait for him to realize something's gone wrong?" she interrupted. "What do you think he's going to do, exactly, when he decides that Lavender isn't coming back?"

I cleared my throat. That was a very good point. I had no desire to be woken up in the middle of the night by one of Phoenix's horrors gnawing on my balls.

"Fair enough," I said. "Just take my arm at least, will you?"

She did, and leaned on me heavily as we made our slow way to the front of Phoenix's apartment building. I buried my free hand in my coat pocket and gingerly fingered the thing I had brought with me from the flat. I really hoped I wouldn't need it, but I was starting to wonder. We climbed the steps to the front door slowly and, in Trixie's case at least, painfully. The doorbell intercom was one of those video jobs, I noticed with a sinking feeling.

"Just stay out of sight," she said, and pushed the button. The machine bleeped.

"It's me," Trixie said, in Lavender's voice.

I looked sharply at her. She was wearing Lavender's face, above my spare coat. I shivered. She was a girl of many talents and no mistake.

"About time," a deep voice rumbled from the intercom, and the door buzzed open.

"Yuk," Trixie said, wiping away the glamour of Lavender with a distasteful swipe of her hand. "He really was not a very nice man."

"No shit," I muttered as I followed her into the tastefully decorated Georgian lobby.

"Third floor," Trixie said.

Thankfully there was a lift, a baroque confection of brass rods and levers that would probably be worth a fortune at one of those poncey Notting Hill antiques places. Good job too, as I really didn't think she would have made it up three flights of stairs. She was leaning heavily on my arm again by the time we arrived outside Phoenix's front door. I stood aside as she put on Lavender's face once more and rang the doorbell. Wellington Phoenix opened the door, filling the opening like an ebony colossus in a dark grey suit and open-necked pink shirt.

"Why has it taken this long?" he said, before he realized the body below Lavender's face most definitely did not belong to Lavender.

"In," Trixie said, and shoved him in the chest so hard he staggered backwards into the apartment and hit the floor with a heavy thud.

I followed her inside and kicked the door shut behind me. Phoenix was on his feet again already, and he was chanting. I remembered the broken sword Trixie had left on my sofa, and prayed she had another weapon hidden somewhere she could get to it in a hurry. Apparently she didn't need one.

"Oh no you don't," she said.

She pivoted smoothly on her bad leg and kicked Phoenix in the side of the knee with the toe of her boot. He howled and went down again.

"I'm not messing around with any more of your vile pets," she said. "This time it's just you and me, Wellington."

She reached down and grabbed him by the throat with her right hand, and hauled him up onto his knees. Phoenix was a huge man, still well over twenty stone even in his old age, but Trixie lifted him with no more than a grunt. She punched him in the solar plexus with her left fist, doubling him over, then followed that up by kicking him so hard he went crashing into an antique writing desk.

It had all been going so well up until then.

Phoenix hauled himself up and wrenched open the desk drawer. His hand dipped inside and came back out holding a long, ornate dagger.

"What are you, woman?" he panted. "Something that can die, I hope."

He had so far ignored me completely, I noticed. I have to admit that pissed me off a bit.

"Not by your hand," Trixie said.

She grinned and twisted her empty right hand through a double figure-of-eight movement. There was a sort of blurry shimmer in the air, and when she finished there was a sword in her hand. A new one. She swung into her guard position and cut for Phoenix's head before he could get his breath back enough to start his summoning chant again. He threw himself desperately to one side and knocked over an occasional table, sending a priceless-looking Chinese vase crashing to the carpet. She held her guard posture as he lumbered back to his feet once more.

Phoenix bellowed and charged.

It was an unorthodox move certainly, and definitely not a gentlemanly one, but it worked – after a fashion. Trixie stepped smoothly out of his way of course, pivoting like a dancer, one foot crossing behind the other as she brought her blade up and over for the killing stroke.

Her broken leg collapsed.

She went down with a shriek of pain and Phoenix fell on her with all his weight. He slammed the sword from her hand, sending it flying across the carpet. The point of his dagger slipped through one of the cracks in her armour and he drove it into her stomach to the hilt.

"Trixie!" I screamed.

My hand plunged into my coat pocket as Phoenix started to work the dagger free from the blood-slick armour. I pulled Lavender's talisman out of my pocket and stared helplessly at it, wishing I'd had time to study it properly before we'd left my flat. There were three glyphs engraved on the disk. One was a fairly straightforward representation of a human figure with thin lines extending from its wrists and ankles which I could only assume was for the paralysis spell. It was going to take a lot more than that to stop Wellington Phoenix, I was sure. The other two meant nothing to me, but in my experience the more complicated a Goetic sigil is, the nastier the thing it represents. I mashed my thumb down onto the biggest and ugliest of the glyphs and focused my Will into it as hard as I'd ever focused on anything in my life.

"Come to me," I whispered. "Come on, you horrible thing, come here..."

The air tore open beside me, and dripping black tentacles boiled into the room from some unseen void of darkness. I have to confess that wasn't the best time to realize I had absolutely no idea how to control a devourer. Often though, in magic as in life, the simplest answer is the right one. I pointed at Wellington Phoenix where he crouched over Trixie's prone body. He had the dagger free at last, and was raising it over her throat for the final blow.

"Kill," I said.

The tentacles surged forwards, accompanied by a stomach-churning slobbering noise from the hole in the air. Phoenix spun around, his dagger raised, but the look on his face told me it was already too late.

"No!" he screamed.

The devourer's tentacles grabbed him, three or four to each arm and leg. Muscles bunched under the slick, rubbery skin as they began to squeeze.

"Kill him!" I yelled at the monstrosity.

Phoenix wailed as the Devourer yanked him off his feet and dragged him through the air towards the shimmering black void. I had a momentary glimpse of teeth in there, thousands of hideous, glistening teeth, then he was gone. The portal closed with a thoroughly revolting noise that sounded a lot like chewing. I dropped the talisman like it was a warm turd and hurried to kneel at Trixie's side.

"Don't be dead," I whispered as I cradled her head in my hands. "Oh dear God please don't be dead."

"She's not," said an aristocratic voice behind me.

I almost died of shock. I leaped to my feet and whirled around to keep myself between Trixie and whoever it was, in the throes of a brief fit of suicidal bravery. I relaxed when I saw who it was. A bit, anyway.

"You're a bit fucking late," I said.

Adam chuckled. "It looks to me like you did just fine without me," he said. "You showed good control of the devourer there, and a very strong will."

"Spare me the man love and help me with Trixie," I said, kneeling beside her again. "I can't lose her now."

He scooped Trixie effortlessly up from the floor and never said a word about the blood soaking into the front of his immaculate suit. He simply nodded at one corner of the room, where it suddenly got very dark indeed until I couldn't even see Phoenix's opulent wallpaper any more.

"Coming?" he asked, and strode into the darkness with Trixie in his arms.

Now I admit that following a self-confessed fallen angel into unknown darkness might not sound like it was one of my better plans, but there was no way I was letting him out of my sight while he had Trixie. I grabbed up the talisman, swallowed hard and went after him.

CHAPTER 16

I can't tell you how relieved I was when we stepped out of the darkness into my office and not into the depths of Hell.

"Bedroom?" Adam asked.

I pointed wordlessly to the door at the end of the hall, trying not to think about how exactly the fuck I had just walked home from South Kensington in a single step. Adam nodded and carried Trixie inside. I was just starting after him when he shut the door firmly in my face. I stared helplessly at it for a moment, then went back to the office and slumped onto the sofa. It might be my flat, but I could tell there was something going on in there that I really wasn't supposed to see. That was fine by me. It had been, to put it mildly, a fucking long day. I let my head sag back and closed my eyes.

Phoenix was dead and in Hell where he belonged, so I was at least reasonably confident I would live to see the morning. Whether Trixie would was another matter – Phoenix's knife had gone into her to the hilt, and there had been a frightening amount of blood. I was far from thrilled at having a fallen angel under my roof but if Adam could save her, I'd be willing to forgive him almost anything.

She'll be back on her feet slaying Furies in no time, I told myself.

I wanted to believe it, I really did. Poor Trixie was desperate to destroy Ally and her sisters so she could finally go home. I could understand that, but how she thought she was ever going to kill something that apparently wouldn't stay dead I really had no idea.

I sighed. Trixie had forgiven me, and fought for me, and tonight she had almost died for me. The least I could do was help her figure out how to kill the Furies once and for all.

"Oi, numbnuts, is that you back?" the Burned Man called out from the workroom.

I groaned and got up again.

"Yeah," I said as I pushed the door open. "Yeah, we're back."

"And?"

"Phoenix is gone," I said. "Adam is back. Trixie is... I dunno. Half dead, I think."

"Who the fuck is Adam?" it demanded.

Damn it. It really *had* been a long day, I was starting to slip up.

"Friend of Trixie's," I said. "Don't wind him up, OK?"

"As if I would," it said. "Are you planning on feeding me today, by the way?"

"Oh for fuck's sake," I muttered, but I opened my shirt and sank wearily to my knees in front of it anyway. "Don't blame me if you nod out, I don't know how much smack there still is in my system."

"Doesn't affect me," the Burned Man said, and sank its

teeth into my chest with a wet slurp of satisfaction.

I groaned and let it feed. I was still kneeling there when the door opened and Adam walked in.

"Oh my," he said.

Oh bollocks, I thought.

"Well now, isn't this interesting," Adam said.

He came into the room and shut the door behind him. The front of his shirt was sodden with blood.

"How's Trixie?" I asked.

"She's asleep," he said. "Don't worry, she'll be right as rain in the morning. We do heal awfully fast you know, and I've helped her along a little."

The Burned Man let go of my chest so fast I thought it had been stung.

"We?" it asked, its eyes glittering eagerly. "What are you then, mate? You and her?"

"They're friends," I said at once. "Aren't you, Adam?"

"We have a mutual understanding I suppose you might say, Don," he said, a wry smile playing around his lips. "I don't suppose I could make myself a cup of coffee?"

"Help yourself," I said. "Kitchen's down the hall."

He nodded and left the room again.

"Bugger it, Drake, what aren't you telling me?" the Burned Man demanded. "You *know* something, don't you?"

"You're done feeding for the night, I know that much," I said, and got to my feet.

"Bastard!" it shouted at my back as I closed the door on it.

I wasn't even really sure why I didn't want it to know what Trixie was, but something at the back of my mind kept telling me it was very important that it didn't find out. It had been the Burned Man that had been so adamant she wasn't an angel in the first place, after all, and something about that was starting to smell bad.

I found Adam in the kitchen stirring sugar into a cup of black coffee. "Thanks for that," I said.

He gave me a level look.

"The Burned Man, Don. I'm impressed. It's no wonder you handled the devourer so deftly if you're accustomed to controlling that."

Controlling *might be putting a bit of a gloss on it*, I thought, but I saw no reason to disillusion him just then.

"Yeah, well," I said. "You know how it is."

"No, I'm not sure that I do," Adam said. "You'll have to tell me all about it some time."

"Look, I don't know about you mate but I'm bloody knackered," I said. I thought of Trixie lying in my bed, and sighed. "I'll take the sofa."

Adam gave me a thin smile. "You do that," he said.

I hate sleeping on sofas but I was so tired I went out like a light. I don't know how long I slept for, but when I was woken up by the sound of raised voices it must have been sometime around mid morning. The shouting sounded like it was coming from my bedroom. I sat up and rubbed my eyes, trying to listen.

"...even he knows that much. Now that I've seen..."

That was Adam's voice, definitely, although I could only make out snatches through the closed door. I didn't know whether he'd gone away and come back again or not, but the thought that he might have spent the night in there with Trixie irritated me much more than it should have done.

"...be done, or I'd have..." Trixie replied, sounding waspish and irritable. "...close to him... your idea in the first place."

"Plans change. You must..."

"...want to go *home!*"

She sounded upset now, there was no mistaking that, but thank God she was still alive. I got up and padded down the hall. The voices stopped abruptly, and Adam opened the door. I looked past his shoulder to see Trixie propped up on my pillows with the sheets pulled up to her chin and her blonde hair spread out in loose disarray. The sight of her in my bed made my insides do something strange.

"Morning," I said.

"Yes it is," said Adam, without much warmth to his tone. "Did you want something?"

Whose place is this anyway? I thought, but it didn't seem like a good idea to say it just then.

"I just wanted to see how Trixie is," I said.

She smiled at me. "Much better, thank you Don," she said. "Adam has quite a healing touch."

Adam's touch was the last thing I wanted to hear her talk about. I cleared my throat, feeling awkward.

"Good," I said. "Good, I'm, um, glad to hear it. Well, um, I'll leave you to it then."

Adam nodded and closed the door on me without another word. After that there was no more shouting, and if they were still talking at all they were doing it quietly enough that I couldn't hear them through the door. I sighed and went to put the kettle on. My stomach felt fluttery, the way it had during my lost week, but I knew she wasn't doing anything to me now. This was my own head playing games with me. I wanted to slap myself.

Have a word with yourself Don, for fuck's sake. I was just missing Debbie, that was all it was. I was missing female company in general to be honest, so I was looking for it in completely the wrong place. As usual. I made a coffee and carried it back through to my office. The huge blood-and-brains stain on the wall greeted me with its presence. *A spot of cleaning will take my mind off things,* I thought. I sat down behind my desk, sipped my coffee, and stared at the telephone. *It's still too soon to call her.* I picked up the receiver and punched Debbie's number anyway.

"Hi, this is Debbie," said her answering machine. "I can't..."

Her mobile went straight to voicemail too. I hung up and sighed. Cleaning it was, then.

I rooted through the cupboard under the kitchen sink for a bucket and scrubbing brush, but I must admit the enormity of the task seemed a bit daunting. I supposed I could scrub the sticky patch off the floor and just buy a rug or something to cover the inevitable stain, but the wall was a bit beyond my meagre domestic skills. There was a crater where the bullet had ended up that would need filling, for one thing. It would probably be easier to just repaint the whole thing, but that would mean going out and buying paint, and a roller, and why the fucking hell was I even worrying about that right now anyway?

I picked up the phone and called Debbie again. The answer machine picked up, and I howled with frustration and hurled the phone onto the floor in a fit of sudden rage.

I stared at it for a moment, then picked it up again and put it gently back on the desk. I sank into my chair and laid my head on the desk. Things were, I think it's fair to say at this point, starting to get on top of me a bit.

I suppose I must have dozed off again like that, because the next thing I knew Trixie was shaking me gently by the shoulder. I looked up at her and frowned. She was wearing one of my old T-shirts and a pair of jogging bottoms I had forgotten I owned. She looked much, much better than she had any right to, all things considered. She looked bloody gorgeous, to be perfectly honest, but I was trying not to think about that.

"Sleepyhead," she said, with a smile.

"Mmmmh," I said, sitting up and rubbing my eyes vigorously. "How are you feeling?"

"Much better," she said. "Look."

She walked slowly across the room and back again to prove it. She was still limping a bit, but for someone who'd had a collapsed femur and a horrific stab wound less than twelve hours ago it was beyond belief.

"Wow," was all I managed to come up with.

"I told you, Adam has a healing touch."

"Where is he anyway?" I asked.

"Oh, he's gone," she said. "He had some things he had to do, but he'll be back later."

"Oh good," I said, trying and completely failing to keep the vinegar out of my voice. "Look, about Adam. Honestly Trixie, I'm not sure he's really the best company you could be keeping at the moment, if you know what I mean."

"Damn it, Don, he's the only one of my own kind who

still even speaks to me," Trixie snapped.

Your own kind? Not any more he's not.

"I'm just not sure Adam has your best interests at heart, that's all," I said.

"Perhaps," she said. "Who knows what's best, these days?"

I shrugged. That, as ever, was the sixty-four thousand dollar question.

"What *is* best for you?" I asked her. "What do you really want, Trixie?"

Her eyes blazed with sudden anger. "I want to go *home*," she shouted at me. "Is that so bad of me? I just want to go home, but I can't, can I? I can't go home until I've killed the Furies, and the Furies can't be killed. I'll be stuck here forever, trapped on Earth on an impossible mission I can never complete. It's not *fair!*"

I frowned at her. It certainly didn't sound very fair to me, but then of course life isn't. "Who would even give you a job like that?"

"My Dominion," she said, and sighed. "My boss, sort of, to put it in words you'd understand. No that's not right, much more than my boss. My king, my father, my... Oh I don't know, it doesn't really translate into English. I'm just an angel, just... a soldier, like I told you. Do you understand how armies work?"

I nodded. "Sort of," I said. I'd watched a lot of war movies. "Enough, probably. Go on."

"Well," she said, "I'm a soldier. Above me are the archangels. They're our sergeants, sort of, then the principalities above them, they're like the officers. They take their orders directly from the Dominions, the top brass. The only ones above them are the thrones and the seraphim, but it starts to get very weird up there by all accounts. I wouldn't really know what they're like I'm afraid, and I don't even pretend to understand how the Upper Echelon actually works. I'm just a soldier, Don, and like most soldiers all I want to do is stop fighting and go home."

"Spending time with Adam probably isn't going to help with that," I pointed out. "If you slipped a bit then he fell right off the bloody cliff, didn't he?"

"He helped me," Trixie said. "When I slipped, I mean. He showed me… well, he…"

She has her own path to follow, Adam had told me. I nodded.

"I'm sure he did," I said. I reached out and took her hand, "and I'm sure you know what you're doing."

I was sure of no such thing, but like I'd told Adam, she was a big girl.

Adam came back later that afternoon, more's the pity. I was still on my knees scrubbing the floor when he appeared in my office, which I have to admit didn't do much for my standing as the alpha male in my own flat. I had taken Trixie down to Dave's for lunch earlier on, but now she was resting again at my insistence. She might say she was fine now, but I don't think either of us really believed it.

"How is she?" Adam said, by way of a greeting.

"Asleep, with a bit of luck," I said. I got up and looked at him. "Look, Adam, I think we need to talk about Trixie."

"Do you?" Adam asked mildly. "I really don't think we do, you know."

He made to walk past me towards the bedroom, but I

reached out and put a hand on his arm.

"Yeah," I said, "we really do."

Adam looked down at my hand on the arm of his horribly expensive-looking suit, and back up at me again.

"I see," he said.

Now I'm sorry, but I really was scared of Adam. I didn't like him one little bit, however cool his teleporting trick might be, but I was scared of him all the same. Admittedly he hadn't really *done* anything except shoot a man, and I was pretty sure I could do that too given the gun. That wasn't the point though. With him, it was a simple matter of what he *was*. I dropped my hand.

"Look," I said again. "About Trixie... I know what you said, and I know what I agreed to, but–"

"But what?" Adam interrupted me, his aristocratic voice turning to ice. "You are out of your depth here, Donald Drake. You are a very long way out of your depth indeed, in cold and shark-infested waters. Do you really want to question me on this?"

I met his eyes. He had very dark eyes, the irises almost completely black. I swallowed hard.

"Whatever," I muttered. "Just... look after her, OK?"

"Of course," Adam said. "I will *always* look after her."

He turned away and went into the bedroom. The door closed softly behind him and I sagged onto the sofa. I realized my hands were trembling. Of all the crazy things I'd done recently, I couldn't help thinking that might just have been the closest to actual bravery I'd ever come in my life. If these were shark-infested waters then he was the biggest damn shark in them, I was sure of that. Damn but he really did scare the living shit out of me.

I rubbed my hands over my face and swallowed hard, then very carefully slipped my shoes off. I tiptoed down the hall as quietly as I possibly could, almost holding my breath. I couldn't help thinking it was faintly ridiculous to have to sneak around my own flat like this, but it couldn't be helped. I pressed my ear right up against the bedroom door. I'd obviously missed the start of the conversation, and damn him for waking her up at all, but I could hear Trixie talking now.

"Will it help me, though?" she said.

"Fear no demon, Meselandrarasatrixiel," Adam replied. "It is they who should fear us. I am a Duke, in Hell. I can command the Legion and the Leviathan, if I but order it. Do not ask, *command*. That is the true way to power. I told you, even this man Drake knows that much."

"But I thought–"

"Command," he said again. "*Use* the power I have shown you, child. Use it, and triumph."

I winced. That didn't sound good at all. I might not be a churchgoing man these days but I'd been raised Catholic as a lad and I knew what temptation sounded like when I heard it.

"Yes, Adam," she said.

There was something in her voice just then, something cowed, something *owned*, that made me want to kick the door in and just flatten the posh smarmy cunt right there and then. If only life was that simple. It went quiet after that, and I eased myself away from the door and sneaked back down the hall before I was discovered skulking outside.

I had promised myself I would help Trixie figure out how to defeat the Furies, but, from the way things sounded right then, I reckoned the most important thing was to get Adam's claws out of her before her little slip turned into a headlong fall into Hell.

Adam was right about one thing, I *was* out of my depth. I needed some advice, and I knew the Burned Man wasn't the right one to give it to me. That, I'm afraid, didn't leave me with a lot of options. I put my coat on, checked my pockets for money and keys and stuff, and knocked on the bedroom door.

"I'm going out," I called. "Don't wait up."

I left without waiting for an answer.

CHAPTER 17

There was a little Italian place a couple of streets away and I went there first for a bit of dinner. I was getting heartily sick of Big Dave's bacon-with-everything menu for one thing, and for another he wasn't licensed. The Italian place was, so I happily killed a bottle of red while I ate my spag bol. It felt good to be on my own for once, somewhere I was no different to any other punter. I almost had a minor nervous breakdown at one point when I saw a woman with red hair walk into the restaurant, but it wasn't Ally. *It's just some redhead girl*, I told myself as I finished my glass of wine in one long, shuddering swallow. *Calm down man, for fuck's sake. Ally's hardly the only red haired woman in London.*

I lingered over dessert and liqueur coffees until about ten o'clock, then paid up and went looking for a taxi. The roll of cash Trixie had given me was still comfortingly fat in my pocket, and I was buggered if I was walking all that way in the dark and the cold if I didn't have to.

The cabbie pulled up where I told him to at about ten thirty, right at the end of the alley. I tipped him too much and waited for him to clear off before I started walking. I was nervous now, and getting paranoid about being seen going in. Fuck knows why, looking back on it. Like I said, things had been starting to get on top of me recently. They must have been, or I would never have thought this was a good idea in the first place.

I walked down the alley and stopped outside the hidden entrance to Wormwood's club. I waved a hand over the graffiti-covered brickwork, and mumbled the words of entry a bit less clearly than usual. I walked into the wall, through the cold, sticky feeling of the glamour, and into the bar on the other side.

There was a sudden hush as I stepped into the dimly lit little bar. Connie was standing at the bottom of the stairs that led up into the club proper, wearing his dinner suit and looming the way a good bouncer should. He was the only person in there that I recognized, though. Well, I say person but you know what I mean. It dawned on me that I was actually the only human in there. Now we're usually in the minority, admittedly, but I don't think I'd ever been the *only* one before. I waved hastily at Connie before any of the patrons decided to make an issue of my being there.

"Yo, Connie," I called out. "How's it going, big lad?"

"All right, Don," Connie said. He nodded at me, and I felt the mood in the room palpably relax.

Bless him, if he hadn't been so ugly I could almost have kissed him right then. I was certainly ready to forgive him the various hidings he'd given me. It's the same in clubs all over the world, I'm sure it is. If you're in with the bouncer, you're OK with everyone. I picked my way through the crowd to talk to him.

"Is the boss in?" I asked.

Connie jerked his head towards the top of the stairs.

"He's upstairs," he said. "Playing cards, I think. You ain't going to go and spoil his night now, are you Don?"

"Who me? Nah, I just want a chat," I said. "I'm after a bit of advice like, that's all."

Connie gave me a dubious look, but in the end he nodded.

"Go on up then," he said. "You know the way."

Connie stood out of the way to let me up the stairs, and I climbed the thick red velvet carpet into the upstairs club. It was smoky up there already, and busier than it normally was this early in the evening. I recognized the hoodoo man over at a table in the far corner, drinking rum and playing craps with something enormous and covered in shaggy brown hair. The old man was wearing his top hat and tails again, and had his arm around a slender blonde who couldn't have been more than sixteen. *You old dog,* I thought. I waved, and he grinned and tipped his hat at me in greeting. There were a few other actual humans up there, thankfully, but no one else I knew other than by sight.

Wormwood was sitting at his usual table with the two decks of cards neatly positioned on the green cloth in front of him, ready for Fates. He had an already full ashtray balanced on the arm of his chair by his elbow. The waitress with the cute tail was nowhere to be seen tonight, sadly, but there was a glass and an open bottle of single malt waiting by the empty chair opposite him for anyone who might fancy taking him on.

I walked up to his table and cleared my throat.

"Evening, Wormwood," I said.

"If you're here about that little bit of business," Wormwood said quietly, "you need to learn some fucking protocol. I mean, well done and all that shit but this ain't the time or the place to be talking about that sort of thing, you understand me?"

"Nah, no business tonight," I said. "I just wanted a little chat. Like I told Connie, I'm after a bit of advice, that's all."

Now I know that going to Wormwood for advice probably makes me sound like I'd gone off my head. Maybe I had a bit, looking back on it, but you have to remember that Wormwood was an archdemon. A bloody horrible seedy one, granted, but an archdemon of Mammon none the less. He was a businessman, not a despoiler of worlds. He was a child of Mammon and a cunning, *ruthless* businessman, who had got where he was through influence and manipulation rather than violence.

If there was one thing Wormwood knew inside out it was how to get people to do what he wanted them to. If anyone could tell me how to get Adam's claws out of Trixie without getting myself into a fight I had no chance of surviving, it was him.

"Nothing's free in this life, not even advice," Wormwood said, with a sour twist of his greyish lips. "Especially not in here, and even more so not when you want it from me. I'll play you a hand for it, if you've got anything to bet."

I sighed. Of course nothing was free – not from Wormwood it wasn't anyway. I knew him that well, so I'd seen this coming. It would have been nice to have been wrong, but there we were.

"I've got one thing," I said. "Just one though, so no raising, OK?"

"It'd better be good," he said, but I could tell he knew it would be if I was even offering it to him.

"Oh yes," I said. "It is."

I took Lavender's talisman out of my pocket and put it on the table between us.

"This summons a devourer," I said. "And does some other shit too, but the devourer's the star prize. That's my bet."

Wormwood's eyes glittered with avarice. From what I had seen of them, I reckoned a single devourer probably represented more killing power than all the other muscle at his command put together. The look on his face told me I was right.

"What's mine?" he asked.

I shrugged. "Against this? That advice I want, for one thing. Then, well, depending what you tell me, either your help carrying out that advice or you wipe my slate clean. And I'm still undervaluing this, and you know it."

"Yeah well, you ain't got anything else, have you, unless I'm wildly mistaken," he said. He sucked his shit-coloured teeth for a moment while he made up his mind. "Deal."

Normal blokes would have shaken hands at that point, but neither of us were exactly normal and neither of us much wanted to touch the other one. We nodded at each other instead, and the croupier cut the two decks and began to deal the minor arcana from the thicker of the two decks.

I poured myself a drink. I'd already done that bottle of red wine in the Italian, and three or four liqueur coffees after that, but now I really felt like I needed a drink. I tipped the first shot straight down my neck and was refilling the glass before I'd even finished swallowing. This was it. This, as I saw it, was pretty much my last chance to get between Adam and Trixie before it was too late.

I picked up my cards and fanned them, looking at a pair of sixes and a mixture of random junk. I kept my face smooth. Except for the uncontrollable tic that was beating under my left eye, anyway. Wormwood looked down at his own cards, his horrible weaselly little face expressionless. The way Fates is played, you have to decide on your minor arcana, your suits, before you draw your trump.

Wormwood plucked a card out of his fan and discarded it on the table, face down.

"Card," he said.

I did the same. The dealer dished us each out another minor card, and I had to fight to keep my face still. Six of Pentacles – this was more like it.

Wormwood said nothing, nodded. He looked at me. "I'm good," he said. "Stand."

I swallowed another shot of whisky and poured again, fighting my nerves. My palms were itching so bad I wanted to scrape them on the side of the table until they were raw. Three of a kind was good, but this was Wormwood I was up against, and tonight I might very well be playing for an angel's soul.

"Card," I said, dropping a useless Three of Swords face down onto the table.

The dealer pushed a new card to me across the table, and I gently eased it up and into my fan. Six of Cups! That gave me four of a kind. I nodded, trying and failing to keep my left eye under control.

"Stand," I said.

"Trumps then," said Wormwood.

The dealer slipped us each a card from the slim deck of major arcana. You can't change your trump card once it's been dealt. That's the "fate" part of Fates. I gently eased mine up and peered at the corner of the card. It was the motherloving Tower again, the very card that had started this whole miserable mess for me in the first place. I cleared my throat. I don't know how well up on your tarot you are, but the Tower isn't usually regarded as exactly what you'd call a good omen.

"We agreed no raising," I reminded him. "This is it, Wormwood. What've you got?"

He raised an eyebrow at me. "Challengers first," he said.

I shrugged and laid my cards out. Four sixes and the Tower was a blinding hand, and I knew it. The Tower might not be an auspicious card in tarot but it's the sixteenth trump so at least it scores well. A smile was already starting to creep across my lips even before I saw the wide-eyed expression on Wormwood's face.

"Four sixes?" he whispered. "You've got four sixes and sixteen, you wanker?"

I nodded. "Looks that way," I said, unable to resist twisting the knife. "It ain't your lucky night, Wormwood."

"Smug little prick," Wormwood muttered as he threw his cards face down onto the table.

I never did find out what he'd had, but it was a safe bet it was a losing hand. Wormwood doesn't have a magnanimous side any more than he has a sense of humour.

"My hand, I think," I said. "So let's talk."

"Knowing what a fuckup you are, as a rule," Wormwood said, "I ain't listening to your tales of woe in front of all these good people. Come into the office with me."

He got up and led me across the club, patting backs and shaking hands as he went, exchanging nods and smiles and generally taking care of business. I trailed in his wake and tried to ignore all the curious stares I could feel following me through the crowd. Hardly anyone got a private audience with Wormwood, I knew that much, and the fact that I'd evidently just won mine at the card table seemed to be making me interesting.

He ushered me through a door and into an office. It was much nicer than the one downstairs where he had received me last time. This looked like it was where actual club business got done, as opposed to the other sort. He sat down behind a huge rosewood desk and waved brusquely at one of the chairs facing him. He lit a cigarette.

"So, advice then," he said. "You won it fair and square Drake, much as it pains me to admit it. What's on your mind?"

I told him all of it. I hadn't meant to, not all of it anyway, but once I started I just couldn't stop. The only thing I didn't mention was the Burned Man. I didn't like Wormwood. I knew damn well I couldn't trust Wormwood, and yet... he was my constant, my anchor, know what I mean? He was the only person of any real influence that I'd known before all this kicked off. He was very old and very clever and... yeah I know, I really have to get over my father issues. Anyway, I clung to him in the way a shipwrecked sailor will cling to a splintered board, and I poured my guts out.

That probably wasn't the cleverest thing I've ever done, truth be told.

"...so, it comes down to this," I said at last. "How the hell do I stop Adam from corrupting Trixie any further, and forcing her fall? How to I help her to go home?"

Wormwood leaned his elbows on the desk, steepled his fingers in front of him, and blew a long stream of smoke in my face.

"So *she* killed Hedgefund Harry, not you," he said. "Is that what you're telling me, Drake? I gave you a job. Out of the misguided goodness of my heart I gave you a way to work off some of your ever-mounting debt to me, and you subcontracted it out to your half-sane pet angel, is that what you're telling me?"

"What? No, no fuck that, that's neither here nor there," I said, coughing as his rancid smoke made my eyes water. "Haven't you been listening to me? The point is–"

"It *is* here, and it's quite possibly also fucking *there* as well," Wormwood interrupted me. "You cheeky bastard, Drake. You cheeky, cheating, lying little wanker. I gave you *respect* for that job, and you never even fucking did it, did you?"

"It got done," I said. "What more do you want?"

"Honesty," Wormwood snarled at me. "Respect. Loyalty. But right now, you fucking cheat, I want that talisman."

"You what? Piss off, I won that hand!"

"You cheated me," Wormwood hissed. "No one cheats me, not ever. Gimme!"

He lunged across the desk towards me, and I leapt backwards out of my chair and pulled the talisman out of my pocket.

"You sure about this, Wormwood?" I said. "You're a big noise maybe, but you aren't a fighter. Can you really face down a devourer on your own? Really?"

Wormwood sneered at me. "How many times has that been used?" he said.

"What? Twice, that I know of. One of them by me, and I fucking ate Wellington Phoenix with it, so—"

"So that's two down," he said. "How many charges did it have to start with, Drake? Do you even know?"

"Charges?"

I could feel the quicksand shifting under my feet again, and I didn't like it one little bit.

"You fucking idiot," Wormwood sneered. "What did you think, someone makes a talisman and you can have instant devourers on tap for ever more? Why hasn't some banana republic headcase already long since conquered the world with one of those then?"

"Um," I said. I had to admit I hadn't really given it a lot of thought, but now that he mentioned it…

"Do you have the *faintest* idea of what it takes to summon a devourer?" he asked. "It makes what you do look like a Sunday school picnic. The enchanter has to carry out one real live summoning for each charge he wants to imbue into a talisman, that's how it *works* you fucknut. How many charges do you think could have been in that thing, realistically? Two? Three, tops. No more than that, I assure you, or the body count would have made the papers."

I looked from him to the talisman and back again. His argument made sense, much as I hated to admit it. Fuck it. *Fuck* it, I was getting well and truly pissed off with everything going wrong for me. Still, I reasoned, he wanted the talisman all the same so he must believe there was at least a fair chance of it still having a charge left in it. I think it was the slimy look of raw greed on Wormwood's face that finally tipped me over the edge.

"So was it two charges, or was it three?" I asked him. "How much do you want to bet?"

"What?"

"I'll call it," I said. "If it was two charges, you win and I'm fucked. You can have Connie kick the living snot out of me again, whatever you like. If it was three though... if it was three then I get to see you dragged screaming back down to Hell. I've already proved it ain't your lucky night, Wormwood."

Wormwood gripped the edge of his desk so hard his knuckles went white. Thin tendrils of smoke rose from between his fingers as the rosewood began to smoulder. Oh yes, he wanted that talisman all right, even if there *was* only one devourer left in it. At the same time, after what Trixie had told me I knew that I had touched on his deepest fear. If there was one thing Wormwood was terrified of, it was being sent back to Hell.

I'm sorry, I just couldn't resist it.

"Are you feeling lucky, punk?" I asked him.

"Oh fuck off!" Wormwood shouted at me. "Just fuck off out of here, and we'll both pretend this night never happened."

"What about my debt?" I asked him.

He gave me a look of pure hatred. "Don't fucking push your luck Drake, or I *will* call your bluff. Just fuck off, and don't come back until you're told to."

Sanity prevailed at the last minute. I turned my back and fled while I still could, the talisman clutched tightly in my hand. I almost ran straight into the hoodoo man. He had left his teenage arm-candy at the craps table and was standing outside Wormwood's office smoking a cigar and obviously waiting for me.

"Don-boy Drake," he said with a wide grin. His accent was so thick I could barely make out what he was saying. "Long time no see."

"Good evening, Houngan," I said.

I'm afraid I had no idea what his name was, but he seemed content enough to be given the respect of his title. Come to that I had no idea how he knew *my* name, but I felt ridiculously flattered that he did.

"*Tout moun fet pou soufri, tout moun fet pou mouri,*" he said, his silk top hat nodding wisely.

"Forgive me, Houngan, my Haitian isn't all that great," I said. "Everyone is...?"

"Everyone is born to suffer, everyone is born to die," he said. "Old proverb."

What an uplifting thought that isn't. "Um, right, OK," I said.

"What it mean is, everyone suffer," he said. "Don't matter. What make the man is what him do when the sufferin' come knockin' on his door. You listen me now, Don-boy, and you listen well. You come here lookin' for advice, I'm hearin'."

"Yeah," I said. "Yeah I was, but... I dunno."

"There be loa fightin' in your house. You draw your *vévés* and speak wit' bad spirits, but time him come, Don-boy, when a man gotta choose what path he goin' walk. That your advice from Houngan Armand. From *Papa* Armand, you understand?"

He chuckled and sauntered off into the crowd without waiting for an answer, trailing cigar smoke in the air behind him. I frowned after him. The only thing I'd really understood from that was that his name was Armand, which I hadn't known. That, and he'd just given me tacit approval to address him as Papa instead of by his formal title of Houngan, which was basically just Vodou for "priest". That meant, to him at least, that he had accepted me as a spiritual pupil. I had no idea whether that was a good thing or not. Probably not, the way my luck had been running recently, but all the same. I liked the guy, you know?

I looked around the club, feeling people watching me. Wormwood was bound to come out of his office sooner or later, and I knew it would be in the best interests of my health if I wasn't still there when he did. It was too hot in the club, and the air suddenly seemed close and stifling. It was fair to say my night had been an unmitigated failure so far.

I pushed my way through the crowd and headed down the stairs. Connie was still standing there like a statue at the bottom of the steps, keeping an eye on the bar and the front door.

"You get your advice, Don?" he asked.

"I got *some* advice," I said. "Not sure I understood it though."

Connie laughed and gave me a friendly pat on the shoulder that almost floored me. "I know that feeling," he said. "You stopping for a drink?"

The funny thing was, for all that Connie had slapped the crap out of me several times in the last couple of weeks, I couldn't help but like him. He seemed so amiable it was almost rude not to, if you know what I mean. I glanced around the bar. There were a few actual humans in now amongst the other patrons, but no one I recognized. There were a couple of young guys in heavy metal T-shirts at the bar, their bare arms covered in Goetic tattoos – and wasn't *that* going to bite them in the arse sooner or later – a red haired girl with her back to me, and a husband and wife exorcism team I'd once been briefly introduced to and couldn't remember the names of.

"Nah," I said. "Think I'll call it a night. Cheers anyway, Con."

"Another time then," he said.

I nodded and made my way to the door. *A red haired girl...* I half-paused in the doorway when someone shoved me through the glamour and out into the alleyway. I stumbled forwards a couple of steps and smacked the palms of my hands painfully against the opposite wall.

"Hello sweetie," she said.

"Oh for fuck's–" I managed, before she kicked me in the kidneys hard enough to send me to my knees.

I scraped a good bit of skin off my face and hands on my way down the wall. Damn but this was really starting to piss me off now. I turned on my knees to see Ally standing over me, glaring down at me with her hands on her hips.

"Oh yes," she said, "I think I like you better on your knees."

"Will you for the love of God please just fuck off," I said. "Do I have to call Trixie again? Really?"

"I heard your pretty little angel was feeling under the weather," Ally said. "She's so under the weather she couldn't even keep me out of that pub, remember? And that was before she hurt her poor little leg."

I *did* remember, and I also remembered how Trixie hadn't had an adequate explanation for that. I didn't like it one little bit, and I even less liked it that Ally seemed to know she was hurt.

"We were both pissed and you caught her off guard, that's all," I bluffed.

Alley smirked at me, her lips twisting into an ugly sneer. How I had ever thought she was attractive was beyond me now. It's amazing what magic can do, and she had definitely been doing something to my head at the time. I was bloody sure she had.

"Little miss goody-two-shoes' pretty angel magic doesn't seem to be working quite as well as it used to, does it?" Ally said. "I wonder why that might be. Maybe she's not quite as angelic as she used to be, what do you think? Maybe she's keeping bad company."

She threw another kick at my head, and I rolled out of the way and pulled myself frantically to my feet. I'd had yet another shit day, I was half pissed, confused, scared, and not in any sort of mood to take another kicking from this horrible cow. She closed in to slap me, and I lost my rag. I'd never hit a woman before in my life, I swear I hadn't, but then Ally was only technically a woman and I was past breaking point by then. I balled my right hand into a fist and belted her in the mouth as hard as I could. Ally's head snapped back an inch, and she blinked at me in astonishment. But that was all. She laughed.

"Is that it?" she said. "Is that the best you can do?"

She hit me in the guts so hard I doubled over, puking spaghetti and red wine all over the filthy ground. At least, I *hoped* it was just red wine and she hadn't actually ruptured something in my guts that time. I clutched my stomach with both hands, and felt the shape of the talisman through my coat pocket.

If there was one more charge left in it, I could set a devourer on her right there and then. That was the beauty of a talisman. Maybe you *did* have to do the summonings in advance when you made the thing, but it still meant you could have the results immediately whenever you needed them. I really had to learn how to do that. If there was just one more charge I could have her. *If* there was.

I staggered backwards a step and pulled the talisman out of my pocket. Ally frowned at me as I held it up, my thumb rubbing at the ugly sigil of the devourer as I focused my Will and prayed for a little bit of luck, just this one time. I had to be owed some luck by now, surely. Something must have been smiling on me for once, though I dread to think what. The air split open beside me, and vile black tentacles burst into the night air.

"No, that *isn't* the best I can do," I said, and pointed at her. "Kill!"

She dropped into a crouch, her claws extending smoothly from her right hand. The tentacles surged towards her and she went into overdrive, seeming to flow bonelessly around them as she slashed and cut and whirled. I watched in dumbstruck astonishment as it started to rain the Devil's own calamari. A tentacle whipped up and opened a long cut across her cheek, then another slashed almost the entire length of her left arm open as the devourer gave as good as it was getting, but she was still going. One of the tentacles wrapped around her thigh and almost yanked her off her feet but she leapt into the pull, her claws slicing down and out as she turned a perfect somersault. The severed tentacle withered and fell away from her leg, and curled into a shrivelled ball on the ground. Ally landed on her feet with a grunt of pain, obviously hurt but still fighting.

Dear fucking God, I thought, *she can't be this good!* But she could, and she was. I backed away in horror, suddenly remembering how Ally had almost faced down Trixie that first time. Ally, it dawned on me somewhat belatedly, was almost as good as Trixie, and Trixie had killed three of these things in one go. She might be hurt, but by then I could tell that she was going to win.

I wanted to run, but they were between me and the street. The other end of the alleyway ended in a blank wall two stories high. That was me well and truly fucked then.

I sank hopelessly to my knees and watched Ally destroy my last chance. She took another lashing cut across the stomach, still fighting her way closer and closer to the source of the tentacles. I could only stare numbly as she plunged her claws right into the hole in the air with a savage grin of satisfaction on her face. Thick black ichor poured out of the void as something down there died screaming. Ally turned to face me just as Wormwood's club erupted like a kicked anthill.

Connie was first out of the door, bless him, with a baseball bat clutched in each massive hand like they were billy clubs. The tattooed heavy metal boys were right behind him, and the huge shaggy thing that had been playing craps with Papa Armand was behind them. Ally backed up a step as still more people jostled out of the club, all of them staring in astonishment at the slimy mess of diced devourer all over the ground and splashed up the walls.

"What the bloody hell's going on out here?" Connie bellowed. "Something big just died, I felt it."

Ally backed up another step, limping and hunched over around her wounded stomach. There was inky black goo dripping from her claws, which was about as incriminating as evidence gets. Her gaze flicked over the crowd as though counting, figuring the odds. She turned and ran. Connie shook his huge, horned head in amazement.

"You do get in some scrapes, Don," he said.

I sagged back onto my knees and let my head rock backwards with a weary sigh. Looking up, I could see through the glamour covering the upper floor of the club. There was a window there, and Wormwood was standing at it looking down at me with a sour expression on his face.

"Don't I just," I said.

CHAPTER 18

I woke up sprawled on the sofa in my office, still wearing my coat. God only knew what time I had got home last night. Connie had called me a cab, and I had been nearly asleep by the time it pulled up outside my front door. I remembered dragging myself up the stairs to my office, but that was it.

I sat up and groaned. There was dried puke all down the front of my shirt. My guts hurt, my head was pounding, the palms of my hands and my right cheek were grazed raw and, not to put too fine a point on it, I stank. I made myself get off the sofa and head to the bathroom.

I felt a bit more human for a shower and a shave. I wanted some clean clothes too, but they were in my bedroom where I assumed Trixie was still asleep. I made do with a towel wrapped around my waist and went to make coffee. To my surprise I found her sitting at the kitchen table instead, drinking coffee and smoking one of her awful Russian cigarettes. She must have been back to wherever she had her base, or wiggled her nose or whatever the hell she did, as she was wearing her own clothes again now. Very nice

250

she looked too, in a pair of eyewateringly tight jeans and a loose white silk blouse. She winced when she saw me.

"What happened to you last night?" she asked.

"I got in a fight," I muttered.

Trixie mashed her cigarette out on the saucer she was using as an ashtray and gave me a cross look. "Who with?"

"Doesn't matter," I said, acutely conscious that I was only wearing a towel. "I'll just go get dressed."

"It was Aleto again, wasn't it?" she demanded as I left the room.

I ignored her and closed the bedroom door behind me. I dug through my wardrobe, thinking it was high time I did some laundry. It's funny how the simple jobs of keeping life going are easy to forget about when things get hectic, but are so quick to turn around and bite you when you suddenly realize you've run out of things to wear, or you haven't got anything to eat or whatever. I normally wear suits but yesterday's had been my last clean shirt, and now that had vomit down the front of it and was splattered with devourer ink as well.

I sighed and settled on a pair of jeans that had probably been fashionable about five years ago, and a plain black sweatshirt. That would have to do. Trixie rapped on the door and barged in without waiting for an answer. At least I was halfway into my jeans by then, that was something. I yanked them up sharpish and turned to face her.

"Don't you ignore me when I'm talking to you," she snapped. "It was her, wasn't it?"

"Yeah, it was," I said. I pulled the sweatshirt on over my scarred chest and looked at her. "She knows you're hurt,

Trixie. I don't know how, but she does."

She knew Trixie was keeping "bad company" too, and that was probably much worse. *Maybe she's not quite as angelic as she used to be*, Ally had said, and that was the very thing I was afraid of.

"I'm fine," Trixie said brusquely. "How are *you*, more to the point?"

I shrugged. "A bit battered, but not too bad. I set a devourer on her, the last one in the talisman I think. The last charge, you know how it works."

Yeah I know, I know, but there was no way I was going to admit to her how naive I had been about how talismans work. A man has to have some pride after all, and I really didn't want to look stupid in front of her. More stupid than I did already, anyway.

"And?"

"And she slaughtered it," I admitted glumly. "Bit of a waste, really."

"Yes, it was a bit," Trixie said. "That might have come in handy for something it actually stood a chance of doing. For heaven's sake, Don, don't you understand how strong Aleto is?"

"I do now," I said. "To be honest I figured it out at the time, about thirty seconds too late."

"Well, it can't be helped now I suppose," Trixie said. "Have you still got the talisman?"

I nodded. "Yeah, it's in my coat pocket."

I went and got it for her, and she followed me through to the office. Her aura glowed momentarily brighter as she examined it closely.

"Yes, the devourers are all used up I'm afraid," she said after a moment. "That's a shame. So is the paralysis spell, by the way."

I coughed. So if I had tried that one on Phoenix first instead of going straight for the big guns he might well have killed Trixie in the time it would have taken me to figure out that the spell wasn't going to do anything. All because I hadn't known how a talisman works. It's times like that when I seriously start to worry about what else I don't know and really should. It was starting to look like the Burned Man had left more than a few holes in my education.

"What does the other glyph mean? Any idea?" I asked her.

She shook her head. "No, sorry, I haven't got a clue. There's still power in it though, whatever it is."

"Well I'm not trying it just to find out," I said.

"No, no, I don't think that would be a very good idea," she said.

She slipped the talisman into the pocket of her jeans, as though to make *sure* I didn't do that. I shrugged. It was no use to me now anyway, and she was probably right. Curiosity was bound to have gotten the better of me sooner or later, and whenever that happens I usually fuck something up.

"I'm going for a lie down," Trixie said.

"Help yourself," I said, again trying not to think about her lying in my bed. "It'll do you good."

She left the room and I sighed and went to make myself a coffee. I stood at the kitchen window drinking it, looking down into the yard behind the grocers where Mr Chowdhury and his eldest son were sitting by their back door on a pair of upturned crates. They were drinking cups of tea and laughing together. For a moment I envied them their normal life. *Good for you, Mr Chowdhury*, I thought. *Make the most of it.*

The phone in my office rang. I hurried through to get it before the noise disturbed Trixie, cursing under my breath as I slopped hot coffee over the back of my hand. I just reached it before the machine picked up.

"Don Drake," I said.

"Don, thank God!"

It was Debbie. I put the cup down in a hurry, spilling more coffee on the desk. Her voice sounded fuzzy, like she was on a mobile somewhere with lousy reception.

"Debs? Debs, what's the matter, where are you? I–"

"Shut up and listen," she interrupted, and now I could hear the panic in her voice. "I don't *know* where I am, Don! She took me away, sometime last night. She's–"

I heard a muffled voice in the background, then there was a sharp crack and a howl of pain. I'd have known that sound anywhere – the evil cow had obviously got herself a new fucking whip.

"Hello sweetie," Ally purred down the phone, her voice like battery acid poured over an open wound. "I've got your little friend. You're actually quite brave in your weaselly little way, aren't you sweetie? Tormenting you will take me years, and to be perfectly frank, I can't be arsed. Still, you have the very devil of a conscience. If I hurt *her*, well, you'll drive yourself crazy over it for me, won't you?"

"You fucking bitch!" I yelled down the phone at her. "Where are you? Where's Debbie?"

I heard another crack of the whip, another shriek, and

the line went dead. I screamed and hurled the phone across the room. The worst of it was, she was absolutely right. I *would* drive myself crazy, more than I already was. That was it. That was just fucking *it!* The bitch was never going to go away, was she? I couldn't stand by while she hurt Debs, that much was for certain. I stormed into the workroom.

"Fuck the cost, how do I kill a Fury?" I demanded, before I really took in what I was seeing.

Trixie was standing over the Burned Man with the talisman in her hand. She was pressing down on the third glyph, and whatever that one did it was halfway through cutting a hole in my altar around the Burned Man.

"*This* way," she said. She turned to stare at me, and something in her eyes looked quite unhinged. "The third glyph is a spell for *opening things*, Don. Locked doors mostly, but this is working just fine."

"Trixie..." I started.

"No! I'm *sick* of this," she screamed at me. "Sick of *waiting!* Get close to him, Adam said. Kill for him, make him owe you, make him love you, he said, and sooner or later he'll give it to you. But you *won't*, will you? You love this... this *fucking* thing more than anyone on Earth, don't you?"

I stared at her in astonishment. That was the first time I had ever heard Trixie swear. *Adam said...* I had a very, very bad feeling about that.

"I'm touched," the Burned Man sneered, but I couldn't mistake the gleeful look in its beady little eyes. "The *angel* says you love me."

"*Adam* said... you want the Burned Man?" I said. "That's what you were after, all along?"

You don't think there's even the tiniest chance she might want something in return? the Burned Man had asked me, but I don't think it had ever occurred to either of us that what she really wanted was the Burned Man itself. And now it knew what she was. That was bad. I still wasn't quite sure why, but I knew that it was.

"I *need* it," she said. "I can do it, with this. I can finally destroy Aleto and *go home!*"

I suppose I should have pointed out that Meg and Tess weren't actually dead so killing Ally wouldn't get her home anyway, but Trixie looked so close to going for my throat right then that I honestly didn't dare. All the same, I didn't dare let her try to steal the Burned Man either.

"Trixie," I said, "you can't–"

"*Don't tell me what to do!*" she shrieked.

She threw out a hand towards me and some psychic outpouring of her rage picked me up and hurled me bodily across the room like a rag doll. My head slammed into the wall with a solid crunch. You can't steal the Burned Man, I had been trying to tell her. It doesn't work like that.

I slumped to the floor in a heap and the lights went out.

I had tried it myself, of course. Davidson had been well on his way to dying of cirrhosis of the liver by then, but he was taking far too long about it for my liking.

"Why the fuck should I wait any longer?" I demanded, pacing Davidson's study with a glass of his whisky in my hand. "I'm sick of waiting."

I had been a student of the Burned Man for almost four years by then, and I was running short of patience. I had learned everything it had to teach me, or so I thought at the time, and there was little more we could usefully do now until I actually owned it. Davidson assured me he had left it to me in his will, described rather obtusely as "a curious statue of which Donald has grown fond".

Fond might not be quite the right word for it. The Burned Man still revolted me and frightened me by turns, but I couldn't deny its power. I had my own keys to Davidson's place by then and I had taken to feeding the Burned Man myself, since Davidson was rarely in any state to do it these days. I had also taken to drinking too much, and not spending as much time with Debbie as I should. She had actually joked that she thought I might be having some sort of gay affair with Davidson. At least, I sincerely *hoped* she had been joking.

He was thoroughly repellent by then, of course, and if I had been gay I'd like to think I could have done a good deal better. He was never sober, rarely functional, and he stank all the time. The university had pensioned him off two years ago, when he started to become too much of a public embarrassment for them to pretend to ignore it any longer. He still steadfastly refused to see a doctor, and, as much as I hate to admit it, I hadn't exactly encouraged him to either. To put it bluntly, I needed him dead.

"They say all things come to those who wait," the Burned Man said.

"Things come to those who reach out and fucking take them for themselves," I snapped at it. "You told me that yourself."

"So I did," it said, and chuckled.

Davidson chose that moment to stagger into the room. He was wearing a stained dressing gown of a sort of dirty mustard yellow that matched the colour his skin seemed to be gradually turning. He smelled horrific.

"Don, dear boy," he slurred. "Lovely... to see you."

It was eleven o'clock on a Saturday morning and he was shitfaced. He stood there for a moment, swaying on his bare feet with a slightly confused look on his face. A moment later he turned and shuffled out of the room again.

"You can't still want to belong to that," I said. "The man's an alcoholic wreck."

"Never said I did," the Burned Man said, "but I *do* belong to him and there it is. He has to give me to you, and he won't while he's still alive. He's said as much. We'll just have to wait for him to finish drinking himself to death."

"How long is *that* going to take?"

The Burned Man shrugged. "I can't see it being more than another year or two, the state he's in these days," it said.

"Oh fuck that," I said. "I'm not getting any younger here. I'm not waiting another *year!*"

I was all of twenty-four by then, after all.

"You'll just have to, unless you want to do him in," it said. "I can't help you with that I'm afraid, not while he still owns me. And if you try to do it by yourself you'll only fuck it up and end up dead or in prison, so that's the end of that."

"No it isn't," I said. "Things come to those who take them."

"I've told you before, I can't be stolen," it said.

"And I'm telling you, bullshit."

I threw the last of the whisky down my throat and stormed out.

My mate Jim had dropped out of university altogether by then and was working locally as a carpenter of all things. I shudder to think what his painfully middle class parents must have thought of that, after what his abandoned education had cost them. I dropped round to see him that afternoon, and borrowed his electric circular saw. I can't remember what line of crap I gave him about why I wanted it, but by the time we'd killed the case of beer I'd turned up at his flat with, he was happy enough to lend it to me for the rest of the weekend. I stumbled home with it over my shoulder in a canvas rucksack.

I let myself into Davidson's place bright and early the next morning, and checked to make sure the old soak was still passed out from the night before. Needless to say he was. I found him curled up on his unmade bed in the foetal position, with fresh vomit staining his pillow. Delightful. I closed his bedroom door firmly behind me and went through to the study.

"Morning," I said, putting the rucksack down in front of the altar.

"I hope you've cheered up a bit since yesterday, you miserable bugger," the Burned Man said.

I grinned and opened the rucksack.

"Yeah," I said, "I have."

I took the saw out and plugged it in.

"Now hold on a minute," the Burned Man said. "If that's for what I think it is, you're a fucking idiot."

"I'm reaching out and taking what's rightfully mine, that's all," I said.

I pulled the triggers and the saw roared into life as I bent over the altar. The shiny new blade chewed through the ancient wood with a satisfying growl, drowning out whatever the Burned Man was trying to say to me. I worked the blade across the altar on the Burned Man's left, then again on its right, cutting out a neat slice of wood with it chained in the middle. I shut off the saw and lifted the chunk of wood free, holding it up until the Burned Man stood level with my face.

"Oh you've done it now," it said.

"Yes I have," I grinned at it. "Come on, you're coming with me."

I put the piece of altar wood carefully in the bottom of the rucksack and closed the bag over the Burned Man's head. I could feel it struggling as I hefted the bag onto my shoulder. It might not be a dignified way to travel, exactly, but what the hell. It would forgive me once I got it home, I was sure.

I'd got maybe halfway down Davidson's hall when my eyes started to itch, then sting, and then really burn. By the time I got to the front door my view of the world had turned into a blurry mist as tears streamed down my cheeks. It was like getting grit blown into your eyes on a windy day, if the grit was made of broken glass. Broken glass that was on fire, at that.

I stumbled against the door almost clawing at my eyes, my teeth chattering uncontrollably. I dumped the rucksack in the hall and dashed into the filthy bathroom, and turned the basin taps on by feel alone. Handfuls of cold water hit my face as I desperately tried to wash my eyes. The pain got steadily worse and worse until it was unbearable.

I threw my head back and screamed in agony, and that's when I made out my reflection in the spotted shaving mirror over the sink. The whites of my eyes were crimson with blood, and my eyelids were burning. Actually, literally on fire. I howled.

"What the fuck have you done to me?" I screamed.

"Told you," came the muffled voice of the Burned Man, from my rucksack in the hall. "It can't be done."

I poured more water over my face, sobbing miserably and ready to slam my head against the wall with the pain. I heard unsteady footsteps behind me.

"Stupid boy," Davidson mumbled. "Knew you'd try it, sooner or later. Damn impatient stupid bloody boy. Stupid…"

I fell to my knees, sobbing, banging my head against the side of the bath, the heels of my hands pressed helplessly against my burning eyes. I heard Davidson shuffle down the hall and mutter something to the Burned Man. I think I was still screaming when I finally lost consciousness.

The miserable old fucker must have just left me lying there on his piss-stinking bathroom carpet, because that's where I woke up some time later. I whimpered, terrified I might have gone permanently blind, but when I finally summoned the courage to open my eyes I found I could see as well as ever. I pulled myself unsteadily to my feet and risked a look in the mirror. My eyes were a bit bloodshot but no more than that, and even my eyelashes were intact. I had *seen* them burning, but there they were none the less.

I washed my face with shaking hands. One look at Davidson's slimy towel was enough to make me decide to just drip dry, sitting on the edge of the bath with my head in my hands. After a while I made myself get up and go and look in the study. The Burned Man was back where it had always been, in the middle of the altar. There were rough seams on the long piece of ancient wood, like half-healed wounds, but it was definitely all one piece again.

"I did tell you, you twat," it said. "That always happens."

I opened my eyes with a groan and sat up on the floor of my workroom. Trixie was gone, and so was the Burned Man. I rubbed my hands over my face and got up, gingerly feeling the lump on the back of my head. There was a neat, perfectly circular hole cut out of the middle of the altar where the Burned Man should have been standing. I stared at that hole and felt... I don't know what, exactly. Empty, I suppose. Lost. And perhaps a little bit relieved, if I'm completely honest about it. I owed everything I had to the Burned Man, but when I remembered the bright-eyed, easygoing twenty year-old I had once been I couldn't help feeling that maybe it had taken away a good deal more than it had given me over the years.

I just couldn't believe she'd done it. I mean, I'd always been a bit wary of Trixie, in between intermittently feeling like I was falling in love with her, but all the same. I supposed I'd had my doubts all along though, from that first moment I saw her standing across from the café, the day after I'd lost that first game of Fates to Wormwood. I... *Well fucking hell!*

Maybe the bang on the head had finally knocked some sense into me, I don't know, but just then I could have cheerfully kicked myself all the way down the street and back again. It had suddenly dawned on me that the first time I had seen Trixie had been the day *before* the Vincent and

Danny job. A day before the Furies even knew I was alive.

I supposed it was beyond doubt now that she really was stuck with this impossible mission to kill the Furies, but she must have already been looking for me independently of that. *No, she wasn't looking for me at all,* I thought with a sudden sick feeling. *She was looking for the Burned Man.* It had just been bloody lucky for her that I had fucked the job up the way I had and brought the Furies down on myself. That, or the Furies had been following Trixie while she was looking for me, and I was lucky for them, I really wasn't sure any more. I kicked the wall in frustration. Whichever way it had gone down, I'd been royally had.

"Fuck it!" I shouted at the empty flat.

I supposed it didn't even matter now which way around it had been. I'd been played good and proper, and that was all there was to it. All the same though... Had she really believed I would ever *give* her the Burned Man, whatever she did for me? *Adam said...* The smell of rat was back in a big way. I had a really deep, really nasty suspicion that Adam at least had never believed anything of the sort. Trixie wasn't stupid by any means, but I did get the distinct impression that she was a little bit naive about certain things. Adam, on the other hand, definitely was not.

Still, that wasn't the point now. The point was that Trixie had done something terrible and, unless I was completely wide of the mark, she was in serious danger of doing something much, much worse any time now. This was all Adam's doing, I just knew it was. I remembered all that big talk I'd overheard from him about command and power and triumph, all the words of temptation. He wanted...

no, he didn't just want, for some reason he was *desperate* to complete her fall.

"You set her up didn't you, you smarmy bastard," I whispered aloud. "You wanted her to do this all along."

She had obviously got it into her head, no doubt from Adam, that she could somehow use the Burned Man to destroy the Furies once and for all. Whether that was true or not didn't even really matter any more. The point was that if she tried it she would fall. I can command the legion and the leviathan, if I but order it, I remembered hearing him say to her. Do not ask, command. That is the true way to power.

If she tried that on the Burned Man she would fall for real, and there would be nothing I or anyone else could do to save her then. Not only that, but I couldn't help remembering the gleeful look on the Burned Man's face as she was cutting it out of the altar. I could only imagine the amount of magical power that might be generated by the fall of an angel. I had a horrible suspicion that the Burned Man believed it would be able to harvest enough of that power to break free of the fetish all by itself, ritual or no ritual. And it might be right. I *knew* there was a reason I hadn't wanted it to find out what she was. It could almost taste its freedom, I knew it could.

All the same, I thought about just washing my hands of the whole fucking mess and leaving her to it, I really did. For about two seconds, anyway. After everything I've done in my life, after all the killings and betrayals I've been responsible for, there was no way I was having a fallen angel on my conscience as well. There was still just enough of that long-gone twenty year-old left in me somewhere that I knew I couldn't live with that. That, and she had forgiven me. I closed my eyes, and saw his face.

I forgive you, she had said, and those three words had meant the world to me. Perhaps more than that. She was an angel, after all. It was just possible that those words had meant my *soul*.

I had to stop her, and I had to rescue Debbie too. I didn't even know where they were but it stood to reason that they'd both be in the same place, and that was wherever Ally was. Unfortunately the only person I could think of who was likely to be able to find Trixie and get me to her in time was Adam himself.

I wanted nothing in the world more than to knock that prick's teeth down his throat, but for one thing I needed him and for another I knew he'd eat me alive if I so much as looked at him funny. A sad fact I know, but there we were. I gritted my teeth and called his name.

"Adam, I need your help," I shouted. "Please Adam, this is important. *Trixie* needs your help."

He might just humour me, with that one. I certainly wasn't about to admit I was wise to his game, and it wouldn't surprise me if he wanted to gloat over her fall anyway. Fuck it but I wished I knew his true name. That would bring him a damn sight faster than just asking nicely was ever going to. Whatever his name was, it obviously wasn't going to actually be Adam – that would be far too easy. Things like him don't give away their true names for free, after all. Trixie had, to be fair, but that was just another sign of how naive she could still be about certain things. She's a child, relatively speaking, Adam had said, and I could tell he was right about that in a way. I paced the workroom for five minutes before

I had to admit to myself that he wasn't coming.

"Damn it," I muttered aloud to myself, "why do you call yourself Adam? Trixie's simple enough, it's just a short form of the end of her bloody unwieldy true name, but you? No, you wouldn't do that. You're clever, aren't you? Oh yes, you're too bloody clever by half you are. You think you're *so* fucking clever no one can touch you, so you leave clues, don't you? It *is* a clue isn't it, you cocksucker, I know it is."

I paced some more, painfully aware of the seconds ticking by. I didn't even know how long I had been knocked out for but the daylight coming into the room didn't seem to have changed so I could only hope it hadn't been too long.

"Basics first," I told myself, still thinking out loud. I do that sometimes, when I'm tense. It doesn't mean I'm crazy or anything. "Adam was the first human in the Abrahamic creation myth, everyone knows that. You're *not* human though, you never have been, so why call yourself that? It's an Abrahamic form though, so that's the paradigm we're working with here. Adam was the first man in both Genesis and the Quran, but you're not a man, so what am I missing? The first something else maybe, but what? So what *are* you? You're a fallen angel. You're…"

Oh fuck me.

"The first fallen angel was Lucifer, any first year occultist or heavy metal fan will tell you that, but that's no fucking use to man or beast is it?" I was starting to rant now, I knew I was, but I really didn't give a toss any more. "That's a title not a name, that's just Latin Vulgate for morning star from a dodgy King James translation of the Hebrew Bible, in which it appears precisely once and is virtually irrelevant anyway.

What's your fucking *name?*"

I tore into my dusty pile of books like a man possessed. I couldn't believe I didn't know the answer, but it had never really come up before, and truth be told I'd never expected to *need* to know it. The first of the fallen was an archangel, I knew that much, although, according to Trixie, that made him a lot less high up in the great scheme of things than most people would have you believe. How had she put it? The archangels are like our sergeants, something like that.

That made sense. Lucifer was still a big deal, don't get me wrong, but he was a long way from being the boss downstairs. Hell was there before he fell into it, after all, and something must have already been in charge down there when he turned up. All the same, it was a start. I read furiously, tossing one book aside and grabbing another, cross-indexing in my head as I went. I hadn't been a student for all those years for nothing, you know.

According to LaVay he was the Torch of Baphomet, which would make him Azazel – but Azazel was a Hebrew goat-demon, and Baphomet is just a corruption of Mahomet which was the Latinization of Muhammad, so that was nothing but medieval bigotry in action and an obvious dead end. In Arabic lore there was Azazil, which as far as I could see was the same goat thing, and that was supposedly the original name of Iblis who was the Islamic devil. Ah, but then Iblis was originally a djinn not an angel so that didn't work either. *Fuck it!*

I made myself take a deep breath and calm down before I lost it and threw one of the precious books through the window. OK, not that then. Back to basics again and try another tack. The name Lucifer means morning star, which equates him with the planet Venus, and therefore by the table of correspondences with the archangel Lumiel. Aha! Lumiel is the archangel of light, which also fits LaVay again who says Lucifer represents enlightenment. The Kabbalah says that Lumiel is sometimes considered to be the angel of the Earth. The name Adam derives from the Hebrew noun *ha adamah* which means... Earth. *Got you!*

"Lumiel!" I bellowed, throwing every last ounce of my will in to the command. "Get in here, you cunt!"

Of course Davidson did die in the end, about three months later as it turned out. It wasn't a moment too soon as far as I was concerned. He never really forgave me for trying to steal the Burned Man, but he was much too far gone to do anything about it by then. The Burned Man wanted to be mine, we both knew that, and as I've said, it ruled the professor with a rod of iron. I kept going to his flat and there was nothing he could do to stop me. I think he'd realized by then that if I wanted the Burned Man badly enough to try and steal it then I must be praying for his death anyway. One joyous morning he obliged and I found him dead on the living room floor in a puddle of the bloody vomit he had choked on. I left him lying there and went straight to the study.

"It's over," I said.

The Burned Man looked at me with glittering eyes, and grinned.

"Oh no," it said, "it's just beginning. You've got real

potential, boy, potential like I haven't seen for a thousand years or more. Do what I tell you and I'll make you more powerful than you can possibly imagine."

The bolt of pure power that shot up my spine from God only knows where almost took my head off. All the same, I couldn't help feeling just a little bit pleased with myself when Adam stepped out of the pitch darkness that had suddenly filled the doorway.

"Oh, very well done," he said. "You're not as stupid as you look."

"I need you to get me to wherever Trixie is," I said. "Right now."

He chuckled. "Oh do you now? You might know my name, diabolist, but you are a very long way from being able to order me about. You are a very long way away from that indeed, especially now that you appear to have lost the Burned Man."

"Why do you think I want to find her?" I snapped at him. "I want it back!"

"Mmmm, I dare say you do," he said. "You aren't all that much without it, are you?"

I gave him an ugly look. Partly because he was right, admittedly. But then again, he was there, wasn't he?

"I'm enough to get you here when I want you, you bugger," I said. "No Burned Man this time, that was all me. I'm *that* much, mate."

I realized that what I had just said was actually true. I never knew I had it in me, to be perfectly honest with you. The enormity of what I had done slowly began to sink in, and right then I wasn't sure how much I really liked it after all. I had managed to summon him without any help from the Burned Man, without any ritual or ingredients or anything, and that was some impressive shit whichever way you looked at it. Only now that I actually *did* look at it, of course, I realized that meant I had summoned him without any protection whatsoever. *Oh shit.*

Adam smiled. A bit, anyway.

"I suppose you are," he admitted after a moment. "Isn't it astonishing what one can sometimes find out about oneself... in extremis. Oh very well, I don't really care if you want your nasty little fetish back. What about Meselandrarasatrixiel?"

Now I don't know how much you know about controlling a summoned demon, but I'm going to take a guess at not much. Even when I'm working with the Burned Man and using the grand summoning circle and the best ingredients available they can still put up a bitch of a fight sometimes. I had called Adam without so much as a basic ring of salt around me. That was sort of like jumping out of a plane without a parachute at the best of times, except in this case I might as well have doused myself in petrol and set myself on fire before I jumped. This wasn't just any summoned demon after all, this was *Lucifer* for fuck's sake. I thought my head was about to split open from the effort I was having to put into this.

"You can have her," I said. "She stole from me, the bitch. I just want Debbie back, and I want what's rightfully mine."

I hurled my Will at him so hard sweat broke out all over my body and my knees began to tremble as my mind ranted at him in desperate fury. *Thou shalt do my bidding Lumiel, I*

*bind thee to my Will Lumiel Lucifer Morningstar, my Will be done
I command you to do my bidding!*

Oh dear God what was I doing? I *command* you? Wasn't
that exactly what he had been trying to tempt Trixie to
do? I could feel that quicksand beneath me again, shifting,
sinking ever downwards. Fuck it, it was too late to worry
about that now.

"Well…" Adam said, and his thin lips slowly twisted into a
cruel smile. "Oh, I suppose it might be fun to watch, at that.
You can have your woman and your Burned Man, and I get
the angel. Deal?"

*My words do not bind me to thee, fallen abomination. I command
thee, Lumiel Lucifer. My Will prevail, my Will be done.*

"Deal," I lied.

"Very well then," he said. "Come with me."

He gestured towards the impenetrable darkness filling
the doorway. Just then I noticed the talisman lying on the
floor beside the altar where Trixie had obviously discarded
it. I had no way of knowing if there was any more of the
opening spell left in it or not, but I picked it up and slipped it
into my pocket anyway. You never knew, it might still work
and if it did there was always a chance it might come in
handy. I nodded and followed him into the shadows.

CHAPTER 19

I stepped out of the darkness and stood beside Lucifer, the first of the fallen. Fuck me, I never thought I'd get to say that.

"Well," he said, "is this what you were looking for, diabolist?"

I stared at the sight in front of me. We were back in the same underground car park or whatever it was that Ally and her sisters had dragged me to when they had kidnapped me that time before. There was even a parked van, albeit a different one. That was all that was the same, though.

The whole space seemed to be burning, and howling with an unnatural hot wind. Trixie and Ally were circling each other like furious lionesses, Ally cutting and slashing with the steel claws of her right hand. She had made up for the loss of the other set with a long, wickedly curved black dagger. Trixie had a flaming sword in her right hand, and in her left she held the Burned Man tightly around its middle. Both of the women had minor cuts and scratches in half a dozen places already, and the look on their faces was pure murder. I watched their steel ballet in stunned silence until

Trixie turned enough for me to see her face properly. Her eyes were on fire.

That always happens.

"Dear God," I whispered.

She must have seen us there, for all that. She gestured urgently for me to keep out of the way. I had no idea how she was withstanding the Burned Man's curse, but somehow she was. Her face was set in a mask of furious concentration as she cut and thrust one-handed with her sword, flames boiling from between her eyelids. I wondered how she could even see at all any more. I started towards her, but Adam put a restraining hand on my shoulder.

"Your woman is in the vehicle," he said.

My woman... *Debbie!* I hadn't forgotten her, honest to God I hadn't, it was just that the sight of Trixie and Ally battling it out like that had knocked all other thoughts out of my head. I wrenched free of Adam's grip and dashed towards the van, dodging pools of liquid fire on the ground as I went, and never stopping to wonder exactly where they had come from. It looked like both the girls had brought out their big guns tonight, and to be honest, the less I had to do with their war the better it was likely to be for the state of my health. I ducked and dived my way to the back of the van, and pulled myself inside. And there was Debbie.

Ally hadn't been gentle with her, that was for certain. She was still dressed, sort of, that was something I supposed. All the same, Ally's bullwhip had cut great bloody slashes through her jeans and T-shirt, and she had been beaten black and blue. She was tied up with the same greasy nylon rope that Meg had used on me when her and Tess had dragged me here the first time.

"Don?" Debbie croaked as she looked up at me through swollen blackened eyes, obviously struggling to focus. "Don, is that you?"

Oh dear God, this was all my fault. I knew it was, and I could see in her face that she knew damn well that it was too.

"Yeah baby, it's me," I said.

She was tied to some sort of crude wooden frame that had been erected in the back of the van, her wrists and ankles bound tightly to the rough, splintery uprights. If I'd been one of those macho guys who carry a big knife around with them I could have slashed through her bonds and carried her dramatically off to freedom, but I'm afraid I've never been that sort of bloke at all. I frowned for a moment, then fished Lavender's talisman out of my pocket.

One more charge, I prayed, *please God give me just one more charge in this fucking thing.* I pressed my thumb down on the mystery third glyph, and focused. The talisman shivered in my hand, and I felt the mental image of a cutting edge appear in my mind. This was obviously the same spell that Trixie had used to cut the Burned Man out of my altar. If it would go through that then I reckoned it could certainly cut through a few ropes.

I moved the talisman carefully in my hand, focusing the image of the cutting edge on the ropes and being very careful indeed to keep it away from Debbie herself. Trixie had said it was for opening things, and I dreaded to think what might happen if you were to slip up and open a person by mistake. The ropes parted like butter in front of a chemical laser, and Debbie sagged forwards as the tension released in her shoulders and legs. I had almost finished cutting through the last of the ropes when the remaining power in the spell gave out. I dropped the now useless talisman on the floor of the van and tore at the last frayed rope with my fingernails until it finally gave way. I pulled Debbie into my arms and held her tightly.

"It's OK, baby," I whispered into her hair. "It's OK, I've got you now. I won't ever let you go again."

I thought maybe I could get to quite like this white knight business after all. You know, rescuing the fair maiden from the foul monster and all that. Right at that moment it had a certain sort of appeal, I had to admit. Debbie wrenched free of my arms and put her whole body behind a right hook that felt like it almost broke my jaw.

"You son of a bitch!" she screamed at me. "Do you seriously think I want anything to do with you after this? Are you fucking *insane?* Your slut *tortured* me, because of you! Get out of my life! Get out of my fucking *sight!*"

Oh dear. So much for the big heroic rescue, then.

"I can't really do that right now," I said, rubbing the side of my jaw where she had belted me. "There's World War Bitch going on outside, in case you hadn't noticed."

I turned to look over my shoulder, and saw that it was still true. Ally and Trixie were raining hell on each other out there while Adam stood back well out of the way with his hands in the pockets of his overly expensive-looking coat, watching with a smug smile on his face.

The Burned Man's curse must have been really taking its toll on Trixie, because Ally was easily giving as good as she got now, if not more so. I watched in astonishment as she raised the black dagger overhead and raked her claws down its blade, striking sparks. Crimson lightning flared along the length of the curved blade, and another pool of liquid fire erupted from the ground at Trixie's feet.

"Damn it!" Trixie screamed as she threw herself out of the way, rolling and coming up to her feet in her guard position with the Burned Man still clutched tightly in her other hand. "How are you so strong, you whore?"

Ally threw her head back and laughed, her long red hair blowing in the hot wind that seemed to be coming from the fires themselves.

"I made a deal," she said, circling Trixie again now with her dagger held low down by her left hip. "Your pretty boyfriend doesn't love you any more, sweetcheeks."

I darted a glance at Adam, but his smooth face still bore the same highly punchable expression of self-satisfaction that it usually did.

"You're lying!" Trixie shouted at her.

"He gave me my sisters back," Ally said. "Oh, you may have destroyed their bodies but they're right here, inside me. Three Furies in one flesh, three times the power. Oh, and he gave me *this!*"

She feinted with her claws and drove the dagger savagely upwards with her other hand. Trixie twisted away at the last moment, but the evil-looking black blade still carved a long scratch in her side. Trixie staggered backwards as red lightning flickered along the length of the wound. She dashed the back of her sword-arm across her burning eyes.

Ally laughed again. "And all I have to do in return is kill you!"

"Adam!" Trixie wailed. "Tell me this isn't true, Adam!"

"Three Furies trapped in one body, my dear," Adam said. He didn't seem to raise his voice, yet it boomed quite clearly over the howling wind all the same. "Destroy her now, and you destroy all of them at a stroke. You can end your war forever, right here and now."

"Oh you *shit!*" Ally said.

"I *can't,*" Trixie screamed. "They can't die!"

Ally attacked again, her face twisted into a livid grimace of hatred. Trixie fell back before the flurry of blows, her sword moving in a blur as she parried desperately. Whether Furies could die or not seemed to be a moot point by then, from what I could see. At this rate, Trixie was going to lose.

"Use the power of Hell, and you can do anything!" Adam bellowed.

Trixie screamed in pain and rage, and caught Ally with a spinning kick so hard it made her fly backwards across the burning concrete.

"I don't know how!" Trixie sobbed. She held the Burned Man aloft, shaking it in her hand. "Kill her, you little monster!"

"Get fucked," the Burned Man said. "You *stole* me, you mad bint. You want me to help you? Fucking make me."

To force your will straight down into Hell and take control of a demon directly without the use of the ritual summoning circle or any of the required ingredients was the very pinnacle of the diabolist's art. This wasn't even just raw summoning, like I had somehow managed to do with Adam. This was total mind control, utter domination. It was the highest level of attainment one could reach, or the lowest level of damnation to which one could sink, depending on your point of view. I had never even attempted it myself, but that was exactly what Adam was urging Trixie to do now – and so was the Burned Man. Oh yes, it thought it could break free if she fell all right, and by then I believed it.

Ally was getting back to her feet now, the dagger held out in front of her like a pistol. She slashed her claws against it once more, triggering it somehow, and lightning flickered and then leapt from the blade and arced through the air to strike Trixie in the chest. She screamed and fell to her knees. Her sword tumbled from her fingers and lay there burning, but she still gripped the Burned Man tightly in her other hand.

"Do what I tell you!" she shrieked at it, almost demented in her rage.

I could see she was focusing the full force of her will into the Burned Man now. The corona of white light around her flared like the sun for a moment, then the illusion collapsed as she lost concentration on it. I gaped as I saw the corrupted horror of her true aura. Her golden glow was streaked with writhing threads of black and green rot.

She's not quite as angelic as she used to be, Ally had said. No shit.

Trixie's hair was on fire now, and molten flames were licking out of the corners of her eyes and running down her cheeks like tears. The Burned Man bellowed with laughter in her shaking grip.

"Do it now!" Adam urged her. "Three Furies in one body – destroy the trinity and you can be free at last. Use the power, Meselandrarasatrixiel! Reach down its throat into

Hell and *make* it obey you!"

"That's right Blondie, *make* me!"

She has her own path to follow, Adam had told me, but you know what? Fuck Adam. Trixie needed my help right then, and I owed it to her. I owed her this much for forgiving me, if nothing else, and the look of naked lust on the Burned Man's face was enough to convince me. I couldn't just stand by and let this happen any longer.

I jumped out of the back of the van and ran to Trixie's side, dodging around the flames and narrowly avoiding a swipe of Ally's claws that would probably have disembowelled me on the spot.

"Trixie, no!" I screamed at her. "Don't! It's not worth it, *she's* not worth it! If you fall now they'll never let you go home. Give me back the Burned Man and *I'll* do it! It's not too late for you. I'm damned anyway, but you... you're not, Trixie. Please, I can't watch you fall!"

I dropped to my knees beside her and reached out my hands for the Burned Man.

"Leave... me... *alone!*" she bellowed.

Trixie swept an arm out and hurled me bodily away from her, sending me sprawling. She turned back to Ally with a look of pure, simple hatred. Flames erupted from her right hand and streaked across the expanse of burning concrete. Ally threw herself out of their way with an expression of astonishment and sudden horror on her face.

"Come and take me, angel!" the Burned Man roared at her, its poisonous black aura billowing around it. "Shitting hellfire but I've been looking forward to this!"

"You..." Trixie snarled, and turned the full savagery of

her insane stare on the Burned Man. "You will... do... as I... *command!*"

"Yes!" Adam hissed.

Trixie's own aura was darkening by the second, the rotten-looking black streaks spreading and expanding as though they were eating what was left of the beautiful golden angel she had once been. I struggled onto my knees, beginning to despair as I watched it happen before my eyes.

"Help her!" I screamed in sheer desperation. "Excelsior Deus trismegistus in nomine Patris et Filii et Spiritus Sancti for fuck's sake someone help her! Please, she's *falling!*"

The very world tore open.

Golden light and thunder and searing heat and freezing, howling terror filled my head to bursting point. It felt as though every nuclear explosion in history had all happened at once, right behind me. A wave of indescribable pressure hurled me onto my face on the stained concrete and pinned me down in obeisance.

A single word shattered the air like a sonic boom.

"*Stop.*"

"Dominion!" Trixie wailed.

I managed to lift my head enough to see the Burned Man tumble from her hands. Its monstrous black aura shrivelled, and all the fires went out at once. Trixie collapsed to the floor in a sobbing, smouldering heap. Adam turned on his heel and disappeared into the darkness. Ally gaped at me, at whatever was behind me. She shrieked. Her mouth stretched wide in an endless scream of agony, opening so far that it tore at the edges. Her long red hair crisped to ashes and blew away. Skin and flesh split open and peeled bloodlessly back from her face and from her hands and her throat and scalp until the blackened skeleton beneath was exposed. Maggots and grave worms writhed in the open cavities of her desiccated flesh as her eyes boiled and collapsed into her head.

The voice thundered and roared behind me, and still I couldn't turn, still couldn't see what it was that spoke. I'm not sure I'm sorry about that, all things considered.

"Thrones and Dominions I show you, furious children," it bellowed. "Your time here is at an end."

Ally exploded like she'd swallowed a kilo of Semtex.

So much for the Furies.

"You have saved my soldier-sister-daughter," the voice rumbled, its volume finally dropping slightly below the pain threshold. "For the first time in your life, Donald Drake, you have put another before yourself. Today, you offered your first real sacrifice. There may yet be hope."

I was speechless with a mixture of awe and sheer bloody terror.

"May I–" Trixie began, in a small, hoarse voice.

"This matter of the Burned Man is not ended, and this came close to catastrophe," the voice cut over her as though she hadn't spoken. "The thrones are watching over you, and I now task you as guardian. Guard your charge well."

And that was all.

The atomic light and crushing pressure vanished as though they had never been. The silence was almost total. It seemed very dark in there, now that the maelstrom of light and noise had disappeared as suddenly as it had come. The Burned Man coughed and muttered to itself, but wisely held its peace for once.

I heard the creak of the van's suspension as Debbie finally climbed down from the back. She stood there staring at me for a moment, at Trixie and the Burned Man and the ragged tatters of what had once been Ally and her sisters. She had a look of dull, shellshocked horror on her face that reminded me of those people you see on the news sometimes, the survivors of disasters and war zones.

She shook her head slowly, and fixed me with a cold stare.

"I *never* want to see you again," she said.

CHAPTER 20

It took some doing, but I eventually got Trixie and the Burned Man back to my place. The car park turned out to be underneath a condemned tower block not far from a parade of tatty shops. It was getting late by then, but eventually we managed to hail a cab on the high street. I don't know where Debbie went. She walked quite deliberately in the opposite direction from us when we finally found our way out of the concrete labyrinth underneath the building, and I haven't seen her since. The last I heard she'd moved to Glasgow.

If the cabbie wondered why Trixie was covered in cuts and blood and soot, or what exactly was wriggling and muttering to itself under my coat, my promise of a fifty quid tip in exchange for a silent ride home proved enough to stop him from actually asking.

I was starting to get worried about Trixie, truth be told. She hadn't said a single word since the Dominion had left, if indeed that's what it had been. She hadn't even noticed when I had picked up Ally's dagger and tucked it through my belt, before covering it and the Burned Man with my coat.

We drew up outside Mr Chowdhury's shop after a long, tense drive. Trixie had spent the whole trip staring straight ahead, her bloodshot eyes glassy and blank looking. I paid off the driver and helped Trixie awkwardly out of the back of the cab, struggling to hold the Burned Man still under my coat with my other hand. The taxi drove off, and I unlocked my front door.

"I really have got to get around to doing something about that bloody sign," I said, hoping to get some sort of response out of her to lighten the mood.

Trixie just looked at me, haunted eyes in an expressionless face, and said nothing. I nodded and pushed the door open with a sigh, and followed her inside. For once I didn't even look at her arse as she climbed the stairs in front of me.

She walked into my office and sat down on the sofa, and still she hadn't said anything. I tossed my coat over the desk and carried the Burned Man through to the workroom. It looked up at me as I set the piece of wood it was still chained to carefully back into the hole in the altar. The ancient wood would heal soon enough. I knew that all too well from my own attempt to steal it, all those years ago.

"We need to talk," I said to it, keeping my voice as low as I could, "but not now. Do me a favour and just keep quiet for a bit, OK?"

It nodded slowly, and mercifully said nothing. It looked too crushed with disappointment to speak anyway. I was halfway out of the door when I remembered the dagger still stuck through my belt. I had seen what it could do, and I knew where it must have come from too. If *Adam* had given it to Ally then... well, let's just say I wasn't about to chuck something like that out without giving it some serious thought first. I opened one of the drawers in the big cupboard under my books and slipped the dagger inside. I stood there for a moment, looking at the chest of drawers, then nodded slowly. I closed the workroom door behind me.

Trixie was where I had left her, staring out of the office window with a vacant look on her face. I went into the kitchen and made coffee for us both. Her cigarette case and lighter were sitting on the kitchen table, I noticed. She still hadn't moved when I came back through a few minutes later and held a cup of coffee in front of her face.

"Here," I said.

She reached out and took it, that was something. I had been starting to get a bit scared that she might have gone catatonic on me. I held her fags out to her as well, and she took them from me without a word. She took a cigarette out of the case without even looking, lit it one-handed and blew a long stream of acrid Russian smoke into her coffee.

I put my cup on the edge of the desk and crouched down in front of her to look her in the eyes. She looked so lost it broke my heart. I wanted to hug her, but I didn't quite dare.

"Trixie," I said gently.

She surged to her feet and hurled her cup across the office with a primal scream of rage. The cup exploded against the far wall, sending a great gout of black coffee bursting across the dried remains of Lavender's head that still decorated the plaster.

"Why?" she shrieked. "Why did he *arm* her? I'd have had the bitch if he hadn't given her that *fucking* dagger!"

I took a wary step backwards. She had stopped bothering

to try to mask her aura. The rotten taint had receded considerably from where it had been when she was trying to command the Burned Man, but it wasn't gone altogether. There were still thin black tendrils running through her golden glow, surrounding a pattern of greenish blooms like mould on stale bread. One of them was moving even now, almost too slow to see, but I swear it was getting bigger.

"Trixie," I said again, "look, um, sit down, yeah? I think I know the answer but... well, you're scaring the shit out of me right now, to be perfectly honest with you."

She looked at me and blinked in surprise as though noticing I was there for the first time.

"I'm sorry," she said.

She sat down and retrieved the cigarette she had dropped on the floor when she hurled her cup. She brushed ash from the end and took a slow drag, looking expectantly up at me. I had a sip of my coffee and sighed.

"Look," I said, "I mean, I'm half guessing some of this here but... well, I think I've got it straight in my head now."

"Go on then," she said.

"So, Adam," I said, and stopped again. "You *do* know who he is, yes?"

"Yes," Trixie whispered. "I know."

I must admit I had rather been hoping that she hadn't, but there we were. I sighed again.

"Right," I said. "So, well, you know he isn't exactly the most trustworthy of people then, don't you? By reputation at least, if nothing else."

"I suppose," Trixie said, almost too quietly to hear.

I nodded. "So, the way I see it, he's been deliberately

trying to make you fall all along, ever since you first, you know, slipped a bit. He's been setting you up, and he's been using Ally to do it. He brought the other two sisters back and put them in Ally's body to make that fight too tempting for you to resist. He gave you the chance to end your war in a single stroke and finally go home at last, if you just killed her. You were never going to be able to turn that down, were you? But you're *good*, Trixie, that was his problem. You're hell on wheels with that sword, if you'll pardon the expression, and he couldn't take the risk that you might actually beat her on your own. That, and he had to make Ally think he was helping *her* if he wanted to get her to go along with the plan at all, so he gave her the dagger to give her an edge in your final showdown. With that in her hand and her sisters' power added to hers as well you couldn't beat her, could you? Not on your own, anyway, not unless you used the Burned Man.

"He might have told you I'd eventually give it to you but he never believed that and he never even wanted me to, because that would have spoiled his plan. No, he needed you to have to steal it, because so long as you didn't legitimately own it the only way you could use it at all was to force your Will down into Hell and attempt to directly command it, which is what he wanted you to do all along because *that* would guarantee that you fell good and proper, wouldn't it?"

Trixie stared at me for a long moment, then nodded miserably.

"Yes," she admitted.

I pushed my hands back through my hair and grimaced. "The only thing I don't get is *why*. Why did he want you so badly in the first place, out of all the angels?"

"Because I'm good at what I do, like you said," Trixie said, her voice flat and numb. "That's why. I'm a soldier. A very good one. He needs soldiers like me, for what's coming."

I blinked at her. "I thought..." I started. "I'm sorry, but you're the only angel I've ever met. I sort of thought you were all like that."

"Oh no," she said. "We are the messengers of the Word. The Word is life. The Word is light and the Word is love, and renewal and growth and healing and peace. Also the Word is law and judgment and justice, and sometimes... yes, sometimes the Word is death. There are a multitude of messengers for all these many facets of the Word, but only a very few of us are soldiers. I'm among the best of them. I'm a killer, Don. That's what I'm *for*. He wanted me for what I can do, that's all."

I swallowed. I had a sudden sick suspicion that Trixie might just have been a little bit in love with Adam, even though she knew who he really was. I wasn't going to ask. I didn't want to know. She leaned forwards and covered her face with her hands, and said nothing.

I sat down behind my desk and swivelled my chair so that I was facing out of the window, staring at the gathering dusk with my back turned to her. She deserved her privacy for a moment, at least. I sipped my coffee and fought the prickly sting of tears at the back of my eyes. It was so... tragic, I suppose that's the only word for it. Tragic in the classical sense.

After a few minutes I heard her get up, and then she put a hand lightly on my shoulder.

"Thank you," she said after a moment.

I turned to look up at her, and she smiled at me. She seemed to be coming back to life, that was something I supposed. I shrugged.

"What for?"

"For being prepared to take the fall for me," she said. "For calling the Dominion. For saving my *soul*, you idiot!"

"I..." I started.

Oh but there was so much there that I could take the credit for, if I wanted to. If I just had the sheer bloody brass neck and cheek to do it. It was tempting, I have to admit. She was so... just *so*...

"Yes, Don?"

I gave her a wan smile. It was no good, I just couldn't quite bring myself.

"I panicked, bullshitted, panicked some more, and fell back on my Catholic upbringing as a refuge of last resort," I admitted. "I didn't really do *anything*, at the end of the day."

"You offered to damn yourself for me," she said, then frowned. "*Can* you do that? Directly command a demon, I mean?"

"Buggered if I know," I said, and grinned at her. "Doubt it. I can't say I've ever tried."

She laughed, and it sounded so good to hear her that I was glad I *hadn't* taken the credit. Well sort of, anyway.

"So I suppose you didn't know how to call the Dominion either," she said.

"Not a clue," I said. "That was a combination of having a rough idea of the right sort of thing to say and sheer bloody desperation, I think."

"And one of the strongest Wills I've ever seen," she said.

I felt myself blushing. "Yeah, well," I said. "I have been doing this for a while you know. You can talk, the way you stood up to the Burned Man's curse like that. I've been there myself, and I'd never have believed it was possible."

"Mmmm, yes well I've been doing this a good few thousand years longer than you have," she said. "I might have picked up a trick or two myself along the way. There's a funny thing, though."

"What's that?"

"The Dominion certainly seemed to think that you could have done it, if you'd wanted to. You wouldn't have been making much of a sacrifice otherwise, now would you? Believe me, it would have known if you were bluffing."

"But I *was* bluffing," I said. "That was twenty-four carat Don Drake bullshit. I just wanted to get the Burned Man off you before you did something you'd regret, that's all."

I wasn't going to tell her how close I suspected she had come to freeing the Burned Man as well. I think we'd *all* have regretted that, if she had, but as far as I was concerned she had enough to feel bad about as it was.

"I'm not so sure about that, Don," she said. "Trust me, if a Dominion thinks you can do something, then it's a pretty safe bet that you can, even if you don't know it yourself yet."

Well now, wasn't *that* an interesting thought. And then there was the matter of how I had somehow managed to summon Adam all by myself, too… thoughts for another day, I told myself.

"There's something else about the Dominion," I said. "It talked about the Burned Man, and it called me guardian.

The Dominion did, I mean. So... what? I'm the guardian of the Burned Man now, is that it?"

"What? Oh good heavens, no," Trixie said, shaking her head with a smile. "The Dominion wasn't talking to you then. I'm astonished it even noticed you at all, never mind that it actually spoke to you. You have no idea how much of an honour that was, Don. Dominions are... well, nothing at all like I am. All the same, a Dominion would no more give a task to a human than you'd be likely to hand out jobs to the individual bacteria in your stomach."

"Oh," I said, feeling a tiny little bit crushed. "So, um...?"

"It was talking to me," she said. "It was giving me my new assignment. I'm not going home just yet, I'm afraid."

"You? What are you the guardian of, then?"

"The Burned Man, of course," she said. "You had that part right at least. And since the Burned Man currently belongs to you, well, I think the boss just made me your guardian angel."

I stared at her.

"You're having a laugh," I said.

"No," she said, and smiled at me. "No, I'm really not."

CHAPTER 21

Well of course it would have been rude not to make the most of that. I took her out for dinner at the little Italian place round the corner and I really did tell her all of it this time. I told her all about Wormwood, and my gambling debt, and about his idea of how compound interest worked. I could see Trixie didn't think a whole lot of that, all things being equal.

"An angel's skull?" she echoed. "That's the sort of thing you people play cards for, is it? Seriously?"

"Ah," I said, feeling slightly embarrassed. Looking back on it, I may not have entirely thought that part though before my mouth ran away with me. "Well, you know how it is. Sometimes, I suppose."

"Well don't go getting any ideas about paying him back," she said. "I like my skull right where it is, inside my head!"

I laughed. "Perish the thought," I said. "All the same though, he's going to be bloody hard to get rid of."

"No he isn't," Trixie said, and smiled at me over her glass of red wine. "What time does this club of his open?"

Oh it was beautiful, it really was. We took a taxi from the restaurant to Wormwood's club, and I showed her where the door was. After that I didn't have to do much more than say hello to Connie so we could get up the stairs, and then it was all her. I think that was the night I really fell in love with her.

Trixie swept into the club like she owned the place, in the long sleeveless white dress she had whistled up from somewhere while I was taking a shower before we went out. The cuts and grazes on her face and arms were still only half-healed, but they lent her an air of dangerous mystique that made me feel like I had somehow stepped into an old Bogart film or something. She snagged a glass of champagne from a passing waiter and strode straight over to Wormwood's table. She sat down opposite him without waiting for introduction or invitation, which was an almost unspeakable breach of protocol. I stood at her shoulder, trying and failing to keep the increasingly smug smile off my face.

"I'll play you," she said.

"What the fuck is this then?" Wormwood said.

He glared irritably up at her, then blinked and took another, longer look. She still wasn't hiding her aura, and I knew he could see it every bit as well as I could. He knew *exactly* what she was. He looked from her to me, and a slightly queasy look crossed his sallow face.

"Look, mate," he said. "We ain't got ourselves into some sort of unfortunate misunderstanding here, have we?"

Trixie lit a long black cigarette and blew smoke in Wormwood's face. I kept quiet, not wanting to break her magnificent spell.

"It's like this," she said, leaning forwards with her elbows on the table. She kept her voice pitched low, so only Wormwood and I could hear her. "I am Don's guardian angel, and I am more than capable of having you for breakfast. In fact I would actually enjoy it a great deal. Now I realize you play an important part in the underground economy of this country, but don't for one moment think that that protects you from me in any way. You could quite easily be replaced."

"I see," Wormwood said, his voice sounding slightly strangled. "What... well, that is... look, well, how can we sort this out then?"

Trixie smiled at him. After a very brief and extremely one-sided negotiation he soon came around to her way of thinking. Yes, of course the debt was paid off in full, and completely forgotten about. He was terribly sorry about having Connie slap me about those times too. Naturally he would continue to supply any alchemical requirements I might have in the future, and at a heavily discounted price too. He even offered me my warpstone back as a sign of good faith, that's how scared of her he was. Now I'm sorry but I'm not that proud, and I really missed that warpstone. I took it.

Trixie stood up and gave Wormwood a cool nod.

"Well then," she said, "I think we're done here. I'll be seeing you."

He cleared his throat in a way that said he really hoped she wouldn't. We were about to leave when I spotted Papa Armand on the other side of the club, engaged in a heated argument with the middle-aged woman with the peacock feather fan. Now I don't know how much you know about Haitian etiquette, but I'm going to take a guess at not much. You see, if you see your spiritual mama or papa somewhere you *always* say hello, even if they're in the middle of something. Even if your mambo is up to her elbows in laundry and on the phone at the same time or your Houngan is having a blazing row with some business rival, you still go and butt in to say hello. Over here it would be rude to interrupt, but in Haiti it's rude not to.

"Excuse me for a moment," I said to Trixie, "I just have to speak to someone before we go."

She nodded and I headed across the club, leaving her sipping her champagne and watching a card game. I knew Houngan Armand was only my papa because he said he was and I hadn't actually agreed to anything, but I felt I needed to be polite all the same. I didn't know a lot about him, but I knew he was heavy. For one thing he was here so he must be, and for another I've always respected Vodou and I've always liked him. I stepped up beside him and the fan lady and cleared my throat.

"…must be joking," she was saying, her voice carrying a hint of an American accent. "You can't possibly expect us to…"

"Um, hello Papa," I said.

He turned and grinned at me. He had a glass of rum in one hand and a cigar in the other. The fan lady looked slightly surprised to see that it was me addressing him in that fashion, but she nodded in understanding all the same and took a step backwards to give us some space.

"Don-boy Drake," he said, his silk top hat nodding as he bobbed his head in welcome, "good to see you. Papa Armand just reasonin' wit' this lady right now, but one thing afore you goin'."

"Yes Papa?" I said, leaning closer to let him whisper in my ear.

"I'm goin' say it again, Don-boy. Time him come when a man gotta choose what path he goin' walk," he said.

He chuckled then clapped me on the shoulder and turned away, back to his argument with the fan lady. I shivered and went to find Trixie.

"Everything all right?" she asked as I took her arm.

"Yeah," I said, although I was no longer quite so sure that it was. "Yeah, I think so."

"I'm tired," she said. "Shall we?"

I led her out of the club and down to the street to look for a taxi, but Trixie suggested walking home instead for the fresh air. Now I'm not a fan of walking at the best of times, or fresh air as it goes, but after her magnificent performance with Wormwood I wasn't about to refuse her anything.

"Yeah OK, why not?" I said.

We were maybe half of the way back to my place when something whistled at me from an alleyway. I turned to look and made out the unmistakable shadowy outline of a night creature. I felt Trixie tense beside me, but I put a reassuring hand on her arm.

"It's OK," I said, "I know these little buggers." I walked to the mouth of the alley and looked at it. "What?"

The night creature looked at me for a long moment, and sniggered. "Don't you ever check your email?" it said. "You've got a message."

I hardly ever looked at my email, or even turned the

laptop on for that matter. I'm not a big fan of technology, as I might have said. Or much of a businessman either, sadly.

"I'll take a look when I get home," I said. "Cheers."

It showed me a few long, crocodilian teeth in something that might have been a smile, and scurried away into the shadows. Of course, it might *not* have been a smile at all. I shrugged and went back to Trixie, and took her home.

"Um," I said when we got inside, feeling slightly awkward. "Sleeping arrangements?"

It was only a one bedroom flat, after all. Trixie gave me a level look.

"You're on the sofa, Don," she said firmly.

I sighed. It was *my* flat but... yeah OK, fair enough.

"Night then," I said.

She stopped at the bedroom door and turned back to look at me.

"Oh, there is just one thing, before I forget," she said.

I frowned. I couldn't believe Trixie ever forgot anything, and this felt like it might just have a sting in its tail.

"Yeah?"

"What happened to Aleto's dagger? The one Adam gave her, I mean?"

"No idea," I lied automatically. "I guess it got blown to pieces when she did."

"Oh," Trixie said. "Pity."

I felt bad about that straight away, but it was too late to change my mind now. Obviously she wasn't going to approve of me having a demonic weapon but, well, a man in my line of work never knew when he might come to need something like that.

"Night," I said again.

"Yes," she said, "it is."

She closed my bedroom door behind her. I sighed and sat down at my desk, and took the whisky bottle out of the bottom drawer.

Time him come when a man gotta choose what path he goin' walk. I was starting to think Papa Armand might just be right about that. I dragged my laptop out of the desk and turned it on to check my emails.

I only had one message, from an anonymous address. It simply said, "You have made an enemy."

It was signed *Adam*.

ACKNOWLEDGMENTS

Writing can be a lonely business, but nothing worthwhile is ever accomplished alone. I would like to thank the following people for helping to make this book what it is:

My long-suffering beta readers, Nila and Chris, for their invaluable feedback.

Alison Clayton for telling me I could do this, all those years ago – thank you, ma'am!

My editor, Phil Jourdan at Angry Robot, for his guiding hand.

My wonderful wife, Diane, for everything else and most of all for putting up with all my shit while I did this. Love you babes.

ABOUT THE AUTHOR

Peter McLean was born near London in 1972, the son of a bank manager and an English teacher. He went to school in the shadow of Norwich Cathedral where he spent most of his time making up stories. By the time he left school this was probably the thing he was best at, alongside the Taoist kung fu he had been studying since the age of 13.

He grew up in the Norwich alternative scene, alternating dingy nightclubs with studying martial arts and practical magic. He has since grown up a bit, if not a lot, and now works in corporate datacentre outsourcing for a major American multinational company. He is married to Diane and is still making up stories.

talonwraith.com • twitter.com/PeteMC666